D0056768

GATHER HER ROUND

BOOKS BY ALEX BLEDSOE

Blood Groove
The Girls with Games of Blood
The Sword-Edged Blonde
Burn Me Deadly
Dark Jenny
Wake of the Bloody Angel
He Drank, and Saw the Spider
The Hum and the Shiver
Wisp of a Thing
Long Black Curl
Chapel of Ease
Gather Her Round

GATHER HER ROUND

ALEX BLEDSOE

A TOM DOHERTY ASSOCIATES BOOK

NEW YORK

This is a work of fiction. All of the characters, organizations, and events portrayed in this novel are either products of the author's imagination or are used fictitiously.

GATHER HER ROUND

A Tor Book
Published by Tom Doherty Associates
175 Fifth Avenue
New York, NY 10010

www.tor-forge.com

Tor® is a registered trademark of Macmillan Publishing Group, LLC.

The Library of Congress Cataloging-in-Publication Data is available upon request.

ISBN 978-0-7653-8334-1 (hardcover)
ISBN 978-1-4668-9155-5 (e-book)

First Edition: March 2017

Printed in the United States of America

0 9 8 7 6 5 4 3 2 1

To Steven Stack, a.k.a. Rex Winters

SPECIAL THANKS

Sheila Kay Adams
Jen Cass and Eric Janetsky
Bartlett Durand
Dan Fuqua
Jay Hunt
Diana Pho
Melissa Roelli and the staff of the Mount Horeb Public Library
Sjölinds Chocolate House, where most of this was written and edited
Paul Stevens
Marlene Stringer
Tuatha Dea

And, as always,
Valette, Jacob, Charlie, and Amelia

GATHER HER ROUND

1

"Y'all give it up for Magda the Story Spider," the announcer said as the woman strode offstage with a grin and a wave. The crowd beneath the huge tent applauded and whooped its approval. Even though it was nearing midnight, they weren't the least bit ready for things to end, especially knowing who was next on the bill.

The announcer mopped his face with a handkerchief; the old-fashioned gesture felt entirely appropriate in this setting. "Reckon it's hot enough?"

A good-natured chuckle went through the crowd. Although it was October in the Smoky Mountains, the weather was unseasonably warm. Almost everyone clutched a bottle of water and swiped at the bugs drawn in by the lights. Many fanned themselves with their programs. The odors of sweat and citronella mixed in the heavy air. This was the midnight cabaret, a special late-night event at the National Storytelling Festival in Jonesborough, Tennessee. Here the festival's normally family-friendly fare gave way to more adult tales that touched on some of the darker, but usually no less humorous, aspects of life.

"Well, I suspect it's about to get hotter with our

next performer," he continued. "Y'all might know her from her world-famous musical group, the Little Trouble Girls. Or maybe her Oscar-nominated role in that movie *Fire from the Heavens.* Well, she's back here tonight as one of us, a storyteller, and I don't think you'll be disappointed. Folks, let's give it up for a young lady who grew up right down the road, Janet Harper!"

A slender black-haired woman in a long Roma-style skirt, with a bright blue electric guitar over her shoulder, strode out to center stage, where a barstool and a microphone waited. She carried herself with the certainty of someone used to being watched by a crowd. She paused to give the announcer a perfunctory hug and kiss on the cheek, then settled on the stool, one leg straight to the ground, the other propped on a lower rung to provide support for the guitar. The announcer slipped discreetly away, the applause ended, and the whole crowd leaned forward expectantly in their chairs.

She looked down at her guitar and strummed the instrument once, a minor chord that rippled through the watchers like waves from a stone, quieting and settling them. At last she looked up and said, "It's hotter'n two squirrels fornicatin' in a wool sock, ain't it?"

Laughter broke the tension, but not the spell.

"As y'all can probably tell from the way I talk, I really am from around here. I grew up in Needsville, which is just over that way as the crow flies. One reason I love coming to this festival, besides hearing all the great stories, is that I also get to go home and see my folks and my friends." She strummed again. "But enough about me. I reckon I should tell you a story, then, since that's why you're here, and what I'm here to do."

She began to pick on the guitar, idly and softly, pretending to think as she went through her carefully rehearsed routine. She let her voice shift into a drawl, a much heavier Southern accent than her normal one. "I think on a night like this, a love story is the right thing to tell. The lady taking this stage after me, Sheila

Kay Adams, likes to say, 'It might be about murder, suicide, dismemberment, or coming back from the dead, but if it's got a man and a woman in it, it's a love song.' Well, the same thing's true about love *stories.*

"This story I'm about to tell you happened back when I was growing up over in Needsville. It didn't exactly happen to me, but I was involved just the same, and most of it is stuff I saw for myself. But it ain't a once-upon-a-time kind of story. It's the kind of thing that's probably going on between and among some of you good people right now. But I ain't judging, understand: it's just a story about some of them fundamental things that make us human. Of course, like Sheila Kay says, it can leave a trail of murder, suicide, and dismemberment behind it, which is why it's powerful and why we tell stories about it."

Her guitar noodling segued into a melody that most of the audience felt like they'd heard before, even if they never had. It was called "Handsome Mary, the Lily of the West." After she'd gone through the music a couple of times, she leaned close to the microphone and began to sing in a high, pure voice.

When first I came to Louisville, some pleasure there to find,
A damsel fair from Lexington was pleasing to my mind.
Her cherry cheeks and ruby lips, like arrows pierced my breast.
They called her Handsome Mary, the Lily of the West.

No one watching would have guessed that another song, with a completely different melody and lyric, ran through her head at the same time, fighting to be heard. But that song was not for this crowd, or anyone else. It had been played once, sung once, and would never be heard again. Its curse was that it also could never be forgotten.

By now the only motion in the crowd was the flutter of fans

and programs trying to move the still air. Every face glowed with both sweat and concentration. Given that this audience came from all over the world, it was doubtful many of them had heard the stories of the Tufa, the allegedly strange and mysterious people who claimed Janet as one of their own. But not knowing about the magic didn't keep it from working.

She continued to pick the melody as she said, "This story begins with a girl. She ain't named Mary, her hair ain't brown, and her eyes ain't either. She's a shapely girl with jet-black hair that you might think came down from some Native American ancestor, kinda like mine. But just so you know, she ain't me; my part comes along later. As the story starts, she's walking alone in the woods. It's a beautiful late-summer morning, the birds are singing, the wind is blowing, and she ain't got a care in the world."

She stopped playing. "Well, that's not strictly true. She does have a care. It's the boy she's been dating. Or I should say, *one* of the boys she's been dating." She began to play again. "This girl likes boys, but no particular boy. She's young, been out of high school for a couple of years, and she's just starting to learn about herself and what her being a woman can make happen in the world. And you know what? There ain't nothing wrong with that, despite what the tight-asses try to tell you."

Some pockets of laughter came from the rapt audience, although a few faces pinched tight with disapproval.

"So this girl's been practicing for a honeymoon she ain't planning yet, with two different boys," Janet continued. "But only one of them two boys knew about the other one. And on this day, that other boy, the one who thought he was the only dipstick checking this young lady's oil, was the one on her mind. Should she tell him? Should she break up with him? Or should she just smile and keep going 'cause it's so much fun to hop back and forth between the two of them?"

She wasn't going to use the real names as she told the story, but of course, the actual people now moved through her memory: Kera, Duncan, Renny, Adam, Mandalay, Bliss, Popcorn . . . they coalesced in her mind, looking just as they had over a decade earlier, and waiting to take part in the reenactment she was about to describe.

"That's what was going through her mind that morning as she strode through the woods. And she might've made her choice that day, one that changed the direction of her whole life, if she hadn't run into the monster. . . ."

2

Kera Rogers sniffed the morning air. There was something new in it, something she hadn't encountered before. It was a pungent, organic smell, like manure but with a musky tang. She'd walked this trail her whole life, and knew it like the proverbial back of her hand, but never before had she smelled something like this. She looked around, but saw nothing.

Her dog, Quigley, a mass of entwined canine genes so thick, hardly any aspect of a specific breed could be identified, stopped suddenly. Kera didn't notice, and kept walking.

Kera was twenty-one years old, wide-shouldered and broad-hipped, with an earthy femininity that meant she'd never lacked for male attention since she hit puberty. She had the jet-black hair, dusky skin, and perfect teeth of Cloud County's mysterious Tufa people, but her Tufa blood wasn't terribly strong, and she never thought of herself as that different from the people in Unicorn or other nearby towns. She was sweet but aimless, content to still live at home, work part-time at Doyle Collins's garage, and indulge her one true Tufa vice: music.

She was in one of the low gullies at the far east end of Cloud County, ten miles from Needsville and an hour's slow walk from her family's farm. She had her pennywhistle in the back pocket of her cutoffs and sought a comfortable and acoustically suitable spot to play. She knew there was a particular outcropping of rock ahead that crudely mimicked the shape of a recliner, nestled in a grove that gave her playing the extra spark that she imagined the great god Pan had enjoyed in the forests of Greece.

At last she noticed that Quigley remained stock-still in the middle of the trail behind her. "What is it?" she asked impatiently.

The dog stared straight ahead, his ears flattened. He was a notorious coward, having once been treed by a squirrel while the whole family watched. But even for him, this was unusual.

"Oh, go on home, you big baby," Kera said. "Git!"

Quigley didn't need a second command. He turned and trotted back toward the house.

Kera shook her head. Quigley was old, and it wasn't fair to expect him to change his ways now. She'd had him since he was a pup, and whatever his failings as a guard dog, he was still her baby. She continued on to Recliner Rock, enjoying the silence without pondering its source.

She recalled the shallow stream that ran beside Recliner Rock, trickling down from a spring somewhere in Half Pea Hollow and cutting through Dunwoody Mountain on its way to, eventually, join the Tennessee River. It had no official name, but was generally referred to as Half Pea Creek, after its origin. Sometimes she stripped naked and sat in the water, imagining herself one of those rural Greek girls, about to be ravaged by their goat-footed god drawn to her piping. Although, as a Tufa, she and Pan were more like equals than anyone might suspect.

There were two groups of Tufa in Cloud County. Kera's family had, as long as anyone could remember, been under the guidance of Rockhouse Hicks, a bastard by any definition of the word. But his death the previous year had resulted in Junior

Damo, a man with no experience in any sort of leadership, taking over.

Kera hadn't had many dealings with Rockhouse before his demise. Mostly she saw him at the old moonshiner's cave, where her family and the rest of his people met to play, drink, and hang out, or at the Pair-A-Dice roadhouse, where they mingled with the other group. The old man had, of course, commented on her physical attributes, saying she was "building herself a career" when she hit twelve and her ass went from flat to shapely, and snickering that she "must've left the air-conditioning on" if her nipples were visible through her bra and blouse. But he did that to every woman and girl, so she neither thought much about it nor took it personally.

And as for Junior, she barely knew what he looked like. Her parents bitched about him, but he didn't impinge on her life any more than Rockhouse had.

Neither of them were on her mind that morning as she hiked the familiar trail and pondered the unfamiliar smell. She couldn't wait to settle in and hear the notes of "The Old McMaynus Goose" twining through the trees from her pennywhistle.

But another song ran through her head right now, and she sang it softly, to herself, smiling at the irony.

Somebody's tall and handsome,
Somebody's brave and true,
Somebody's hair is dark as night,
And somebody's eyes are blue. . . .

The irony was that the song could apply to either of two young men in her life. Or for that matter, to almost any Tufa boy.

On impulse, she texted Duncan Gowen. Duncan was twenty-one, a Cloud County Tufa even though his family's blood, like hers, wasn't terrible true. But this was no Romeo-and-Juliet romance, or even a Hatfield-and-McCoy one; the Gowens, just like the Rogerses, were part of Junior Damo's group of Tufa families.

In some ways, Duncan was more Tufa than her, because he took his Dobro-playing very seriously, and had even—or so he said—once been able, however briefly, to manifest Tufa wings and ride the night winds.

Kera wasn't sure she believed him, but she also didn't discount it. The Tufa as a whole—a few dozen families clustered around Needsville, Tennessee, at the center of tiny Cloud County—had a history that most people considered myth at best, mere tall tales at worst. That didn't mean it wasn't true that they were descended from an exiled band of Gaelic faery folk, just that they could keep that secret, like so many others, right out in plain sight. After all, who in the twenty-first century believed in faeries?

Duncan was also as close to a boyfriend as she had these days. A Tufa woman, at least one who chose to take her amorous partners from within the community, was not bound by the outside world's morality. She was free to fuck anyone who wanted to fuck her, as often as both of them agreed to do it, without judgment from the other Tufa. And she'd sampled what Cloud County offered. But only Duncan seemed to know her rhythms without being taught, and could match her with every moan, gasp, and cry. They always managed to climax simultaneously, and that was a gift she appreciated. She wasn't in love with him, certainly; but she wasn't done with him, either.

Not that there was anything actively wrong with Duncan. It was just that outside the bedroom, he lacked the spark she sought in a partner. He was good-looking enough, talented enough when he sang and played his Dobro, and certainly skilled enough when they were intimate. Yet she couldn't shake the sense that something *more* waited for her. And that made her touch the old buffalo nickel hanging on a chain around her sweaty neck, an heirloom from her grandfather. She smiled at a thought that had nothing to do with Duncan, but with the other boy.

Her phone buzzed with Duncan's reply. MORNING. WHERE ARE YOU?

She replied, GOING OUT TO RECLINER ROCK TO PLAY MY TIN WHISTLE.

He shot back, I KNOW A TIN WHISTLE YOU CAN PLAY.

She rolled her eyes and giggled. ARE YOU IN SEVENTH GRADE?

I PROMISE, I'M A FULL-GROWN MAN. YOU SHOULD KNOW THAT BY NOW. WANT TO GO TO THE PAIR-A-DICE TONIGHT?

WELL, I'M PROLLY GOING 2B LATE GETTING BACK.

I CAN WAIT.

YOUR RIGHT HAND KEEPING YOU COMPANY?

IF THAT'S WHAT YOU LIKE. YOU WATCH ME, I'LL WATCH YOU.

She laughed out loud. *This* was what kept her around him: his outlandishness, which popped up when she least expected it and sent irresistible little intimate tingles through her. She knew she'd have to tell him the truth soon, and that he'd take it badly. But ultimately that was his problem, not hers.

She glanced down past her phone at the ground and saw something even more outlandish, something that made her stop dead. In the dirt beside her tennis shoe was a huge three-toed animal track, like some dinosaur had passed this way. It was easily six inches across.

She instantly recognized it: the track of an emu, one of the huge Australian birds released by her uncle Sim when his attempt to farm them failed. After getting one last warning from the bank about his delinquent loans, he'd simply walked to the pen, opened the gate, and shooed the immense birds into the woods. He expected them to die during the first winter, but they survived, or at least enough of them did. Now they were breeding, and making these foreign hills their new home. They mostly avoided people and minded their own business, a stance the Tufa could respect.

She recalled her last visit with Uncle Sim. Since his stroke, he'd become convinced that the emus he occasionally saw in the woods were the ghosts of the ones he'd released. No one could persuade him otherwise. He worried that they were plotting revenge, like the haints of murdered wives or husbands.

Ahead she saw the rock, already in comfortable shade. Beside it, the little creek emerged from the ravine before disappearing downhill into the woods. She texted Duncan, I'M JUST NOW GETTING STARTED. WHY DON'T I—

The odor she'd caught earlier suddenly washed over her like a noxious wave. She scowled, turned, and screamed.

The enormous wild hog, nine feet from snout to tail, snorted in surprise as he caught her scent. He stepped out of the woods onto the trail, between her and the way home.

She knew wild hogs were dangerous, and this one seemed to be the size of a Volkswagen. Yellowing tusks curled out from the lower jaw, sliding against the upper whetters that honed their razor-sharp edges. It had high shoulders with ragged skin that had grown thick enough to stop most bullets before they reached anything vital, and bristly hair tapered along its backbone. Its eyes were small, black, and malevolent, set above a wet, flat nose that seemed as large as her own head.

She looked wildly around for any place that might get her out of its reach, but there was nothing. None of the trees had branches low enough for her to grab.

Panicked, she dropped her phone and ran for the chair-shaped boulder. If she could get atop it, she'd have a chance: the hog, even as large as it was, had hooves and couldn't climb.

She slammed into the rock so hard, the pennywhistle fell from her pocket. She didn't notice.

She raised one leg and tried desperately to find a foothold. The edge of her tennis shoe caught on a tiny outcropping, and she prepared to haul herself up.

The hog's tusks slashed upward at her other leg just above her knee, cutting through flesh, tendons, muscle, and her femoral artery. Then its mouth closed on her ankle.

The pain was nothing compared to the irresistible strength that yanked her from the rock and tossed her to the side so hard, it separated the rounded top of her femur from its hip socket. The mouth crushed her lower leg bones, and as she lay on her back in shock, blood surging from the torn artery, she caught sight of a dozen smaller hogs emerging from the woods like a gang of junior high bullies supporting their leader.

The last thing she felt was the hog's hot breath, tinted with the coppery smell of her own blood, as it came for her head.

Duncan Gowen stared at his phone. It was unlike Kera to drop off in the middle of a text.

He looked at her last words: WHY DON'T I

At last he texted, WHY DON'T YOU WHAT?

As he waited for a reply, he went to the refrigerator and got out the iced tea. He was at his parents' house while they were at work; this was his day off from both Old Mr. Parrish's farm and his weekend job as a barista at the convenience store in Unicorn, so he was particularly irked when Kera said she wasn't available. Here he was all alone, the whole house to himself, especially the carpeted stairs that Kera loved to be bent over, as they'd discovered during a tryst back in high school. He'd even done fifty sit-ups and push-ups so his abs, which Kera liked to kiss her way down, would be good and tight.

After he poured his glass, he looked at his phone. Still no reply, and no dots indicating she was typing.

He took a drink and texted, ARE U THERE?

Dots appeared. Then came the reply: DFSGSJDGHKK

He texted, WTF?

He had no way of knowing that a hog had stepped on the discarded phone as it carried away a hunk of Kera's flesh.

Later that day, Duncan stopped at the Fast Grab convenience store in Needsville. It was nothing like the relatively upscale Traveler's Friend he worked at in Unicorn: there the crew wore uniforms with their names on their visors, and corporate sent a representative around every six months to put them through a customer-relations refresher. Here, though, the Fast Grab clerks got loud polyester shirts that were probably trendy around the same time as disco, and nobody got a name badge until they'd passed their first month.

Lassa Gwinn had her name badge. She'd been working here for six years now, through two pregnancies and a divorce. She knew everyone in the county, and remembered anyone traveling through who stopped more than once. She was three-quarters Tufa, part of Duncan's group, and his third cousin.

Now she looked up at him and said, "What's the matter with you?"

He put the bag of chips and bottle of Mountain Dew on the counter and said, "Who said anything was wrong?"

"Well, for starters, you're not drinking beer."

"It's not even eleven o'clock in the morning yet."

"And you got that scowl on your face."

"What scowl?"

"That frowny look you get when you're worrying about a problem. You've gotten that since you were knee-high to a grown man's ball sac. Did you lose your job over in Unicorn?"

"What?"

"'Cause if you did, there's a part-time shift open here. Midnight to six A.M., three nights a week. And I hear that Cyrus Crow and his NY boyfriend are reopening the café down at the Catamount Corner."

"I haven't lost my job."

"Then what's the frown for?"

"You ain't seen Kera come through here, have you?"

"Kera Rogers?"

"Have I got another girlfriend named Kera?"

"She's your girlfriend? I knew you two went out some, but I didn't think you'd made it exclusive. When did that happen?"

He leaned across the counter and said through his teeth, "Have . . . you . . . seen her?"

"Don't get your drawers twisted around your nuts, Duncan. No, I ain't seen her today. Why?"

"We were texting each other this morning and she just dropped off in the middle of it."

"Where was she?"

"She *said* she was out looking for a place to practice her pennywhistle. But I know that spot, and she ought to get a signal the whole way."

"Have you been out there to look for her?"

"No," he said like a pouty child.

"Well, if you're so worried, why not?" When he didn't answer, Lassa said, "Oh, 'cause maybe you don't want to know she ain't there."

"Can you please ring these up before my Co'-Cola gets warm?"

Lassa rang up the purchase and took his money. "If I see her, I'll tell her you're looking for her."

"Thanks," he said, and went outside to his car, an old Altima with a cracked windshield. He cruised around, eating the chips, drinking the Mountain Dew, and trying not to dwell on his suspicions.

Kera was out of his league, and he knew that, but he loved her anyway and tried not to let his paranoia get the best of him. Yet if she'd been texting from somewhere else and only pretending to be in the woods, that would explain the sudden loss of signal, if not that strange last text.

Of course, if she'd butt-texted, especially as she was squirming out of her jeans . . .

He glanced at his phone on the truck's seat beside him. Still nothing.

When he looked up, he stood on the brakes, rose in his seat, and locked his arms to hold the steering wheel steady as the truck screeched to a halt. A half-dozen wild pigs crossed the highway ahead of him. The noise from his tires made them scurry in all directions, and he waited until two that ran back the way they'd come finally went across and joined the others. The whole herd disappeared into the woods.

Duncan tried to calm both his startled heart and his seething temper. He hated himself when he felt this way, helpless to his own emotions and desires. He wanted Kera so badly right now, mainly because the thought of her being with someone else—no, the thought of her *wanting* to be with someone else—was more than he could handle.

And then he inevitably thought: Who could the other guy be? He began mentally listing all the boys she might be fucking at this moment.

Duncan sprawled naked on the couch at his apartment. It was a subdivided old house just off Main Street, and he had three neighbors: two single men who worked construction and were often gone, and a woman who was a secretary at the elementary school and had an eight-year-old son. For the most part, they all got along, since they all knew each other's families, and they all ultimately answered to Junior Damo.

He was half-asleep in the drowsy summer heat when his cell phone finally rang. It was Kera's landline number. "Where have you been?" he said, his voice thick.

"I got up, took a shit, blew my nose, and started my day," said a male voice he instantly recognized. "Where the hell have *you* been?"

"Sorry, Mr. Rogers," Duncan mumbled. "Thought you were somebody else."

"I hope so," said Sam Rogers, Kera's father. "Is Kera with you?"

Duncan shook his head to clear it. Why was Kera's dad calling him? He checked the clock on the cable box: 3:47 in the afternoon. "No, sir. I haven't heard from her since this morning."

"Neither have her mother and I. She went out to practice her pennywhistle and ain't come back."

He sat up. He was damp with sweat from the vinyl couch, and his skin peeled off it like the back of a sticker. "I don't know where she is, either."

"It's not like her to miss lunch, especially when she's working this afternoon out at Doyle's garage. You planning to gather her round from there this evening?"

Duncan waved at a fly that, drawn to his sweat, tried to land on his face. "No, sir. Have you tried calling her?"

Sam Rogers sighed the way parents do at the stupidity of the young. "No, son, that hadn't occurred to me. Glad you're here to remind me of these things. What did I ever do before you came along?"

Sam had never really cared for Duncan, and Duncan knew it. Sam had been a trucker since he turned eighteen, and he felt the boy was too aimless for his daughter, whom he cherished. He'd even tried to fix Kera up with Whitey Crowder, who'd been born without his right arm, when she started dating Duncan. While Duncan had nothing against Whitey, it meant that Kera's father preferred him to someone like Duncan, who had all his parts. That was humbling.

Still, Sam wasn't one of those men who kept his daughter locked away from life. He let Kera make her own mistakes, and was always there to wipe her tears and help her sort things out. So Duncan secretly worried that Sam was, deep down, right about him.

"Sorry," Duncan said, "I just . . . I was asleep."

"In the middle of the afternoon?"

"It's my day off," he said defensively.

"Huh. Must be nice. Well, if you hear from her, tell her to

call home. Her mama's worried, and it ain't doing my blood pressure no good, either."

Sam ended the call, and Duncan stared at the phone. He almost screamed when it suddenly buzzed in his hand again.

"Hey," his friend Adam Procure said. "Is Kera with you?"

"What?"

"I just got a call from her dad, looking for her."

"Why would he call you?"

"I think he's calling everybody."

"No, she's not with me. Have you seen her?"

"Not in days."

"I talked to her this morning, but we got cut off."

"Do you think we should be worried?"

"I dunno, man. I was asleep."

"In the middle of the afternoon?"

"It's my day off!" he repeated, more vehemently.

"Whoa there, slick, calm down. I didn't mean anything by it. When she turns up, let me know, okay?"

"Yeah," he said, and Adam disconnected. Duncan made himself get up, went into the bathroom, and started the shower. He left the water fairly cold, so it would wake him quickly.

For the first time today, he wasn't annoyed or pissed off. Now he was a little scared.

3

It was late afternoon by the time Duncan got ready to go look for Kera. Following his shower, he'd started drinking beer to calm his nerves after talking to Sam and Adam. Then he'd stopped, realizing things might be serious, and was now halfway between a sour-stomached buzz and a hangover. He was also in that middle ground between worry and anger. If something had happened to her, he was going to hate himself for waiting so long to go help; and if nothing had, he was going to be furious with her for yanking his, and everybody else's, chain.

And if he was angry, he knew just how she'd apologize. And that had him intensely aroused. So he was a miasma of conflicting feelings as he drove toward the last place she'd supposedly been.

The Rogerses lived at the base of Dunwoody Mountain, along a winding gravel road. He stopped just before the turn to her house so hopefully Sam wouldn't spot him; he could see the man's trailer-less Peterbilt in the front yard, the truck's chrome gleaming through a coating of road dust. He cut through the forest to reach the trail Kera would've taken to Recliner Rock.

He was no woodsman or hunter, but almost at once he spotted a fresh track from a tennis shoe that looked about the right size, and was pointed in the right direction. He looked around, but there were no similar tracks coming back. So either she'd continued on the trail past Recliner Rock, or . . .

He tried to recall where that trail finally came out. Was it behind Briar Hancock's place, near the old gravel pit? Why would she go there, unless it was to meet someone else?

His already iffy stomach began to churn. He walked as quickly as he could, wishing he felt well enough to run.

He stopped again when he found the ground torn up along a good ten feet of trail. Something had come out of the trees, crossed the trail, and headed uphill into the forest. Again, he wasn't experienced enough to recognize the tracks. They looked like hooves; were they deer? He'd never seen deer agitate the ground like this. This looked like something had rooted around in the dirt in search of something. He flashed back to the wild pigs he'd nearly run over. Could it have been the same herd?

"Kera?" he called out. "Hey, Kera! You out here?"

He stayed very still, listening for any movement. A bird trilled and insects hummed, but there was no human answer.

He picked his way over the torn path, wishing he'd changed out of his new tennis shoes. Ahead, the trail grew wider, which meant he was close to Recliner Rock.

"Kera!" he called again. "C'mon, answer me!"

He stopped when he saw the first splash of red at the trail's edge.

It was a thick liquid, deep crimson and heavy, and its weight bent the grass where it oozed along the blades toward the tip. He touched it, his heart suddenly thundering in his ears with a mix of panic and horror. When he saw it on his fingertips, he knew immediately what it was.

"Kera?" he called out again as he rushed forward. His voice trembled and grew high-pitched. *"Kera!"*

He reached Recliner Rock and stopped dead. A waist-high smear of blood marked its surface. The unmistakable tracks of fingers ran through it, making parallel lines of red down to the ground, which was torn up even more, the mud and blood mixed as thoroughly as if they'd been through a blender.

Duncan couldn't breathe.

"Kera?" he said, his voice barely getting out.

And then, like that scene in *Jaws* when the police chief sees the shark eat the little boy, Duncan's vision shifted until all he could see was the pennywhistle lying discarded on the ground.

And then he knew Kera was gone.

Bliss Overbay, in her capacity as an EMT, draped a blanket around Duncan's shoulders. He looked up from his seat on the Rogerses' front steps and said numbly, "I'm not cold."

"I don't want you going into shock," Bliss said. She looked to be in her thirties, with the long black Tufa hair braided and bundled on her head. She was far more than what she appeared to be, but at that moment, what was needed was simply a compassionate paramedic. "It can happen even in the summer."

"Too late," Duncan said. "I'm pretty fucking shocked."

"I know what you mean," she said, and briefly touched his cheek. She was from the other group of Tufa, guided by a totally different leader, but she had broad responsibilities to the Tufa as a whole. "Let me know if you need anything else, okay? I can call your parents for you."

He closed his eyes, petty annoyance in his voice. "I'm a grown man, Bliss. You don't have to call my folks. I live by myself, I work, I wipe my own ass."

"And you need somebody here with you," she insisted gently.

As if in response, old Quigley padded over and plopped down on his stomach at Duncan's feet. "I've got somebody," Duncan said. "See?"

"Yes, but I don't trust his judgment in a crisis. Is there someone else you'd rather I call?"

He tried to think of someone, but no one came to mind. Certainly not his parents. He could call Adam, but he didn't want his friend to see him so shattered. "No," he said at last.

"There you go, then." Her walkie-talkie beeped, and she took it from her belt. "Overbay."

"Come on up here," a male voice said. "We need you to take a look at something."

"On my way," she said, and clicked off.

Duncan looked up at her. "What did they find?"

"You heard as much as I did."

He started to rise. "I'm coming with you."

She pressed him back down. "No, you're not. I promise, I'll tell you as soon as I know."

He swallowed hard. "If it's her—"

"Then I'll tell you. Do you really want to see it?"

He couldn't meet her steady, no-nonsense gaze. "Okay," he mumbled.

Bliss tousled his hair the way she had when he'd been a boy, only a few years ago, and walked around the house.

Like many of the homes in Cloud County, the Rogers house was built on a hillside, with a small backyard that sloped sharply up to the tree line on Dunwoody Mountain. There were a birdbath and a little herb garden in the more level side yard, both kept neat.

Standing apart from the house, arms around each other, were Kera's parents. Sam and Brenda Rogers had their eyes closed; those unfamiliar with the Tufa might think they were praying, but as she got closer, Bliss heard their faint, light humming.

Bliss walked over to Chloe Hyatt, who stood a respectful distance away, ready to help if needed. The Rogerses' other two adult children, Spook and Harley, were on their way, but it would be hours until they arrived. A few years earlier, Chloe had lost her adult son, so she understood what they were feeling. She also knew that at the moment, she could contribute nothing but her sympathetic presence.

"Did you get news?" Chloe asked softly.

"I think so. They called me up there."

Sam and Brenda's eyes snapped open. Bliss's heart ached for them; they *knew,* but they still had hope. That was the saddest part of all.

"You heard something from Alvin?" Sam asked.

"Yes," Bliss said as she climbed on the four-wheeler that she'd brought here in the back of her truck. She'd strapped a thorough first aid kit, borrowed from the fire station, on the back.

"Did he say—?" Brenda began.

"I don't know anything yet." Bliss started the ATV and headed up the trail before they could ask anything else. She hoped some of the other friends she'd called showed up soon to sit with Sam and Brenda. This would be the worst day in their lives.

It took her ten minutes to reach Recliner Rock. The whole way, she kept glancing into the woods, knowing that something horrible must lurk there, wondering if it was brave enough to attack her atop the roaring machine. She knew the animals that usually lived in the area, as well as the more unique creatures that hovered around the Tufa. Most were contained, either by particular words sung in a specific way, or by the Tufa's ingrained wariness. But things could change, and one of them might have broken free. Then again, it could be something wholly mundane, like a bear or a cougar. Despite what outsiders thought, not every Tufa tragedy had to involve their magical side.

When she'd arrived at the Rogers farm two hours ago, Duncan had told her the basics of what he'd found, and the Rogerses said that they'd called State Trooper Alvin Darwin. Darwin was the only Tufa law enforcement officer, and his usual job—unofficially, of course—was to make sure no crime that occurred in Cloud County attracted any outside attention. Sometimes that was easier than others.

When she reached Recliner Rock, Darwin was there, looking paler than Bliss had ever seen him; Deacon Hyatt and Eldon "Gittem" Sands, both armed with their hunting rifles, gazed at something on the ground. Deacon was middle-aged, with classical gray at the temples of his neat, short hair. Gittem looked like what he was: a wild-haired hillbilly moonshiner, barefoot and clad in patched overalls.

"Do you know what happened to Kera?" Bliss asked as she shut off the ATV and dismounted.

"There ain't much doubt now," Darwin said, "but we need a professional to say so."

He led her over to the others, who stepped aside. Gittem used the tip of his rifle's barrel to indicate something on the ground.

It was part of a woman's hand, the thumb and forefinger. It had been chewed off at the wrist, and the rest of the fingers were likewise missing. The flesh was pure bloodless white, which made the black nail polish appear that much more vivid.

"I don't guess it *fell* off, did it?" Darwin asked.

"Reckon not," Bliss said.

She looked around at the other two solemn men, who waited for her pronouncement. To Darwin, she said, "I can officially confirm those are human remains, all right."

"Kera's?" Deacon asked.

"Is anyone else missing?"

"Not that I've heard anything about," Darwin said.

"Then I'd say yes. I saw her at the post office a couple of days ago, and she'd just painted her nails." Bliss sighed, struggling to maintain her professional distance. "She was showing them off."

"Where's the rest of her, then?" Gittem asked.

No one answered, but Gittem swung his rifle barrel until the tip pointed at another spot on the ground. A huge cloven hoofprint sank deep into the ground.

Deacon looked around at the woods, the ravine with its bubbling little creek, and the mountains that overshadowed them. "Then we got a monster," he said.

Duncan knew the truth when he heard Bliss's ATV arrive in the backyard, and it was confirmed by Brenda's long, ululating wail. He tossed off the blanket and ran around the house as the sound echoed off the trees, for a moment coming at him from all directions and enveloping him in her pain.

Chloe Hyatt and Bliss stood close to the couple, their eyes downcast. Sam held Brenda so tightly, he must've been worried that she'd collapse. She let out another long cry, one that carried all the suffering a mother could possibly feel.

Duncan grabbed Bliss's arm harder than he meant to. "What did you find?"

Bliss looked at him sadly. "I'm sorry, Duncan. She's gone."

Chills took hold of his legs and crept up his whole body. Now he wished he had that blanket.

Darwin, Deacon Hyatt, and Gittem emerged from the trail. None of the Tufa thought anything about the fact that they'd made almost as good time as Bliss on the ATV. Darwin stopped to quietly say something to Sam, then announced, "I've got to go call this in."

"To who?" Gittem asked.

"My dispatcher, for one thing."

"Will other police come out?" Deacon asked.

"I don't think so. It's not a murder, it's what we call 'death by misadventure.' I'm qualified to handle that."

"You know who you need to talk to first," Bliss said, soft but firm.

Darwin nodded. "I'll do that right after I leave here. Reckon I'll find 'em at the post office?"

"I imagine."

"I'll also have to call the wildlife officer for this area."

"Jack Cates," Bliss said. "I've worked with him a few times. He seems like a good guy."

"Nosy?" Deacon asked.

"Only when his job requires it."

"Was it a bear?" Duncan choked out.

Everyone fell silent and turned to him. Ordinarily he'd be embarrassed at the sudden attention, but not today.

"Did a bear kill her?" he asked.

"I don't think so," Darwin said.

"Then what? *What?*" he demanded, his voice cracking.

Darwin paused before speaking, considering how to phrase his words with Kera's parents right there. "I think it was a hog."

"A . . . a *hog*?" Duncan repeated, almost shouting. "You mean someone's fucking *hog* got loose and killed her?"

Brenda cried out and buried her face in Sam's shoulder.

"Shush, son, that's her mother right there," Darwin said. He pulled Duncan aside and said, "Nothing but wild hog tracks around the site; no bear or mountain lion sign at all. That's pretty clear. And we found . . . partial remains."

That word echoed around inside Duncan's head. *Remains.*

He swallowed hard. His mouth was dry, and his eyes burned. "M-maybe they just ate her a-after the bear . . ." Now he really wanted that blanket, and a place to sit down. And a bucket to puke in.

"Son, this is awful, I understand that," Darwin said. "I wish the news was better. Bliss?"

Bliss left Kera's parents and came over to Duncan. "This is what I warned you about," she said as she put her arm around his trembling shoulders. With surprising strength, she walked him back around to the front porch, where she sat him down and again put the blanket around him.

He looked up at her, numb and cold. "W-was it really a hog?"

"It looks that way."

"When I f-find out whose it was—"

"I think it was a *wild* hog, Duncan."

"W-where did it . . . did it . . ."

"Calm down. I don't *know* where it came from. That's not important right now, is it? But I do know it won't be here long." She looked out at the woods that surrounded the house, past the vehicles crammed into the dirt driveway and yard. "No, wherever it is, it's crossed a line."

"It's just an animal, right? I mean, it's not . . . it's not . . ." He hesitated, not wanting to mention the words for things that the Tufa whispered about, afraid that speaking the names aloud might somehow manifest the things themselves.

"No, it's just an animal," Bliss said with an assurance she didn't feel.

Trooper Darwin parked his police cruiser in the post office parking lot. The building was considerably newer than the other structures that constituted downtown Needsville, since the federal government had both insisted it be built, and paid for it. But one very important holdout from the old building had been ported over: the four rocking chairs now lined up along the porch. And at the moment, two of those were occupied.

In one sat a man of about thirty, with Tufa-black hair and a permanent expression of annoyance, which deepened when he realized Darwin was approaching them: Junior Damo. In the other sat a thirteen-year-old girl, her attention apparently all on her smartphone. She didn't even look up. She was Mandalay Harris.

Between the two of them, they governed the Tufa.

Darwin stood on the grass in front of the porch, waiting to be acknowledged. At last Mandalay turned off her phone and said, "Hey, Alvin. Sorry, was in the middle of a conversation. What can we do for you?"

"You mean you don't know?"

She glanced at Junior. "We're not genies, Alvin."

Junior nodded.

"Kera Rogers was killed up on Dunwoody Mountain today."

Neither spoke for a long moment. Then Mandalay said, "How did she die?"

"Appears to be a wild hog."

"A wild hog big enough to kill a person?" Junior said.

"I said it appears to be," Darwin said. "Fair plain enough that a bunch of wild hogs consumed her remains."

"They *ate* her?" Junior said.

"Hog'll eat anything. Hair, bones, clothes, the works."

Junior sat back. Mandalay said, "Who else knows?"

"Nobody outside us yet. I have to tell the wildlife people. If that hog gets out into one of the neighboring counties and kills somebody else, it'll draw a bunch of eyes to us."

"Go ahead and call him," Mandalay said.

"Wait, how can you be so sure?" Junior said. "Game wardens are always traipsing around where they got no business, just looking for excuses to give out tickets. Just like—" He caught himself, aware he was about to say, "like highway patrolmen."

Mandalay turned to him. "Because I am."

"You want state people poking around in the woods?" Junior persisted. "There's no telling what else they might find."

"They won't find anything they're not supposed to," the girl insisted calmly. "Kera's folks are yours, Junior; they'll be needing you."

"I know that," he snapped.

"You should head out there."

"Don't tell me my job."

Darwin thought how odd it was to see a teenage girl bossing a grown man around like this. But this was no ordinary teenage girl; she was the latest in a line of Tufa women that went back farther than most would believe, and in her head she carried the history of all those women, and thus all the Tufa. She and Junior each led half the community, but there was no doubt who had seniority. She was thirteen only on the outside.

"I'll be getting back," Darwin said. "If you need anything else from me, let me know."

He touched the brim of his hat and strode back toward his car. When he glanced back, the girl sat alone on the porch, again looking at her phone. She sang, so softly, he barely heard, "There is a wild boar in this woods, he'll eat your meat and suck your blood, drum-down-rum-dee . . ."

For Duncan, the rest of the afternoon and evening passed in a haze. At some point, he gave an official statement to Trooper Darwin, explaining what had happened and how he'd come to discover the crime scene. He showed him the texts from Kera and how they abruptly stopped. He also told about the herd of pigs he'd nearly hit on the highway. He knew that Darwin, being part Tufa himself, would run interference for them, ensuring that all the paperwork was in order so it wouldn't draw the attention of other law enforcement officers. The Tufa zealously guarded their secrets, even when they didn't need to.

Bliss followed Duncan home in her truck, and once he'd parked his car and reached the door of his apartment, she left. He didn't want her to stay, but at the same time, he didn't want to be alone.

His parents would find out, and they would show up, all concerned and trying to be supportive. Even his big brother, Poole, might come over. He dreaded that more than anything.

He didn't turn on any lights, and it grew dark as the afternoon dissolved to evening. As he sat on his couch, staring at the blank rectangle of the TV screen, he tried to force the new reality to take hold in his brain. Kera was gone. Her laugh, the way she rolled her eyes, the way her breasts bounced when she went without a bra, the sighs she made when he kissed the small of her back . . .

No, stop that, he told himself.

He got up, went to the front door, and made sure it was locked. He checked all the curtains and blinds to make sure no one could see in. Then he sat on the couch again, turned on the reading lamp, and reached into his pocket.

He pulled out Kera's cell phone.

Dirt and bits of grass still covered it from where it had been half-trampled into the torn-up ground. He'd found and pocketed it without really thinking about it, as he waited for Darwin to show up at the bloody scene. Now he stared at it and wondered why he hadn't told the patrolman about it.

He swiped it on, then typed in her security code. He'd learned it over time, by surreptitiously watching her do it. *5-3-7-2.* It was the numerical code for her name.

The screen lit up with her apps. Behind it, the wallpaper was a photo, not of the two of them as it had once been, but of a generic sunset. Duncan wondered if she'd taken it herself; no, she'd never shown any interest in visual art. She must've found it online.

He opened the Messages app. The texts were the last ones she'd sent to him, her last words to another human being on this earth. He read them and before he even realized it, tears streamed down his cheeks, dripping onto the glowing screen. He sniffled and wiped the phone against his shirt.

Then he noticed a little *(3)* symbol at the top. She had three unread messages left, and they weren't from him, since he had that conversation open.

He hesitated. This was a betrayal of a dead girl's trust, her confidentiality, of her life in general. Whomever she was talking to, or ignoring, it was none of his business.

But it was also the last new thing he would ever learn about her.

He carefully touched the little arrow that would show him all her conversations.

4

Long after dark, Duncan remained on his couch. He sat very still and stared at Kera's phone. He had no tears, or rage, or anything left to respond to what he'd found. He hadn't begun to come to terms with Kera's death; her betrayal would take even longer to process.

The three messages that he'd found had been fairly innocuous on the surface. CALL ME LATER, one had said. Then, ARE YOU OKAY? But the final, damning one had been the last: ARE WE STILL ON FOR TONIGHT? CAN'T WAIT TO SEE YOU AND MAKE THAT BUFFALO ROAM.

And the name attached to these texts was even more damning. *Adam.*

Adam Procure. He was taller than Duncan, lean-bodied, and had natural six-pack abs that never needed sit-ups or dieting. He'd heard Kera mention those more than once, but it had always been in passing jokes: "Do you think he can make them clack together?" So Duncan had never been jealous.

Besides, he and Adam had been friends since they met in elementary school. They'd never competed over women, because they had such different interests: Adam preferred blond women from nearby Unicorn or Pea

Station, which is one reason he took a job there, even though he continued to live on his parents' farm. Duncan had, from the first time they met, had eyes only for Kera, although he'd dallied with others as their relationship waxed and waned.

And yet, here was incontrovertible evidence that Adam and Kera had been sneaking around behind his back. The "buffalo" was an old buffalo nickel that Kera wore on a chain, and "making the buffalo roam" meant moving it with your tongue around her neck, before carrying on to other places. Duncan had thought it was something she did only with him.

Tufa women weren't bound by Puritan rules, and he understood that. She did nothing wrong in fucking Adam. But to do it behind his back, and for them both to then hide it from him, and to *keep* doing it . . . that felt like a real betrayal, whatever the rules of their society.

He finished the latest beer and put the bottle on the floor with the others. Then, after twisting the top off a fresh one, he began to look through her photographs. It didn't take long.

There they were, in a selfie on Redford's Ridge, him behind her and their faces close together. Then they were in his truck, with her scooted back against him in the driver's seat. Their smiles were bright, full of hope and promise.

And then there she was in a selfie, nude except for her panties and that necklace, doing a duck-face and standing in her bathroom. She hadn't sent that one to Duncan, so it must have been for Adam.

He turned off the phone and considered throwing it into the opposite wall as hard as he could. But before he could muster the energy, he began to cry. In moments, he was curled up on the floor among the empty bottles, sobbing so hard, it felt like a torque wrench twisting the middle of his body.

Beneath his couch, amongst the dust bunnies and discarded beer tops, he saw a small pink sock rolled up in a ball. He reached for it, and caught it with just his fingertips. She'd looked for this sock for an hour one morning, although neither of them had thought to check that far back under the couch. He pulled it close to his face, studying the weave of the fabric, wondering what had appealed to her about this sock that day. He realized he had no idea what her taste in clothing really was. Did Adam?

He pulled the sock to his face, inhaling dust and lint. He didn't care, though. He just wanted to go back in time far enough to put it back on her dainty little foot, with the nails always painted a bright rainbow of mismatched colors.

His cell phone rang. He looked at it long enough to see that it was his mother, then turned off the ringer. The loss of everything important to him in so short a time was more than he could bear, and he realized he had only one place to go. It was the only place a Tufa in his position *could* go, as much as he hated the idea.

And so, later that night, exhausted and half-lit, he'd gone to his people's refuge: the old moonshiner's cave deep in the hills.

The Tufa were one people, but two tribes, and each had its own place of sanctuary, where only the right people were allowed. The other faction, the one led directly by Mandalay Harris, met in an old barn with SEE ROCK CITY painted on the roof. Duncan's group, led by Junior Damo since the demise of Rockhouse Hicks, met in this cave.

First discovered prior to the Civil War years, it had been used to hide runaway slaves, then deserters who saw the war as none of their business. Cloud County's standing on slavery was really moot: no one was rich enough to own any slaves, and with their black hair and slightly dusky skin, they were often mistaken for mixed-race escaped slaves themselves. So they waited out the war, not getting involved and really not caring about the outcome.

Bootleggers set up shop in the cave after the war, and during the years of Prohibition, it had been a haven for those sought by the "revenuers." Cloud County paint thinner, as it came to be called, had a reputation for getting you roaring drunk almost at once, but with no hangover the next day no matter how much you drank. That wasn't strictly true, but the songs the moonshiners hummed and sang over the sour mash did have an effect on the final result.

Now it was a social hall, although both moonshine and methamphetamine were brewed in various subchambers of the central cave. In the big main room, with its hole in the center of the cave's roof to let out smoke, people milled about in groups and gathered to play music. Smaller "rooms," closed off with curtains, were available for the men and women who wanted privacy. Duncan knew it was considered a degenerate, lower-class hole by those from the other group, with their pristine family-friendly barn; but he'd always loved it, and even though he'd never taken advantage of those little rooms, he felt at home and safe in it. These were his people, and that connection went deep.

Old deer skeletons hung as warnings at the entrance. With a few simple, strategic modifications, they resembled partial human skeletons. Or perhaps they really were human remains; Duncan just assumed they weren't, but he didn't really know for sure. He stopped and stared at one of them; he couldn't tell.

The path into the cave was narrow, and the power lines that provided light and heat had been bolted along the join of floor and wall. He had to step over someone who had evidently been leaving, but passed out before making it out. In the dimness, he couldn't recognize the person, or even tell for certain if it was a man or a woman. At another time, he might have hoisted him, or her, onto his shoulders and carried them back down. But tonight he couldn't be bothered.

There weren't many folks there when he arrived. These were the lifers, the ones who seldom left the cave and even more seldom sobered up. Nearby leaned their banjos with grimy old heads, guitars with whiskers of broken strings, and other instruments that needed just as much attention as their owners, and were just as unlikely to get it. The music they produced was ragged, cacophonous, and cruel to both the ears and the heart.

"Hey, there, Duncan," old Snobie Marks said. He had long hair tied back in a haphazard ponytail, still jet-black despite his advanced years and weathered face. He had exactly two teeth left in his head, which made him smack his lips between every other word when he spoke. "Did I hear something happened to that girl you was seeing?"

"She got killed," Duncan said numbly.

"Ain't that a kick in the head." He shook his head, spat at the ground, and made a swinging gesture with his hand to acknowledge death. "Sure enough is a kick in the head," he muttered when he finished.

"Have you seen Junior?"

Snobie waved toward one of the tunnels. "He's back there holdin' court, trying to make everybody think he's the boss."

"Ain't he?"

Snobie snorted, and ignored the spittle that caught on his chin whiskers. "He got a long way to go before he's another Rockhouse, that's for sure."

"Maybe we don't need another Rockhouse," Duncan said.

"Hey, you know what a pussy hair sounds like before it hits the ground?" When Duncan didn't answer, Snobie made a quick spitting sound. Then he laughed and wandered away.

The tunnel had a line of light sockets along the low ceiling, and Duncan had to dodge them as he walked. As he turned a corner, a female voice said suddenly, "Who the fuck are you?"

Flint Rucker emerged from the shadows of a small side passage, clumsily twirling like a dancer. She wore cutoffs despite the cave's chill, *My Little Pony* tennis shoes, and a T-shirt with a sparkling rainbow across it. Her black hair was tangled into dreadlocks, and her wide eyes were just as black, the pupils huge and almost obliterating the iris. She sang, her voice high:

As I went forth one bright shiny day,
A dainty young couple were coming my way.
The one a fair Damsel of beauty most clear,
The other a . . .

She stopped and looked him up and down, as if measuring him for a new suit of clothes.

. . . mourner, as it does appear.

"Hello, Flint," Duncan said. "I'm here to see Junior."

Flint shuffled closer. She looked barely twenty, but everyone, certainly Duncan, knew better. Flint Rucker had been accidentally trapped in a cave for over forty years, living on lichen, insects, and blind fish. When he heard that some spelunkers had found and rescued her, Rockhouse Hicks laughed and said, "Yeah, I probably shoulda tole her family about that forty years ago."

But the time had altered her. She looked exactly the same age as the day she'd been caved in. She preferred darkness, and her eyes could see not just in the dimmest light, but some said into your very soul. Now Junior had installed her as his assistant, serving the same function for him that Bliss Overbay did for Mandalay Harris. To get to him, you had to get past her. And not everyone could stand up to those penetrating black eyes.

Certainly, drunk and exhausted as he was, they gave Duncan the willies. They were almost insectlike in their unblinking intensity.

"Here to see Junior," Flint repeated in her singsong way.

"Is that okay?"

"Is that okay?" she repeated.

Duncan gritted his teeth. "Flint, please. This has been a horrible day. I really need to see Junior."

"You shouldn't be here," she said. "You should be with her. To gather her round."

"Gather *who* round?"

"Flint!" Junior yelled from far down the hall. "Stop being a damn psycho and let him through."

Flint shrugged, smiled her enigmatic smile, and twirled back into the darkness down the little side tunnel.

Junior had turned one of the small chambers into an office. He had a desk, made of an old door and four milk crates, and sat behind it, watching porn on his laptop. Luckily he didn't have his pants down around his ankles this time, and Duncan loudly cleared his throat before he stepped into the open.

Junior snapped the laptop closed, shutting off the video in mid-squeal. "So what's so damn important, Duncan Gowen?"

"Sorry, sir," Duncan said. He made the elaborate hand gesture he'd learned as a child to show respect to a Tufa leader. It had seemed appropriate for the larger-than-life Rockhouse Hicks, but far out of proportion for his successor. Junior was smaller in every sense.

Junior knew it, too. His own responding gesture was curt and perfunctory. "I asked you what you want."

"Did you hear about what happened to Kera Rogers today?"

"Yeah, I did. I was real sorry to hear that. She was a mighty pretty girl."

"She was my girlfriend."

"That ain't what I heard. She wasn't steady with you."

"No," he had to agree. "But I loved her."

"Then I'm sorry for you, too. Is that all?"

Duncan could tell this would go nowhere. Any justice he asked for, any revenge he demanded for his shattered honor, would be granted only at the cost of what little self-respect he had left. The only remotely good thing was that this wasn't Rockhouse, because that old man would've known exactly why Duncan was here, probably before he knew it himself. Rockhouse had led the Tufa for longer than anyone could remember, and his passing was as traumatic to the community as it was to him. Junior, on the other hand, was one of those people who advance to positions of authority they neither deserve nor can handle.

Duncan said, "Yeah, that's all. I just wanted to make sure you knew about it."

"Wait a minute," Junior said as he got to his feet. He gave Duncan a narrow-eyed measuring look. "That's bullshit. You didn't come here just to tell me that."

"Sure I did."

"Uh-huh. You want something. What?"

Duncan thought fast. "I want to be the one who kills that motherfucking pig."

Junior looked him over, judging his sincerity. "Why tell me?"

"Ain't you the man?"

"What makes you think I can control that? Hell, I ain't the god of pigs or nothing."

"In that case, then, like I said, I'll be going." Duncan turned to leave, trying to ignore the creepy feeling of Junior's eyes on his back.

"You sure that's what you want, Duncan Gowen?"

The voice was not Junior's, and Duncan froze. There was no one else in the room, and there was certainly nowhere for anyone to hide in the ragged stone walls. Yet he was certain the voice wasn't Junior's, and equally as certain whose it was.

He'd heard the stories, whispered over swigs of liquor or between choruses of songs, that Rockhouse Hicks might be dead, but he wasn't *gone.* He haunted Junior Damo, lurking around him and whispering advice, especially when Junior was in this cave. Some claimed to have actually seen him; except he wasn't the old, white-haired monster he'd been at his death, but young, in his prime, his hair as black as the mocking hatred in his eyes.

Duncan's mouth went dry. Did he dare turn around and see if Rockhouse's haint stood behind Junior? He'd never seen a haint himself, although many of his friends had, and he'd heard all the stories.

"I'm sure," he croaked out. Then he left as fast as he could without actually running.

Bliss Overbay sat at the kitchen table in the volunteer fire department. She was alone in the building, and worked on the paperwork she'd need to give Alvin Darwin to close the investigation into Kera Rogers's death. Among the Tufa's many skills was staying off any official radar, which meant that all deaths were natural, all property sales were routine, and all taxes were paid on time and with few eye-catching deductions.

Sometimes, though, things were so strange that they couldn't be glossed over, and Bliss worried that this was one of them. A natural death could be hidden; a murder could be minimized. But slaughtered by a monster? That was much harder to hide.

"Hey," a new voice said. Bliss looked up.

Mandalay Harris stood before her. She wore old-fashioned bell-bottomed jeans and a tank top, with her Tufa-black hair pulled back in a ponytail. There had been no sound of the heavy door opening or closing.

"Hey," Bliss said, the sudden appearance as normal to her as the air around them. "So you heard."

"Yeah. Alvin Darwin came by and told me and Junior."

"How did Junior take it?"

"Same as he takes everything."

"He didn't send Flint Rucker out to bring him the hog's head on a pike?"

"I don't think he trusts Flint with anything but ankle-biting folks who try to bother him."

"How long are you going to put up with him?"

Mandalay wouldn't meet her eyes. "He does his job."

"With Rockhouse gone, it should be your job. There's no need for two tribes anymore."

"I disagree," the girl said simply. And Bliss knew that was that. After a moment, Mandalay asked, "Was Kera really killed by a wild hog?"

"That's what it looks like. An absolutely huge one. Feet this big." She held her hands about six inches apart to indicate the size.

Mandalay sat at the table. She folded her arms, rested her chin on them, and said, "That's got to be one of the worst ways to die I've ever heard of happening around here. Even worse than Ellis Parker dying after being buried under thirteen tons of peas."

"He should've told somebody he was working in the silo," Bliss said.

"Oh, how shall I, this wild boar see? Look left, he'll come to thee, drum-down, rum-down," she sang softly. Then she asked, "So where did this giant killer pig come from?"

"I don't know. Alvin's calling Jack Cates. He's the game warden for this region. Maybe he'll know."

Mandalay nodded. "And Alvin will handle the police?"

"Yeah."

She paused thoughtfully. "There's something else going on here."

"What do you mean?"

"I don't know. If I knew, I wouldn't have to be cryptic, would I?" Her little smile defused any snarkiness.

"It crossed my mind that if someone were to kill a young woman and feed her to the hogs, it'd look a lot like what we saw today," Bliss said.

"That's true. But that sort of thing would make the night winds rattle the trees. Or at least, that's what it usually does."

"The night winds are changing. That's what you've said."

Mandalay was silent, staring into space across the tabletop.

After centuries of passive steadiness, the last few years had seen the night winds exhibit extraordinary activist behavior. The return of Bronwyn Hyatt after she left to join the army. The fall of Rockhouse Hicks, brought about by an outsider guided here by the winds. The rise of Bo-Kate Wisby, and the destruction that followed. So not even Mandalay, who understood clearly what everyone else heard only as indistinct whispers, could say what the night winds truly wanted anymore.

At last she said, "You have to be thinking the same thing I am."

Unbidden, the image of Rockhouse Hicks, with his six-fingered hands, came vividly to her mind. "Him?"

"Yes."

"He's dead. More importantly, dead and gone."

"You think."

"Do you?"

"I haven't sensed even a whisper from him since he died," Mandalay said. "And it wouldn't be like him, even as a haint, to hide away. He'd want everyone to know he was back. That nothing we could do could stop him."

"So it's not him."

"I don't know."

"So what should we do?"

"Keep our eyes open. Try to catch it before it gets out of hand and draws too much attention. And hope I'm wrong."

Bliss tugged a stray strand of the girl's black hair in mock annoyance. "You've really got that 'inscrutable visionary' thing down, don't you?"

Mandalay smiled. "It's no fun for me, either. It's something like a bug crawling on you in the dark: you know it's there, but you can't see it."

"Speaking of, how are things with you and Luke Somerville?"

"All right. We see each other when we can. We play at the Pair-A-Dice a lot. School just started back, so I hope it won't be weird for him. Kids talk."

Luke was from the other half of the Tufa, the ones under Junior. His relationship with Mandalay mirrored the one between Bo-Kate Wisby and Jefferson Powell, the only two Tufa ever to be banished from Cloud County. Bo-Kate and Jeff's return had wreaked chaos the previous winter, and a lot of the Tufa saw the same potential in Mandalay and Luke. So far, though, it had been nothing but a mutual teen crush.

But that was a secondary concern at the moment. Right now, the most urgent matter was the killer animal still out there roaming the hills and hollows of Cloud County.

"We need to know if this monster is real," Mandalay said at last, "or just a way of hiding something."

"That'll be the game warden's job. I'm sure when he gets here, he'll want to see Kera's remains."

"So you'll keep an eye on him?"

"Might even keep both," Bliss said, matching Mandalay's little smile. "Jack's a good-lookin' fella."

5

The next morning, Jack Cates answered the phone at the Tennessee Wildlife Resources Agency's Morristown office. Jack was thirty-six, with short blond hair that turned almost white after any time in the sun. He looked older than he was because of so much time spent outdoors. He was tall, lean, and wore his green uniform with ease and comfort. He *was* comfortable: he liked who he was and what he did, and was content to make that most of his world.

Normally the receptionist, Georgina, answered the phone, but she was away from her desk, and Jack was the kind of guy who pitched in and didn't worry about how it looked. "TWRA," he said.

"May I speak to Mr. Jack Cates?"

"You got him."

"Mr. Cates, this is Alvin Darwin from the highway patrol. I'm up outside Needsville, in Cloud County, investigating a death. I'm pretty sure the victim was killed by one of them wild hogs, so I figured you'd be interested, too."

Cates sat down behind the desk and reached for a pen. "What makes you say that?"

"Hog tracks everywhere around the body, for one thing."

"Hogs might eat a dead body if they found one, but they wouldn't—"

"One of them tracks was a hoofprint six inches wide."

Cates sat up straight. "Six inches?"

"I can e-mail you pictures with a ruler beside it for scale."

"Please do. And you're sure it's not deer tracks? They can look awfully similar."

"I've been hunting deer since I was eight; I'm pretty sure. We also found some partial remains."

"Partial?"

"Part of a hand. Two fingers and a thumb."

"And that's all?"

"That's all. So far."

"So was it a child, or—?"

"Grown woman. Well, she was twenty-one. Attacked about a mile from her home. Fair number of other homes scattered about the area, so it's sort of an emergency."

Cates let out a long, slow breath. He wasn't entirely surprised someone had finally been killed by a wild hog; he'd seen them do plenty of damage, and always assumed it was just a matter of time. He expected it to be a child, though; a hog big enough to take down an adult was more dangerous than he liked to imagine. "When did this happen?"

"Yesterday."

Jack had seen nothing on the local news sites about it; he checked them every morning, and had Internet alerts set up that would let him know when any story appeared that might fall under his purview. He definitely tried to keep up with damage done by wild hogs, the most pernicious and insidiously destructive invasive species he knew. "That a fact? I didn't hear anything about it."

"You are now, I reckon."

"Then I reckon," he said, slightly mocking Darwin's drawl, "I need to come over there and take a look."

"We'd sure appreciate it if you did." Darwin passed on his cell phone number, and the Rogerses' address.

Cates hung up. Georgina, having returned from her errand, stood waiting for him to move so she could sit down. "You can't do every job around here, Jack."

"Sure I can," he said as he stood. "I just wouldn't look as pretty as you doing it."

"Not when you look that serious. What was that about?"

"Another feral hog problem."

"Oh, dear."

"Worse than that. If they're right, this one might've killed somebody."

"What?" she said, eyes wide.

"I know."

"I didn't hear anything about that, and I always watch the news while I'm making the kids' breakfast."

"Me, neither. But that was the highway patrol, and they wouldn't call if they weren't pretty certain."

She sat down at her desk. "That's a first, isn't it?"

"As far as I know." Wild and feral pigs were a large and growing problem, but Jack had never heard of a fatal attack before, let alone one in which the pig had consumed an entire adult body. But if the trooper was right about the size of the track, then the pig in question was bigger than anything he'd ever encountered, and definitely posed a danger. Not to mention a number of questions as well, beginning with, where did it come from?

"So what are you going to do?" Georgina asked.

"First I'm going to drive over there and see what they've got."

"Where is 'over there'?"

"Cloud County."

Georgina looked up sharply. "That's where those emus got loose, isn't it?"

"Yeah." Against all odds, a feral population of emus had settled there, living in the hollows and small valleys and by all accounts thriving. Cates couldn't imagine how they survived the mountain winters, but there was no denying their presence. At least, unlike wild hogs, they hadn't spread beyond the county boundaries, and hadn't yet attacked anyone.

"That's also where the Tufa live, you know," she almost whispered.

"Is it a secret?" Jack whispered back.

"No, it's just . . . I always heard it was bad luck to talk about them out loud."

"Bad luck," he repeated skeptically.

"You're not from around here, Jack. There's some strange stories about them. They say they're part black, and that they brought a bunch of magic from Africa when they came over here. My grandpappy used to tell me that they'd steal children and eat 'em if you didn't say your prayers at night."

"Okay, first, I don't care what their race is. Second, I'm from Covington, which is not exactly a foreign country."

"It's West Tennessee, not East," she said seriously.

"And third, do you really believe in magic?"

"I don't know about that, but my cousin Beaurine told me she knew a woman who tried to cheat a Tufa man who'd done some work for her. The Tufa made some kind of hand sign at her, and told her she'd soon die from choking on her lying tongue. Well, about a month later, that woman dropped over from a heart attack, and when the doctors got to her, they found out she *had* swallowed her tongue. What do you say about that?"

"I'd say that I need a little more than thirdhand gossip to get my worry up." He headed back to his office.

"That isn't all I've heard, Jack," she called after him.

"That's all I've got time for," he responded.

Jack closed the door and nudged the mouse on his computer. The screen came alive with the TWRA home page, which featured an image of a feral hog in one corner. Clicking on that link took you to a page that contained history—the story of how the animals were never native to Tennessee, and had been illegally introduced all over the state for hunting—and the little video that explained the state's approach to eradicating them. Mostly it involved setting up corral traps that captured whole herds, which were then destroyed. In fact, it was illegal to do anything *other* than kill a trapped wild pig.

But there was another contingency plan, one Jack had put together on the sly with a few trusted friends, then presented to his TWRA superiors when it was ready to go. He opened his e-mail and typed in three addresses, then in the subject line, put *WHOMP.*

In the body of the message, he put a photo of an eye-patched David Hasselhoff as Nick Fury, from a TV movie long before Samuel L. Jackson had made the role his own. Beneath that he added the line, *WHOMP, Assemble.*

Ten minutes later, he looked at his computer screen, where a Skype conference call had been set up. Two men and a woman looked back at him.

"It's finally happened," he said. "A goddamn wild hog has killed somebody."

One of the men let out a low whistle. The other said, "Are you sure?"

"I am," the woman said. "I know the family. My mama went over there to sit with them yesterday right after it happened."

"I'm going there right now to confirm it," Jack said. "But assuming it's true, we'll need to get right on it. Are you all available?"

They nodded.

WHOMP—the Wild Hog Offensive Management Program—was a semiofficial organization Jack had set up when he first took this job. Experience told him that, with growing populations of both feral pigs and human beings, it was inevitable that someone would be seriously hurt or killed. He recruited these three for their expertise, knowing that if a hog did kill someone, it would need to be found, and eliminated, as quickly as possible.

So he had Dolph Pettit, the man who used to hold Jack's job before he retired to Gatlinburg; Max McMaynus, a veterinarian and expert on Tennessee wildlife from Jackson; and Bronwyn Chess, an army veteran in addition to being a full-blooded Tufa, something that now seemed like a huge asset, since they'd be operating in Cloud County.

Together, they would efficiently track, contain, and eliminate any porcine threat to human safety. And they'd do it discreetly, to avoid attracting other hunters who might be less diligent about hunting near people. In their previous four times in the field, eliminating hogs that had killed dogs, cats, and livestock, things had gone perfectly. They'd killed over three dozen feral hogs, and actually driven them completely out of certain areas. At least for a while.

"I'll be in touch tonight after I know for certain what we're up against," Jack said. "We'll make plans for tomorrow."

"Have to be a mighty big hog to kill someone," Dolph said. He was African American, with silver touching the temples of his hair and deep smile lines. In his career with the state, he'd personally killed over a thousand wild and feral pigs, and plenty more since retiring. "I knew some folks who got their legs and feet tore up good, but never anybody killed. I reckon if one of them tusks hit an artery and she bled out, that might do it."

"Not enough body found to tell," Jack said. "At least according to what the police told me."

"She was twenty-one years old, and hiking a trail that went through her own backyard," Bronwyn said. Her anger was palpable. "She was a sweet girl who had a whole life ahead of her. Let's not forget that with all this clinical talk about bodies and remains, okay?"

"Apologies, ma'am," Dolph said sincerely. "I meant no disrespect."

"And I'm not mad at you, Mr. Pettit," she said. "Just at a universe that would let this happen. Jack, I may see you out there today. We're taking some food over to the Rogerses'."

"Got it," Jack said. "The rest of you, keep your ears open. I'll be back in touch as soon as I know more."

They all signed off, and Jack sat back in his chair thoughtfully. He jumped as his phone rang. "Cates," he answered.

"Sounds like we got a problem, young man," Dolph said.

Jack did his internship under Dolph back in the early 2000s, and the experience taught him more than any class or textbook. He watched how the older man interacted with people, especially the ones he gave tickets and summons. Many white hunters weren't happy about being caught by an African American, but Dolph had a natural authority and common sense that either defused their racism or intimidated them into not expressing it.

"Remember one thing, young man," Dolph told him on his first day in Dolph's old job. "You have to live with these people long after that fine is paid or that suspension runs out. Treat 'em that way."

And even though Jack had held the post for several years now, he still treated Dolph as a superior, both in work and their personal relationship. "We do, indeed," he said. "A big problem, and a pig problem."

"How sure are you about this?"

"The trooper who called me sounded pretty sure."

"It ain't that ole Pafford boy, is it?"

"No, his name was . . . let me see . . . Darwin."

"That's good. Trooper Pafford was a piece of bad news on rye bread. Come to think of it, I think he's dead. Which is good news for everybody except maybe his dog, if he had one."

"I'll know more about the situation after I see for myself."

"I didn't want to say this on the conference call with the others, but I'd be more inclined to think it's a *long* pig rather than a wild pig."

"What's a long pig?"

"It's what cannibals call human beings."

"Ah."

"Might be hard to come up with a better way of disposing of a body than feeding it to the hogs. If there was a bullet in there, or a knife wound, or even poison, that'd make it pretty hard to find."

"Yeah, that crossed my mind, too. But since the state troopers say it's a pig, I wanted you guys on alert." He started to say something else, then stopped.

Dolph sensed it. "What?"

"Well . . . this all happened over near Needsville. You know what that means."

"Ah. Them Tufa."

"Yeah. I haven't dealt with 'em much before."

"That army girl you had on your conference call is a Tufa."

"And that's the only one I know." He'd met Bronwyn at a shooting range outside Unicorn, where she'd been teaching her tiny daughter how to handle the smallest bolt-action .22 rifle Jack had ever seen. The little girl, beneath ear protection that looked as big as her, had taken the whole thing very seriously, and Jack had struck up a conversation with her mother. When he asked her why she'd come all the way to a range instead of just going out behind her house, she'd said she wanted the girl, whose name escaped him at the moment, to hear lots of other gunfire so she wouldn't be afraid of it. "I don't know that I've been over to Needsville five times in the last six years," Jack added.

"Hell, I stayed away as much as I could, too."

"Why?"

There was a pause while Dolph mustered his answer. "You may think less of me for this answer, Jack, but they flat-out give me the creeps."

"Even Bronwyn?"

"Well, all pretty girls make me nervous," he chuckled. "But yeah, even her."

"How so?"

"They won't tell you shit, not really. They make these weird hand signs to each other when they think no one's watching. And they sing all the damn time."

"Sing? Like hymns, you mean?"

"Naw, ain't you ever noticed? There ain't a church in that county. Not even one of them snake-handling churches like they have over in Campbell County."

Jack bit back most of his sarcasm and said, "Thanks, Dolph. If I get cursed, I'll be sure to let you know."

"Now, don't be a smart-ass, youngster. I can still turn you over my knee and give you the whuppin' your daddy should've given you."

Jack smiled. "I bet you could, Dolph."

"You just watch yourself, and keep in touch."

"That I'll do. Thanks a bunch."

He hung up and leaned back in his chair. The more he thought about it, the more he suspected that this situation did not actually involve wild pigs, or if so, only tangentially. They were unpleasant invasive creatures who needed to be eradicated for the damage they did to the environment, but as a rule, they weren't killers. If a woman had died, he suspected there was ultimately a human hand involved in that.

But luckily, if that turned out to be the case, then it was not his problem.

6

"Did you hear about Kera Rogers?" Ginny Vipperman asked as she opened her locker at the Cloud County Consolidated High School. Classes were about to begin, and she loaded the textbooks she'd need for first period into her backpack. It was still early in the school year, and she hadn't gotten the routine down yet.

At the locker beside her, her best friend, Janet Harper, said, "Yeah, I heard she was killed."

"Oh, that's not the juicy part. She was *eaten*."

Janet's eyes opened wide. "What? Like, by a bear?"

"No, by a pig. A giant wild pig killed her and ate her." Ginny was almost gleeful with the news, not because she lacked empathy, but because it was so rare that she was able to impress her friend.

Janet was, even by Tufa standards, a musical prodigy, possibly on a scale with Mozart; she could play anything, had written songs and operas and even symphonies, and although she was only seventeen, was the best picker in the county. Her all-female band, Little Trouble Girls, was a growing YouTube sensation, and as soon as they all turned eighteen, Janet planned for them to start gigging all over the Southeast. Ginny, who played bass in the band, could hardly wait.

Janet had also been named editor of the school's newspaper, the *Raven's Caw*. Ginny expected her passion for that to fade just as every other nonmusical interest had done, but it hadn't happened yet. Janet had seen *His Girl Friday* on cable late one night, and now fast-talking, no-nonsense Hildy Johnson was her role model. Janet said, "So where did this happen? Who found the body? What are they doing?"

"You left out 'why,'" Ginny said.

"Come on, spill."

"That's really all I know. I heard my parents talking about it this morning. They shut up as soon as I came downstairs."

The five-minute warning bell sounded, and the hallways began to empty as students went to their classes. Janet growled her frustration. "I should be tracking this down, and instead we've got stupid algebra in five minutes."

"They offer stupid algebra? And here I was thinking it was the smart kind," Ginny deadpanned.

Janet wrinkled her nose at her in mock annoyance. "All right, thank you for the tip. Maybe during study hall, I can find out some things. The *Caw* has to cover this."

"Why? Kera hasn't been here in years. She was a senior when we were freshmen."

"Because there won't be anyone else writing about it. No one will talk to the *Weekly Horn* over in Unicorn, so it'll just be a form obituary."

"And you think people will talk to you?" Ginny said dubiously. "Why?"

"Because I'm a fucking charmer," Janet said, then turned on her heel and headed to class. Ginny shook her head and followed.

Jack Cates felt his stomach churn at the sight of the remains, small and insubstantial as they were, resting in a plastic bag on a table in the fire station kitchen. From the time he was a boy running shirtless and barefoot through the woods, he'd trained himself to imagine the entire animal based on the smallest clues: footprints, scat, tufts of fur, stray feathers. It was a skill he couldn't turn off, even when he wanted to. In college, he made an internal game out of identifying who left items of clothing behind in the dorm laundry room, and got so good at it, people started calling him "Sherlock." So now those two fingers and a thumb grew, in his mind, into the young woman whose pictures he'd been shown beaming proudly at her high school graduation, waving with a beer in her hand, and looking pensive in close-up as she hugged her dog. It made him sad, and angry, and sick.

But at least it settled one thing. Whatever killed her, pigs definitely *ate* her. And that meant they had to be dealt with at once.

The phone beside the door rang. It was an old rotary design, one of the few things that survived the fire that ironically destroyed the previous fire station.

"Excuse me," Bliss said, and answered it. "Fire department," she said softly, as if it would be rude to speak too loudly.

After listening for a moment, she said, "Okay, Mrs. Bundy, let me ask you one thing. Is the snake in your basement on fire? No? Then you should probably call Mr. Castellaw, he handles animal control for the county. Okay. Bye."

She returned to stand beside Jack. "Done?"

"More than."

She put the plastic bag back into the fire department freezer.

He looked back down to his phone. Bliss's photographs of the tracks took on an ominous feel, like something lurked in the woods just outside the station, waiting to strike. Again, he had no trouble imagining it in the flesh, scaling up from the hoof to the foot, all the way to the entire beast. The only surprise was accepting just how massive this particular wild pig must be.

"So it's a wild hog?" Alvin Darwin asked. He stood against the wall, his hat in his hand, watching the wildlife man with some skepticism. Jack suspected that Darwin was like other highway cops he'd encountered: he considered game wardens to be little more than parking enforcement officers who worked in the woods, meter maids with manure on their shoes.

"I'd say," Jack agreed. "With a whole herd along for the scraps." That was unusual, too; the big ones were usually solitary.

"How many?"

Jack gestured at the photo. "That's hard to tell. Ten pigs can root up the ground as bad as fifty if they're at it long enough."

"That ain't too specific."

Jack's eyes narrowed at the trooper's tone. "If you've got a crystal ball, you're welcome to look into it and be more definite."

Darwin didn't respond to the sarcasm. "So what do you think we should do about it?"

"I don't think we have any choice but to go out and hunt it down. It's like a bear that's hurt someone; once it's lost its fear of man, it's too dangerous to ignore."

"Do you think you can find it?" Bliss asked.

"I think I can lower the odds," Jack said. "I have some trained experts on call. I alerted them last night, and they can be here later today."

"Thanks," Bliss said.

"And what about you?" he said to Darwin.

"What, you want me to arrest a pig?"

"Well, it's a death. I assume some forms need to be filled out, at least."

"The paperwork will all been taken care of," Bliss said, stepping between the two men. "There's just the matter of this animal to deal with, and then the case can be closed."

Jack frowned. "This just happened *yesterday.* How can you say that?"

"Because it's true," Darwin said. "I've talked to everyone

involved. A long investigation won't change things. Unless you think the pig was framed?"

Jack *really* didn't like this guy. He had long-standing issues with traditional law enforcement treating their position as a license to brutalize and intimidate, and Darwin seemed no different from his predecessor, the notorious Bob Pafford.

Darwin was also clearly a Tufa, and he knew they were experts at misdirection, which might mean Darwin was deliberately trying to make him angry, to keep his attention focused anywhere other than the community where the girl had died. "I think," Jack said carefully, "that some people may ask questions if this is swept under the rug."

"You think there's a cover-up? A Hog-gate?"

"Guys," Bliss said, and snapped off her blue vinyl gloves. "I don't think it's the right time for this sort of pissing contest. We have a dead girl and a dangerous wild animal. Those are what we should be focusing on."

Darwin nodded. "Agreed. Sorry for getting off track."

Still seething, Jack also nodded. "All right. I'll get my people together, and the first thing we'll do is set up a bait trap at the incident site. We might get lucky and catch our boy right off the bat."

"If he's as big as you say, do you think a trap would hold him?" Darwin asked.

"Alvin," Bliss said quietly. "This is Jack's area. Let's let him plow the field with his own mule."

Darwin put on his hat, then touched the brim in salute. "Fair enough. I'll leave you to it, then, unless you call me."

Jack waited until Darwin had sauntered out of the station before saying, "That guy flat gets on my nerves. I imagine I'll be getting lots of tickets now that I've pissed him off."

"He's not like that," Bliss said.

"Yeah?"

"Yeah. Now—what sort of trap have you got in mind?"

Jack forced his mind back to work. "What we usually do is put up an automatic corn feeder first, then let them get used to it for a few days. Then we put a pen around it and a drop gate. We let 'em get used to that before we drop the gate. That way we hope to catch the whole herd."

"How do you know when they're in the trap?"

"Use a trail cam with a live feed." He paused. "Did you know the girl?"

"I did. Known her since she was little. Used to play with her at our local roadhouse. She played the pennywhistle."

"What do you play?"

"I play the guitar, mostly. You?"

"I've been known to annoy a piano."

She smiled, and Jack suddenly realized how pretty she was. He'd met her on several occasions before, always in her capacity as an EMT, with her long black hair braided and piled up on her head. But here she wore it loose, and it framed her high cheekbones and bright, intelligent eyes. He'd heard some odd stories about Tufa women and girls, and not just from Georgina; but he couldn't imagine Bliss Overbay as the source of anything so extreme and, ultimately, ridiculous.

"I'll admit I share your concern that perhaps her death was more suspicious than Alvin thinks," she said. "Would a hog really kill someone?"

"One that's big enough and feels threatened, yeah. It's rare, but it has happened. That's why we're trying to wipe them out."

"If you catch it, will you be able to tell if it was the killer?"

"If we catch it soon enough, I can tell what it's eaten based on its stomach contents. But no, I can't tell how that meal died."

Bliss got herself a paper cup and some water. After she drank, she said, "This is one of the most awful conversations I've ever had, do you know that?"

"It's right up there for me, too. Or down there, I should say."

"Come on," Bliss said as she opened the door. "You can follow me out to the scene of the crime."

And he did follow her, admiring her feminine silhouette.

First the tune penetrated his consciousness, then the words.

I found the trail of the mountain mist,
the mountain mist, the mountain mist
I found the trail of the mountain mist,
But ne'er a trace of baby. . . .

Duncan snapped awake to find his mother, Bobbie, singing softly as she looked down at him. He jumped.

"Sorry," she said. "I didn't mean to scare you."

He sat up, then immediately regretted it. His head thundered, and his stomach churned. At first he thought he was back in his old bedroom, but then he realized he was, in fact, in his apartment. How had she gotten in?

"What are you doing here, Mom?" he croaked. She'd even opened the blinds, flooding his aching eyeballs with bright morning sun.

"You didn't answer your phone, and after what happened yesterday, I was worried."

"Me, too," a new voice said. He turned toward it, glad the hangover hid the rush of emotions that flew through him.

Adam Procure.

"I heard you were down at the old 'shine cave, and got pretty wasted," Adam continued. He was freshly scrubbed, his black hair still damp from a recent shower, and wore a faded Skrillex T-shirt over his enviably muscular torso. Duncan was filled with jealousy, resentment, and rage.

However, he was also filled with the dregs of whatever he'd

drunk last night, and that took priority. So he said, "Y'all might want to back up," and gave out a warning burp.

"Come on," Adam said, grabbed him by the arm, and heaved him upright. He carried him the few feet across the bedroom to the bathroom just in time.

Duncan threw up, long and agonizingly deep, the physical pain made worse by the knowledge that both his mother and the man his dead girlfriend had been cheating with watched him. His body wrenched tight, then relaxed, then seized up again, and his fingers scraped against the porcelain as they sought a steady grip.

"Oh, son," he heard his mother say. "I didn't raise you to be the kind of man who drinks that stuff."

"That stuff" was the moonshine they brewed right there in the cave, made in ways so unsafe, almost everyone involved in its manufacture had burn scars—or worse. Cloud County paint thinner, indeed.

At last, his throat on fire and his stomach still in knots, Duncan rolled onto his back and looked up at the water-stained ceiling. "I think I'm done," he choked out.

"Can you stand?" Adam asked.

"Turn off the turntable I'm on, and maybe."

Bobbie said, "I'll get some coffee brewing. Adam, can you help him into the shower?"

"I don't need help," Duncan muttered, and rolled over. He pushed himself up onto his hands and knees, then used the toilet for support as he got to his feet. The room spun, as he expected, and he stumbled back into the wall. He braced his legs and grabbed the edge of the sink. "Do not," he said with great care, "try to undress me, Adam."

"Man, if I had a nickel for every time I'd heard that," he chuckled. "Always been from girls before, though."

Not here, Duncan told himself. *Not now.* But his anger and hatred burned even worse than his esophagus.

The shower did help clear his head and settle his stomach, and when he finished, his mother had a fresh cup of coffee for him. He sat down at his little bistro table opposite Bobbie and sipped the hot liquid. His throat and stomach protested, but the caffeine did its job. Adam stood beside him, radiating sympathy.

"There's no real news about anything," Bobbie said. "I reckon the wildlife people are going to try to kill the hog that did it."

"That's good," Duncan muttered.

"I wish I could go get after it," Adam said. "It'd be better if a Tufa got it, and sang its little ham hock soul to hell in the process."

A little bell went off in Duncan's head, the germ of an idea, but he was far too fuzzy-brained to pursue it. He said, "I need to get back out there and see Brenda and Sam. They must be feeling terrible."

"I'm not sure you're up to going anywhere," Bobbie said.

"I'll be fine once I get something greasy in me," he said, and got to his feet. "I've got some sausage in the fridge, and—"

"And nothing," Bobbie said. "You sit down, I'll cook you something. Adam, you hungry?"

"I can always eat, Mrs. Gowen," Adam said genially, and took the seat that Bobbie vacated. "And sausage feels appropriate."

A joke, Duncan thought. *The smug SOB is making a joke about this.*

As Bobbie puttered in the kitchen, Adam leaned close and said, "How are you, man? Really?"

"I'm pretty fucking shitty," Duncan said honestly.

"Yeah. I know you can't talk with your mom here, but . . . what did you get into last night?"

He had a vague memory of encountering Flint, then talking with Junior, and of sitting on a bench in a corner, moping and drinking moonshine. At some point, he must have been screaming, because he also recalled being shaken awake, a circle of concerned faces around him. Things got blurry again after that.

"I just drove around," he said. "I know, drinking and driving, blah blah blah. But," he added snidely, "it was a special occasion."

"Well, you can hang out with me today. I got my banjo in the car. We'll play a little when your hands stop shaking. Get back to normal."

What normal? he thought. *The normal where I have a girlfriend who loves me, or the normal where she's cheating with you behind my back?*

Suddenly he sat up straight. Adam said worriedly, "What?"

The phone. Duncan looked around, terrified that he'd left Kera's phone out in the open. But it wasn't on the table, or on the nightstand. Where the hell was it? Had he left it in his truck?

"Nothing," Duncan said. More images from the prior night came to him. He had, at some point, screamed at Flint, demanding to see Junior again. Why had he wanted to do that? He recalled Flint's ethereal voice singing . . . something. Then nothing else until he woke up.

Before Adam could press him, Bobbie brought two plates of scrambled eggs and sausage to the table, and he began to eat. With each bite, his stomach settled, and that little germ of an idea began to grow.

He managed a tired smile at Adam. His ostensible friend smiled innocently back. *Yeah, just keep grinning, asshole,* he thought. *Just keep grinning.*

Jack let the pocket tape measure snap back into its little case. Bliss's photograph had not exaggerated things. The print was truly gigantic, and all the implications that it carried filled Jack with a kind of dread he'd never felt before. He'd hunted most animals in these mountains, including bear, but even a bear print didn't scare him like this did. The ramifications of its size, and the certainty of its ferocity, set a cold knot in his belly.

Bliss stood back beyond the yellow crime scene tape and let

him do his work, measuring and photographing, while she kept watch with a rifle in her hands. The woods were solemn, with even the birdsong muted, as if in respect. Or terror.

He stood, wiped his hands on his pants, and said, "I don't know if this hog did kill that girl, but I know he damn well could have." He looked up the hill, where the woods closed in and provided the kind of dark shadowy spaces that might very well hide monsters. "I reckon this one weighs around eight hundred pounds, based on the size and depth of those tracks."

"Eight hundred pounds?" Bliss repeated. "How is that even possible?"

"Unlimited feed," Jack said. "This hog didn't grow that big in the wild. He got loose from somewhere."

"Where? I mean, everybody around here pretty much has a few pigs, but I haven't heard of anyone raising one that big."

"Would you? Hear about it, I mean."

"It's a small town. I think I would."

"That's something I'll be looking into, then. This beauty would be about seven feet long. Probably have tusks about like this," he said as he held his hands about nine inches apart.

"Even if it was raised on a farm?"

"Depends on how long ago it got loose. Pigs go feral within six months. They grow hair, tusks, the works. That's how thin their domestication is."

"Jesus." She peered into the forest shadows, searching for any sign of movement. Normally wild hogs wouldn't come near a human scent, but anything this big was decidedly not normal.

"I don't want to waste any time," Jack said, and took out his phone. "My team will be in here this afternoon to set up the trap. Pigs are creatures of habit: they like to use the same trails, so it's pretty likely they'll be back around here tonight."

"I hope it's that easy."

He began to text his photographs to the members of WHOMP. "You and me both."

7

Janet skipped her after-lunch study hall and cornered Mr. Pirtle, the English teacher and de facto sponsor for the student paper, alone in the faculty lounge. He wasn't a Tufa, but he understood them after teaching there for twenty years, and knew more about them than even they suspected. He had curly brown hair, a mostly gray mustache, and absolutely no patience with teenage nonsense. Janet adored him.

"I've got a line on a big story, Mr. Pirtle," she said as she sat down opposite him.

"Janet. Please, sit down. The sign on the door says 'Absolutely No Students,' but I'm delighted that you've realized that couldn't possibly apply to you."

She waved her hand as if his sarcasm buzzed around her face. "I'm serious. This story is the best thing ever."

"I assume you don't mean 'A Rose for Emily'?"

"There's been a murder."

"Oh, so you *did* read the Faulkner?"

"*Stop* that," Janet said impatiently. "Kera Rogers was killed yesterday."

"I heard about that. I believe it was an accident, and will no doubt be thoroughly covered by—"

"How are you *accidentally* eaten by a pig? 'Whoops, I tripped and fell into that pig's stomach. How embarrassing.'"

Pirtle took off his glasses and smiled despite himself. "You definitely have the attitude of a real old-school reporter, Janet, I'll give you that. Lois Lane and Carl Kolchak are no doubt smiling down on us at this very moment. But that story, while certainly sensational and tragic, has nothing to do with the school. And therefore the *Caw* has no interest in it."

"Kera is an alumni. She has a lot of relatives who still go here."

"Janet, everyone in this county has a lot of relatives who go here. And I'm sure they'll hear all about it from their families. And one female person is an 'alumna,' with an *a*."

"Really? I never heard that word before."

"Then I've taught you something despite yourself."

She leaned forward in her chair "Come on, Mr. Pirtle. This is huge. We have to write something about it. Hell, it should be on the front page." When Pirtle's eyebrows rose at her profanity, Janet quickly added, "I mean, 'Heck, it should be on the front page.'"

Pirtle sighed. The only thing worse than an apathetic student was a crusading one, and he'd expected this ever since Janet was named editor. Everyone warned him that all that mattered to her was music, and that journalism would not hold her interest for long; it was Pirtle's bad luck that the Rogers girl had decided to get eaten so close to the beginning of the school year.

And then he felt terrible for that thought. He'd taught Kera Rogers, had watched her go from a lanky freshman to a beautiful senior, had heard her play her pennywhistle in the school's jam band so sweetly, it once brought tears to his jaded old eyes. He remembered the way she helped the younger kids find the more complex chords on their guitars, delighting in their progress just as any teacher would. Just as *he* should with Janet.

"All right, see what you can find out," Pirtle said seriously. "But it goes through me. With a crime like this, there are some details that just won't fly in a student paper."

Now Janet's eyebrows rose. "Are you censoring me? Is this prior restraint, because I'm pretty sure we learned in civics class that that doesn't fly."

"This is common sense," Pirtle said. "If you give the people more than they can stomach, they won't absorb any of it. And all the grisly details are not what they want, or at least not most of them. There's that whole Gwinn clan who'd probably love it, but for the rest of us, we'll try to stay dignified and above it all."

"I don't remember 'dignity' being a concern of Woodward and Bernstein."

"They just didn't talk about it, because in those days, it was intrinsic. Do you know what that word means?"

"Of course," she snapped back. "Just because I live on a mountain don't mean I'm dumb as a rock. *Doesn't* mean," she corrected quickly.

"And remember: Kera was a human being, just like you. She had the same dreams, the same desires, the same hopes for the future. She lost all that, and so did the people who loved her, the people who are going to read what you wrote. Be truthful, but be kind when you can."

"Yes, sir," Janet said, barely able to contain her excitement. She jumped up and ran out to use the computer in the library.

When he was sure she was gone, Pirtle laughed. Everyone knew that Janet Harper was destined for great things, and most people were content to just stay out of her way. But even genius needed to be pointed in the right direction. With Janet, he always imagined a billiard ball careening off all the bumpers and scattering the rest of the balls before finally landing in the right pocket.

When Duncan arrived at the Rogers house, there were a dozen cars and trucks parked in the yard and along the gravel road.

Death was a big deal to the Tufa. There were rumors outside

Cloud County that Tufa didn't die unless you killed one, but that wasn't true. Well . . . not for everyone. What *was* true was that when one of them did die, it affected them all. There were so few of them left, any loss sent ripples through the community. Songs were lost, secrets never revealed, and the night winds blew with one less rider. The circle might stay unbroken, but it grew smaller.

The first person he saw as he approached the house was Gerald Parrish. They had lost their son Rayford last year, while he was working in New York City. Gerald stood beside Deacon Hyatt, who had also lost a son a few years earlier in a rare incidence of fatal Tufa-on-Tufa violence. Their presence meant that their wives were inside with Kera's parents.

"Duncan," Gerald Parrish said. "I know you was sweet on her. I'm real sorry for your loss, son."

"Thank you, Mr. Parrish," he said, and shook the man's hand.

Deacon Hyatt patted him on the shoulder. "It'll get easier. Not better, but easier."

"I appreciate that, Mr. Hyatt." It was rote politeness, the kind of social interaction that smoothed over the jagged edges no one wanted to acknowledge.

He went inside. The living room was filled with people, all seated, with Brenda and Sam on the couch, holding court. Page Paine sat in a corner playing her fiddle. The sound seemed to gather all the sadness in the room into long, faint notes.

Brenda's eyes were red from crying, and she clutched Kera's graduation picture in its plain black frame. Despite himself, Duncan looked at the picture's image of her bare shoulders in the black drape. How many times had he kissed the little hollow there, or run his fingers lightly along that collarbone? That thin chain was even still around her neck, the buffalo nickel hanging out of sight beneath the drape.

Make the buffalo roam.

He looked around for Adam, but he wasn't here.

"Bless your heart, Duncan," Brenda said when she saw Duncan. "Thank you so much for coming."

He bent down and hugged her. He felt shudders go through her body, the aftershocks of sobs. She was too exhausted to cry right now; he knew that feeling.

He shook Sam's hand and said, "Mr. Rogers, if there's anything I can do, you just let me know." Then he took a deep breath and added, softly so the others wouldn't hear, "If you've got a second, I sure would appreciate a moment of your time."

"Sure, Duncan," he said numbly. He squeezed his wife's hand reassuringly, then got to his feet. They went into the kitchen, where the table was laden with food, including an absurd amount of potato salad. The three people gathered there discreetly slipped out, sensing the two men wanted privacy.

"Cyrus Crow sent us all this," Sam muttered. "Reckon he figures we're a might short on tater salad." He worked one finger beneath the cling wrap and dipped into the bowl.

"Mr. Rogers, I want your blessing for something," Duncan said.

"What's that?"

"Me and Adam Procure are going to go kill that damn pig."

Sam smiled, but it was so weak, it barely touched the corners of his mouth. "Duncan, I think you best leave that to the folks who know what they're doing. I done spoke to the game warden, and he's going to take care of it. But I sure do appreciate you wanting to do it."

"I'm serious, Mr. Rogers. I've got nothing against them wildlife folks, but they ain't lost anybody. We have. I want to even it up as much as I can."

"You think a pig's life will balance out Kera's?"

"No, sir, that ain't what I'm saying. I'm just saying that fucking . . . excuse me, that *damn* animal needs to go down by the hand of someone who suffered from what it did."

"And how will that help?"

Duncan had no real answer for that.

"Duncan, I know it always seemed like I didn't care for you, and to tell the truth, I didn't. I wanted better for Kera."

Again Duncan had no response.

Sam licked the last of the potato salad from his meaty fingertip. "But I can't deny that I know how you felt about her, so I know that right now, me and you, we're closer than family. We're men with our hearts broke."

Duncan nodded.

"Last night I stood out in that backyard, my old deer rifle loaded, and dared that hog to come out. I sang to it, I called to it, I begged the night winds to send it my way. They didn't. And this morning, when I woke up to a house without my baby girl in it, I understand why."

"Why, sir?"

"Because it ain't my place to do it. Just like it ain't yours. Killing that hog won't spackle over that crack in your heart. Only time can do that. And if you let yourself get all righteous and angry about it, then all that stuff will stay in your heart once it does heal up. Kera wouldn't want that for either one of us."

He patted Duncan's shoulder and went to rejoin his wife. Duncan didn't mind. His whole purpose in coming here was to establish that his motives for hunting the pig were pure, and in a sense, they were: despite Sam's warning, he did want to be the one to put a bullet in its stinky, bristly hide.

But his other plan, the one that began to form over breakfast that morning, involved another bullet. And even though he doubted he had the nerve to follow through, he still enjoyed thinking about it, and planning it, and imagining it coming to fruition up there in the dense forest on Dunwoody Mountain, or over the hill in Half Pea Hollow.

8

It was midafternoon before the WHOMP team gathered at the site of Kera Rogers's death. They were grim and single-minded, as befitted an elite force.

Dolph Pettit wore camouflage pants with many pockets, and carried a Sako Finnlight .260 Remington. Max McMaynus dressed in a bark-pattern jumpsuit and toted an Ambush 300 Blackout rifle slung by a strap over his shoulder. Bronwyn Chess wore black, with her dark hair tucked up into a black baseball cap marked with the WHOMP logo: the letters in white stitching, except for the *O,* which contained a snarling boar's face crossed with a red line, like the *Ghostbusters* emblem. She carried a Hoyt Spyder Turbo compound bow.

Jack faced them like a commander briefing his troops, his own 20-gauge Savage M220 Stainless camouflage-patterned shotgun loose in his hands, the barrel pointed at the ground. "I want to thank y'all for coming out here today. If we're lucky, the pigs will come back through here tonight or tomorrow morning. They came around here last night, or at least a few of them did, according to the tracks."

"Any sign of the big one?" Max asked.

"Nothing conclusive. But we'll assume he's running with them."

"Why?" Dolph asked. "The big ones—"

"I know," Jack interrupted. "But the tracks were all made at the same time. For whatever reason, he's with a herd."

"Damn," Max said, and shook his head.

"Normally we'd put up the feeder for a few days before setting up the corral," Jack continued, "but under the circumstances, I don't think we can wait."

"If we mess up," Dolph said, "that'll trap-spook 'em. We'll never get 'em in one."

"We'll have to take that chance. This is about a lot more than property damage."

Bronwyn said, "How big is the one we're after again?"

"I estimate around eight hundred pounds," Jack said. "Seven- to nine-inch tusks. I assume it's a farm escapee, since it'd be hard to find enough food to grow that big in the wild. But I could be wrong."

"You might need something more heavy-duty than that pot sticker," Max said teasingly to Bronwyn.

"All depends on where in the pot you stick 'em," she said.

"I'm hoping it won't come to that," Jack said. "If we can get him in the trap, we can put him down quickly. I admit it, I don't cotton to hunting him down on foot."

"We could set up a blind here, instead of a trap," Dolph said. "What do you think, Max?"

He shrugged. "Yeah, I could put up in a tree blind. I've got a seat in my truck. If it looks like it won't go for the trap, I can tap it."

"Let's do that," Jack said. "We'll come get you out, whatever happens, so you don't have to come back by yourself in the dark."

"That's appreciated," Max said.

"We'll set up a trail cam we can watch on my laptop from the Rogers house," Jack said.

"Yeah, but I don't know if we should just assume it's okay to use their place," Bronwyn said. "The wake's still going on. And I mean, would you want to see the animal that killed and ate your child?"

"Will you ask them?" Jack said. "If you're right and it bothers them, then we'll just take turns sitting and watching in my truck down the road a ways."

"Sure," Bronwyn said.

They headed back down the trail toward the house, each of them calmly watching the woods for something they knew lurked out there. A wild hog would normally never hunt a human being, but this was no normal animal, and none of them were taking any chances. This beast already had enough blood on its tusks.

Adam looked at Duncan in disbelief. "No way."

"Why not?"

"Well, because I ain't no hunter, for one thing. If it's bigger than a squirrel or a rabbit, you can have it. I've never even shot a deer. And for another thing, I hear the game warden's got professionals already out looking for it. We can't compete with that. I'd rather just wait and spit on its carcass."

They sat across a table at the Pair-A-Dice, the local roadhouse that served as a neutral gathering place for both sides of the Tufa community. The beer Duncan sipped deadened the last of his hangover, and gave him the courage he needed to move his plan forward.

On the little stage in the corner, an old woman sawed away at her fiddle. Her technique was crude, but there was no denying the ache that sailed forth from her instrument. She was the last of eleven children, the only sister, and you could feel the loss of each and every brother in her playing. It was like she was tapping into the very feelings Duncan was doing his best to suppress in himself.

She sang in a high voice that trembled with age,

And once they gave Arete as bride in the foreign lands
and years of misery and months of anger came
and death fell upon them and the nine brothers died
the mother was left all alone. . . .

Duncan closed his eyes against a sudden fresh rush of nausea. Or was it revulsion—at himself, at what he planned, at a world that let such thoughts exist?

He stood up and threw his coaster at the old woman. "Goddamn, ain't we depressed enough? Play something about somebody alive, will ya?"

He dropped back into his chair. For a moment, there was dead silence; then the old woman resumed her song, and conversation returned all around them. He didn't listen to see if it was now all about him.

"Wow," Adam said quietly. "You're awfully wound up."

"My girlfriend just died," he snapped back. Then he watched for any response.

Adam only nodded. "Yeah. I'd probably be wound up, too."

The nerve, he thought. *The sheer nerve of this asshole. How can he just sit there like that?* He started to ask him about it straight up, demand the truth about him and Kera. But he'd seen the pictures and read the texts; there could be no doubt. It wasn't one of those TV-movie misunderstandings. There had been a selfie of the two of them in bed, bare-shouldered and tousle-haired; what else could it be? And now here was Adam complaining that *he* was too "wound up."

I'll show you wound up, he thought. *Just wait.* "So are we on for tomorrow?"

"Duncan, it's crazy. It won't accomplish anything."

"It might settle her haint."

"Her haint?" Adam repeated, a little too loudly. More softly, he asked, "Holy shit, man, have you *seen* her?"

"No," Duncan said quickly. Haints were nothing to joke about in Cloud County, and he couldn't believe he'd been so clumsy. "I'm just saying, if she *is* restless, she'll stay that way until someone who—" And here he caught himself, but there was nothing for it, he had to keep plowing ahead. "—loves her," he continued, "avenges her death."

"But you don't know that she *is* restless."

"And you don't know that she's *not.* Come on, Adam, grow a pair. Let's go find this fucker and put him down."

"Where do we even look?"

"Down in Half Pea Hollow."

"Why there?"

"It's just over Dunwoody Mountain from Kera's place, and nobody ever goes there."

"You know why, too."

"You believe it's haunted?"

"I believe it's a bad idea to go traipsing through it to find out."

"We're not going there to find out if it's haunted. We're going to find a wild pig. Look, just come with me. We come in from each end of the hollow, catch whatever's in there between us, and wipe it the fuck out. Then we bring that sucker's head back on the hood of my car."

Adam thought it over. "Well . . . I wouldn't mind seeing it dead, that's for sure."

"That's right," Duncan said, keeping his elation in check. "You bring that Nosler your daddy's got up on the wall, and it wouldn't stand a chance. That thing would stop a buffalo."

Adam tapped his fingertips on the tabletop, thinking. It took all Duncan's self-control not to try to persuade him more, but he wanted to make sure Adam had time to choose this path himself. Then whatever happened would be Adam's own fault.

"All right," Adam said at last. "When?"

"First thing tomorrow morning."

"What time?"

"Four."

"Jesus. Does the world even exist that early?"

"We want to be out there at first light. I'll call you at three thirty to make sure you're awake."

"No, I'll be awake. Just be quiet when you drive up, and don't gun your engine or anything." Adam lived above the detached garage at his cousin's place; Duncan had been there many times, and now fought down the image of Kera naked on Adam's old trundle bed.

Adam drank from his beer and turned to listen to the music. Duncan watched his handsome profile, the way his chin jutted out just enough, the way his black hair swept back from his face. *Soon enough, you smug* GQ*-looking SOB,* he thought. *Soon enough.*

Mandalay Harris sat at the desk in her bedroom and waited for the other end of the phone call to pick up. Her homework was spread out before her, but that could wait; it never took her long, anyway. Right now, she needed to speak to the person who refused to pick up his damn phone.

It rang many times, too many, and never went to voice mail, but she knew he was there. She tapped the beaded fringe around the shade of her desk lamp, enjoying the way the afternoon sun sparkled on the little aluminum beads. Her concentration had been lacking at school, and her teachers noticed it. Ms. Ogletree, whose New Age hippie past meant she never got upset, had pointed out that Mandalay "seemed to be awfully bummed out." Mandalay put it down to Kera Rogers's death, which was the talk of the school. But while that might be part of it, it was far from all.

Which was why she grew more and more annoyed with each ring.

At last he picked up. "What?" Junior said.

She responded, "It's me."

"Who?"

She sighed impatiently. "Jesus, Junior, don't tell me you don't have my name programmed into your phone."

"All right, whatever. What do you want?"

"Something's in the wind. Do you feel it?"

"Yes."

"No, you don't. That's why I'm telling you."

"If you're so goddamn smart, tell me what it is, then."

"If I knew, I would. I think it's got something to do with Kera Rogers's death."

"A pig ate her. No mystery about that."

"Maybe. But keep your eyes open, will you? And if you suspect anything, tell me. We have to work together, remember."

"Is this how you worked with Rockhouse?"

"No. And you see how it turned out for him."

"Hmph," Junior said. He knew perfectly well what had happened to Rockhouse, now buried on Emania Knob: first robbed of his voice when his own betrayed daughter tore out his throat, then mutilated by Bo-Kate Wisby when she tried to claim his position and take over the Tufa. "Well, I'll let you know."

He hung up. Mandalay gazed at her phone, pondering once again how such a weak, sniveling loser could have ended up in the place of the monumentally cruel Rockhouse Hicks. Was she being too hard on him? she wondered. Or was there more at play here than she knew, things and plots going on behind the scenes? Rockhouse, whatever else Mandalay might have thought about him, was all on the surface. He wanted power, and respect, and fear; he had no interest in outmaneuvering anyone. If he came after you, he came at your face.

Junior, though, was different. Mandalay had honestly expected him to implode by now, to give up his position and return to his miserable life with his unpleasant family. But he'd hung on, and his people seemed satisfied with his leadership. He deferred to Mandalay whenever she insisted on it, but each time, he did it with less and less alacrity. Soon he might actually stand up to her. Then what?

If he was building to something, she'd have to watch for it. As unlikely as it seemed, she'd hate to be caught off guard, especially if it was due to her own overconfidence.

A noise made her turn suddenly, but there was nothing behind her. It had sounded like a laugh. No, like a *particular* laugh. The laugh of a cruel old man.

She'd done all she could to ensure that Rockhouse Hicks stayed buried. His blood had been drained and disposed of separately, and every song she knew that would keep the dead where they belonged had been sung over his grave. So he couldn't come back, not as a Tufa, not as a haint.

Then why, she wondered, did she keep imagining she heard the bark of his cold, cruel, malicious laughter? And what if it wasn't her imagination?

After sundown, Jack Cates, Bronwyn Hyatt, and Dolph Pettit sat around the old table on the Rogerses' back porch. It had once been in their dining room, but Sam had built a new one when this one began to wobble. An old romance paperback titled *Wickedly Dangerous* was stuck beneath one leg, providing stability if no one leaned on it too hard. The chairs had all-weather seat cushions.

Fireflies dotted the yard and the trees that surrounded it. Inside the house, the Rogerses still visited with Bronwyn's parents, the Hyatts, as the soft music of fiddle, guitar, and mandolin drifted out. Playing music together was how the Tufa dealt with everything, and death was no different.

The night was cool and humid, and the mist grew thick in the forest. Jack's laptop screen glowed in the darkness, and he swiped at the insects drawn to its light. On-screen, in the grainy black-and-white of night vision, they watched the trap they'd set up earlier in the day, positioned on the relatively flat area of the trail downslope from Recliner Rock.

It was a small corral about thirty feet across, with a six-foot-tall grain feeder on four legs in the center. Corn formed a trail from the pile beneath the feeder through the gate, which could be dropped remotely.

Although they couldn't see him, Max McMaynus sat in a tree about ten yards away, with a clear view of the area around the trap's gate. He was fifteen feet off the ground, his back against a trunk big enough to block the edges of his silhouette. He was practiced enough to have the necessary patience for this sort of hunting.

He had the 300 Blackout across his lap. It was not, as they say, a "sport" weapon; it was a killing rifle, made by the sporting division of a national defense contractor, but there was no sport to it. A silencer made the rifle quiet enough that, if needed, he could hopefully get off a second shot before the monster had even registered the first.

The clip was loaded with .300 Barnes TAC-TX cartridges that, if he got the right shot, should pierce the hog's hide and tear mercilessly through its organs. It was a problematic shot in the best of situations, and at night, from a tree stand, it would be especially tricky. The area around the trap was lit with red light invisible to the hogs, but hopefully it provided enough illumination for Max's aim through his night-vision scope. He wanted to put this fucker away with the first slug.

The watchers drank iced tea provided by the Rogerses; old Dolph had spiked his, but only lightly. The other two were wide awake and stone-cold sober.

The music paused, and a muted sob came from inside the

house. Bronwyn glanced up and saw, through the window, her mother, Chloe, with her arms around Brenda Rogers. The women were bound by the shared pain of losing a child, and for Bronwyn, a relatively new parent, it sent a jolt of terror and despair through her. She could imagine nothing worse; even losing her big brother, Kell—the worst thing that had happened to her so far—would pale beside it. "How long you reckon this might take?" she asked softly.

"I guess it depends on how hungry they are," Jack said. "The corral and feeder might spook 'em, like Dolph said. I'm hoping since they ate something here already, they'll be more amenable to finding more food."

They fell silent. The old dog Quigley walked to the edge of the yard and stood gazing up into the dark woods. He gave no sign that he smelled or heard anything; he just remained there with his head raised. To Jack, it was a little spooky.

After another few minutes of nothing, Dolph said, "Y'all ever heard of a *barghest*?"

"Sure," Jack said dryly. "I'm a bar guest any chance I get."

"I have," Bronwyn said. "It's a British thing, I think." She knew exactly what he meant, but also knew better than to claim that, because more questions would inevitably follow, and the answers were not for non-Tufa ears.

"That's right," Dolph said.

"No need to sound so surprised," Bronwyn said dryly.

"My apologies."

"Well, I haven't," Jack said. "What is it?"

"It's an animal that acts as an omen of death," Dolph said.

"We've got plenty of those," Bronwyn said, thinking of the owl that heralded her brother's passing.

"It's usually a big black ghost dog, like the *Hound of the Baskervilles,*" Dolph continued. "But sometimes it can be a pig."

"You think this an evil ghost pig?" Jack said dubiously.

"I'm just passing on something I read." To Bronwyn, he said,

"Has anyone mentioned seeing this thing before it attacked that girl?"

"I asked around," she said. "Nobody has."

"That's not exactly evidence," Jack said skeptically.

"And I ain't exactly a lawyer," Dolph said. "I'm just sayin'."

"Hey," Jack said suddenly. "Look."

On the screen, a single hog now stood at the entrance to the corral, nosing at the ground and rooting up the fallen corn. In the unseen infrared illumination, its eyes glowed white and vaguely demonic. Using the gate as a scale, it was no bigger than a normal pig, certainly not the monster they sought. It might even be someone's livestock, broken free and wandering. It betrayed no hesitation about the metal pen, as if it knew exactly what it was and where it came from.

As they watched, two more joined it, along with a half-dozen piglets. One of the babies followed the corn trail into the pen.

Jack had spent many tedious nights watching this sort of thing, waiting for the right moment to drop the gate. Yet this time, his hands were damp with nervous sweat.

Four adult hogs were in the pen now, and another three foraged outside. None of them was larger than average, nor did any of them show the slightest hesitation about the trap. If they were wild, they were first-generation feral.

"Maybe it's a different bunch," Dolph said. "Are you going to trap them?"

The automatic dispenser whirred, dropping fresh corn from the feeder. The hogs scurried away, some outside the pen, some up against the fence.

"Shit," Jack muttered.

Once the corn finished dispensing, though, the pigs resumed feeding as if nothing had happened. Many of them had no doubt encountered feeders before, especially if they had escaped from farms before going wild.

Now eight were inside. Jack moved the cursor over the button that would drop the gate. Even though this herd didn't include the one they sought, these animals needed to be taken out of circulation.

"Dolph," he said quietly, "text Max and tell him I'm about to let 'er rip. We can get a few more hogs out of circulation, at least."

"Got it," Dolph said, and pulled out his phone.

Jack was about to click the button when Bronwyn gasped, "Wait! Look."

Something moved out of the darkness. At first Jack didn't even realize it was an animal; he thought it was just a shadow artifact from the video camera, a pixilation of the image due to the light source. Then he caught the glint of one eye blazing infrared-white in the darkness.

"Jesus Christ," Dolph whispered.

"Jesus didn't have teeth like that," Jack said.

The hog was enormous, easily three times as big as the others. It moved across the camera's field of vision the way a distant mountain moves when you're driving fast on the interstate. The smaller pigs ignored its presence and continued to root at the spilled corn.

"Looks like something from *The Late Late Show,*" Dolph said.

"More like the SyFy Channel," Bronwyn said. " 'Mega-Pig.' Don't suppose that size is a trick of the lens?"

"Nope," Jack said. "It's really that big."

She looked back inside the house. She'd hate for Brenda or Sam to emerge and catch sight of the monster that killed and ate their daughter. She moved to the side to block any accidental glimpse.

The huge hog strode slowly back and forth in front of the pen's gate, momentarily scattering its smaller brethren. Jack had to zoom out to get the whole creature in the image. He'd never seen anything like it, or even imagined he would; and the knowledge that it was now his responsibility filled him with a level of fear he'd never experienced at this job. Bears, poisonous snakes, mountain lions . . . they were all dangerous, and all part of his work. He had respect for them, but didn't fear them. This animal, though, terrified him.

When it presented its rear to them, they saw its huge testicles. "Well, hello, handsome," Bronwyn said.

"Why isn't it eating?" Jack asked.

"Maybe he isn't hungry," Bronwyn said.

"Never saw a hog that wasn't hungry," Dolph muttered.

The animal finally tipped its huge snout down to the corn and nosed up a mouthful. By then even more of the others had moved into the pen, leaving only dregs on the ground. The monster tried to follow them, but it was too broad to get through the gate. Apparently oblivious, it pushed until the metal began to bend, and the whole pen started to wrench up from the ground.

"Holy shit," Dolph whispered.

"We drove those posts down two feet," Bronwyn said.

"So much for that plan," Jack said. "I hope Max takes his shot soon."

The claustrophobic sense of being trapped made the monster hog panic, and it tossed its head, wrenching the chain-link sides of the pen from their posts. Although there was no sound, it was easy for the watchers to imagine the great squealing panic, and the *T.rex*–like vibrations of the giant hog's feet.

Then it bounced in place as if stung, and they all saw a puff of dust rise from the hide near the top of its shoulder, followed by a tiny trickle of black blood. Max had taken his shot, and the soft-tipped bullet failed to penetrate the thick cartilage shield that lurked just under the skin. The only thing damaged was the animal's temper.

The other hogs scurried around inside and outside the pen. A group of them bumped up against one of the feeder's tripod legs and knocked it to the ground. They rooted through the spilled corn, then ran in a circle again, then rooted some more.

The giant hog, unable to free itself, at last panicked, lurching to one side and then the other. It popped free of the gate and ran off into the woods, followed by the others. In moments, all that remained on-screen were the ruins of the trap.

Jack dialed Max's number. "I know, I blew it," Max said as he answered. "I just couldn't get the right angle once he got stuck."

"That's all right, Max. You did the best you could. We're on our way to get you." He ended the call, then looked at the other two. "We go after it again at first light. And we don't stop until it's dead."

"Should we maybe bring in Gamera?" Bronwyn said.

"Who's that?" Dolph asked.

"A giant Japanese monster turtle. Who eats fire."

"Bring in anyone you think will help," Jack said. And he was serious. He stood, and started to close the laptop.

"Look!" Dolph almost yelled.

Once again, they couldn't make out anything at first. They saw the two pinpoints of reflecting eyes deep in the forest, too high off the ground to be one of the smaller pigs. The lights grew larger, and brighter, and the bulky shadow separated from the surrounding gloom.

It walked slowly, deliberately, right up to the tree where the camera was mounted. The head grew sharply defined, until the porcine face took on almost human proportions. When it got too close, the head disappeared beyond the bottom of the frame, and they were treated to a view of its high, bristly back.

The image shuddered. Then it shifted slightly, tilting off the horizontal. The animal's back moved out of frame, and again, all was silent.

"He moved the tree," Dolph said in wonder. "That tree was two feet around. We couldn't move it with a damn backhoe."

"He was sending a message," Bronwyn said.

Jack called Max again. "Are you all right?"

"Holy shit," Max said, his breath quick and panicky. "*Holy shit.* It almost uprooted the tree with the camera. I couldn't get a shot, either; it's like it knew exactly how to stay out of my range. That is pure ADR."

"ADR?"

"Something we use at my clinic: 'Ain't Doin' Right.' "

"We saw. Just sit tight—we're on our way."

"Be careful. I mean, be really careful."

"We will."

When Jack hung up, Dolph leaned close and said softly, "You still want to go after it tomorrow?"

Jack had to swallow once before speaking. "Yes." He hoped he didn't sound nearly so apprehensive as he really was.

9

The next morning, a Saturday, the sun rose on a clear, warm day over the mountains around the Needsville valley. Even the notorious mist that gave the Smoky Mountains their name was conspicuously absent. The dregs of the night wind tickled the treetops. Birds twittered, rabbits returned to their dens, and two groups of hunters, unaware of each other, prepared to seek out a monster.

Across the valley, in her family's trailer home, Mandalay Harris stood at the kitchen sink. Still in her T-shirt and pajama pants, she looked out the little window at the morning. Something intangible was in the air. She couldn't discern anything more detailed, and that bothered her the most. She'd had this feeling before, and about half the time, it amounted to nothing. The other half, though, it turned out to be something awful.

She knew her sort-of boyfriend, Luke Somerville, would be awake now as well, so she called his house. Luke didn't have his own cell phone, so his father, perpetually cranky and tense, answered the house line. "Yeah?"

"It's Mandalay," she said, letting her authority shade her voice for the sake of expediency. "I'm calling for Luke."

"Hold on." Luke and his family were part of Junior's group, and ordinarily would have had nothing to do with Mandalay. But their budding romance had forced both sides to new tolerance, something Mandalay appreciated and wanted to cultivate. The accumulated wisdom of generations of Tufa women ran through her head, but her emotions were all her own, and she often wondered if she was doing the right thing with Luke.

But all those doubts melted away as soon as his voice came over the phone. He was so clearly glad to hear from her, she could practically see his grin when he said, "Hey."

"You have *got* to get your own phone," Mandalay said.

"Daddy says we can't afford it."

"Well, he always sounds angry when he finds out it's me on the phone."

"He always sounds angry, period." There was a pause; then he said, "What's wrong?"

"I got that feeling again. The one that says there might be trouble brewing."

"Better than the one that says there *is* trouble brewing."

She closed her eyes and let the relief of his presence settle on her. He was always so supportive, even when he was teasing her. "Yeah, true enough," she said. "You haven't overheard anything from your people about anything on the horizon, have you?"

"All anybody's talked about is that Rogers girl being killed. Do you think it has anything to do with that?"

"Maybe."

"I'll keep my ears open for anything else."

"Thanks."

"So we're doing one-word answers?"

She smiled, and knew he did, too. "Yes."

"Okay, I can play that. Want to hang out at the Pair-A-Dice later?"

She was glad he couldn't see how happy this made her. She loved playing with him, harmonizing and jamming until her fingers cramped and her voice grew raw. "Yeah, that'd be nice."

"That's four words."

"I'm feeling epic."

"See you there around eleven. We can play and have lunch."

"Okay." Then, with no forethought, she added, "You care if Janet Harper comes along?"

"I guess not," he said after a moment, his disappointment obvious. "She's so much better than us, though, it's hard to really enjoy it."

"You don't get better if you don't play with better players. And . . ."

"What?"

"I promise we'll go for a walk, just the two of us."

She felt his excitement return. "That'll be nice. But what will Janet do?"

"Play. That's all she ever does anyway. She doesn't need us around for that."

They said their good-byes, and Mandalay again looked out the window. That uneasy feeling did not lessen, but now she had a new problem. How would she invite Janet to come along without either sounding weird or making it an order?

She knew the sudden urge to bring the girl along had come from the night winds, and that they always had a reason for things like this. But she wondered if all the prior women in her line, from Radella to Ruby Montana, had watched the tops of the trees wave just as she now did and wondered what the holy hell those reasons could possibly be? Because she did that a lot.

Still, it was better than the one time the winds had spoken to her directly, in human words. That had been the scariest moment of her life, and she'd lacked the courage to turn and see who or what was actually speaking behind her. So when it came right down to it, she supposed living with hints was probably the best way to go.

Adam checked over his Marlin 336 rifle, an older and more battered version of the one Bliss Overbay used, as they stood beside Duncan's car on Dunwoody Mountain, looking down on Half Pea Hollow. This ridge was opposite the one that overlooked the Rogers house, and far enough away that no one would hear them approach.

Adam hadn't gotten his dad's Nosler, as Duncan suggested, because his dad would've known why without him having to say a word. The Marlin would be plenty of firepower, he was sure; he'd seen the way it shattered beer bottles and watermelons on the fencerow behind his house.

As Duncan put on his orange safety vest, Adam said, "Can pigs see color?"

"I don't know," Duncan muttered. His fingers fumbled with the Velcro, making the extra .30-30 shells in his pocket rattle. Sweat trickled down his neck under his hair, despite the cool morning. "I reckon not. Most animals can't."

"*Wild* animals, yeah," Adam said as he slid the last of the four cartridges into the magazine. "But pigs aren't technically wild, or at least not all-the-way wild."

"Well, if we don't find him, then we'll know."

Adam paused and gazed out over the hollow below. "You know this is a wild-goose chase, right? The chances of us finding this thing are fucking slim to none."

"Too scared?" Duncan said, deliberately mocking.

"I'm just not sure why we're doing this, man. Yeah, it sounded great over a table full of beers yesterday afternoon, but now—"

"We're doing it for Kera," Duncan said. "For what she meant to both of us."

Adam nodded. He looked out at the woods, let out a breath, and said, "I need to talk to you about something."

"What?" Duncan said, barely getting the word out past his suddenly constricted throat. Was Adam about to confess? If so, what would Duncan do then?

Adam looked down for a long moment, then said, "Ah, forget it. I promised I'd keep it a secret, so I reckon I better."

"Does it have anything to do with the pig?" Duncan asked.

"No," Adam said honestly. "Not a thing."

"Then it ain't important right now."

Duncan slowly loaded his own Winchester 94, making each motion deliberate so that his trembling fingers didn't drop the cartridges. "I'll go around the rim and come in from the other end of the valley. You start down, and we'll meet somewhere in the middle."

"I've been thinking about that," Adam said. "Shouldn't we stick together?"

"We'd make too much noise," Duncan said without looking up. Three shells were loaded, but it took him two tries to get the last one into the chamber. "And this way if he smells one of us and runs, he'll run smack into the other one."

Adam leaned against the fender of his car. "You know what they say about this place, don't you? About all the ghosts and haints and whatnot."

"You think that pig is a haint?" Duncan snapped.

"Jumping Jesus on a pogo stick, Duncan, I'm just talking. I mean, there are so many stories about this place. Some say the Yunwi Tsundi still live here."

"The Yunwi Tsundi aren't real."

"I heard some of them came to Bronwyn Chess's wedding."

"Did they catch a ride with Santa Claus and the Easter Bunny?"

"What about the story of Lorena Minyard?"

Duncan knew that story well enough; when he and Adam had been about eleven, Duncan's older brother, Poole, had sent them screaming for the house during a night of backyard camping. Lorena Minyard had been a young mother living in Half Pea Hollow who grew sad and depressed after the death of her baby. She fell into a coma and supposedly died; however, when several other people experienced the same symptoms, only to recover, the family realized they might have buried Lorena alive. They exhumed her and, sure enough, it was clear she had awakened inside the coffin and tried to claw her way out. Now her ghost, as insane as she herself must have been in the last moments of her life, allegedly roamed Half Pea Hollow. Encountering her could send you into a similar deathlike coma, after which you were liable to wake in your own coffin.

"I think we've talked enough," Duncan said. "Let's get to hunting." He hoped Adam mistook his nervousness for eagerness. He looked his friend over, imagining those casual motions stilled, that mobile face in a rigid mask of death. Could he really do this? Sure, his friend had betrayed him, but then again, so had his girlfriend. But he couldn't avenge himself on her, not anymore. And didn't his honor demand this?

"How big do you think he is?" Adam asked as he fastened the straps on his own orange vest.

Duncan held up his rifle. "Not so big a .30-30 won't send him to that great barbecue smoker in the sky."

Adam nodded, then gave Duncan a long, serious look. "You sure about this? You sure this is what you want to do? You'll remember this all your life, whenever you think about Kera. Is that what you want?"

It took all Duncan's self-control not to shoot the smug bastard right there. *What will* you *remember?* he wanted to ask. *Those pictures she sent you? Fucking her in your truck while I trusted you both?*

"It's what I want," he said without meeting Adam's eyes.

"All right." The forest was now visible, but there were still plenty of pockets of shadow down in the valley. "I'll text you when I get to the other end. Then we can start toward the middle. Hopefully one of us will flush it out pretty quick." He half saluted with the barrel of his rifle.

Duncan watched Adam proceed down through the briars and finally disappear into the thick trees. Duncan gave him time to get out of both sight and hearing; then he moved, almost running, along the trail that ran along the top of the ridge. He wasn't planning to wait for Adam's text; he intended to be there at the mid-valley rendezvous much, much earlier.

Half Pea Hollow was, geographically speaking, a fairly standard little sub-valley off the main one that held Needsville. A spring-fed creek ran through the middle of it, but most of its route was hidden by thick greenery, so it was seldom fished. There were a few trails, mostly deer paths wide enough for hunters to use if inclined, but the land belonged to no one. On paper, he knew someone held the title, but like a lot of Cloud County, it couldn't be bought, or sold, or inherited. It simply stayed the way it had always been.

The air filled with gnats as he ran, spattering against his face. He spat out those that touched his lips, and wiped at the air with his free hand. He also disturbed a flock of wild turkeys crossing the trail, and sent them gobbling and squawking in every direction. So much for sneaking.

As he ran, the rifle clutched against his chest, a song rose in his mind over the sound of his breathing and his beating heart. It wasn't one he'd listened to in months, maybe years, but it had been a favorite: Crooked Still's version of the old chestnut, "Flora, the Lily of the West."

Of course, as a Tufa, he knew the song by its older variation, "Handsome Mary." But it was the same tune, and although it was told from a male perspective, Aoife O'Donavan's plaintive voice carried more genuine ache than any man he'd ever heard sing it.

When first I came to Louisville, some pleasure there to find,
A handsome girl from Michigan, so pleasing my mind.
Her rosy cheeks and sparkling eyes, like arrows pierced my breast,
They called her Handsome Mary, the Lily of the West.

He was exhausted by the time he reached the other end of Half Pea Valley. Running with a gun was harder than he thought, and finally he had to sit down to catch his breath. He knew he was losing precious time off his plan, but he just didn't have the endurance, and his residual hangover didn't help.

Crows cawed overhead, and a cool breeze swept up out of the shadows below. At last he got to his feet, worked the lever to move a cartridge into the chamber, and started down the hill toward his rendezvous.

10

At about the same time, Jack Cates and the WHOMP team inspected the destroyed corral trap in the cool morning. Dolph wrangled two dogs on leashes, while the others finished readying their weapons.

In person, the damage was even more significant than it had appeared on the computer monitor, and drove home the power of the animal they sought. The metal was not only twisted, but in places torn like tissue paper, as well, the remains ground into the churned-up dirt. The automatic feeder had been toppled, and they startled a bunch of crows feeding on the spill.

"That sucker must stand four feet high at the shoulder," Dolph said, holding the leashes on two mountain cur mixes who sniffed the ground and looked up the slope in silent expectation.

"That ain't far off," Max said. He was still upset about blowing the chance to finish this the previous night.

"Maybe we should go over to the National Guard armory and ask about borrowing a bazooka," Dolph added.

Max looked at the tree where the trail cam was mounted. It leaned a few degrees to one side, and the ground was disturbed where one of the major roots had tried to pull free. "If I hadn't been sitting right there watching it, I never would believe a hog could do this."

He ran his hand over a spot where the bark had been rubbed away. The surface was sticky from exposed sap, and thick bristles adhered to it.

"It's just an animal," Bronwyn said. "It's big, but it's not that tough."

"Say that after them tusks get ahold of your legs," Dolph said. "When they run past you, they shake their heads, like this. They'll cut you up good."

"I ain't saying it's not dangerous," she continued. "A brown recluse is dangerous, but it can't stop a well-placed shoe, now, can it?"

"Just remember this: If one gets after you, jump up in a tree and make sure you pull your legs up after you."

Dolph passed the dogs' leashes to Jack and pulled a plastic squirt bottle from a side pocket of his camouflage pants. "Everyone rub some of this on your exposed skin."

Max took it, opened the lid, and sniffed. "Good gravy, Dolph, what is that shit?"

"Not shit," Dolph said. "Piss. Pig piss."

"I ain't rubbing pig piss on my skin," he said, and handed the bottle to Bronwyn. "Here, honey. Tell me this don't stink."

"Call me 'honey' again, Max, and pig piss will be the least of your problems." She handed it to Jack. "I washed all my clothes in baking soda last night, and showered in it this morning. I'm neutral."

Jack handed the bottle and leashes back to Dolph. He indicated the Key-Wick scent dispenser hung on a leather thong around his neck. "I got a whole bagful if anybody else needs one."

"I reckon I'll take one, then," Dolph grumbled. "Don't want to be the only one who smells like a pig wet his pants."

When they were ready, with walkie-talkies distributed, all their cell phones on vibrate, and anything that jingled out of their pockets, Jack faced them. "We'll follow the creek up into Half Pea Hollow. The tracks lead back up that way. When we spot it, don't hesitate, and don't ask for permission. If you have a shot, take it."

"Absolutely," Bronwyn said.

"I know we're also supposed to kill any and all wild pigs we run up on, like we have in the past," Jack continued, "but on this particular trip, we don't want to scare off the reason we're out here. If we spot the big one and take him down, then you can pick off any of the others dumb enough to stick around." To Dolph, he said, "You reckon them dogs are ready?"

He rubbed their heads with familiar affection. One, Random, was a light brown, while Hobo was darker, with a hint of pit bull in his broad head. Like most mountain curs, they waited in total silence, the same way they would pursue any animal they were set on. Typically Dolph knew they'd cornered their prey when he heard the hog's distinctive panicky squeal. "Any readier and they'd be dragging me after 'em."

"You really think they're up to tackling that monster?" Max asked.

Dolph was actually worried about that, but he wasn't going to cast aspersions on his dogs. "Better worry if the hog'll last until we get to him."

"Let 'em go, then," Jack said.

Dolph unsnapped the leads, and the dogs took off along the stream, Hobo running along the bank, Random splashing through the water. One of them let out a lone bark that echoed in the morning silence. In moments they'd vanished around the bend into Half Pea Hollow.

"Reckon where this creek starts?" Dolph asked as he straightened up and rubbed his lower back.

"A spring up in Half Pea Hollow, I suppose," Max said.

"Anyone ever seen it?"

They turned to Bronwyn. "Not me," she said.

"You're a—" Max stopped before he put his foot in his mouth. "Local."

"I don't know every square inch of the place. I've only been up there once, with Tony Cator, and we were . . . otherwise occupied." She smiled a little at the memory.

"Ever hear about the King of the Forest?" Dolph asked.

No one said anything until Max inquired, "The what?"

"Story I used to hear when I was the warden. They say the biggest deer in the world, big as an elk, lives in this area. They call him the King of the Forest. He has two female coyotes who follow him around."

"Never heard that," Max said.

"On nights when everything's right, they can turn into people. A man with the antlers of a stag, and two beautiful women. Sometimes they trick people into coming into the woods, and they're never seen again."

"That sounds like an old wives' tale," Bronwyn said. "And I know some old wives."

"So you've never heard about it?"

"I've heard about the Tooth Fairy and leprechauns; should I believe in them, too?"

"I ain't saying I believe in them, just that it's interesting." Dolph let it drop at that, but he did note that Bronwyn had not, at any point, denied their existence.

Jack said, "Let's go," and they headed off after the dogs.

Duncan paused. Had he just heard a dog bark? Over the thundering of his own heart, he listened for anything else: the crunch of leaves, the snap of a twig, the flap of wings as startled birds took to the sky. He heard nothing except the distant, soft keening of a cicada.

He tried to slow his pulse with long, deep breaths, but it wasn't racing because of his exertion. He was excited, but not in a good way. This was close enough to terror that he couldn't tell the difference, and if he stopped to think about it, he might never get moving again.

Was he really planning to murder one of his best friends? There could be no colder blood than this, elaborately setting Adam up to walk right into his sights, innocent and unaware. He thought back to their childhood, attending the old schoolhouse before the big county school was built. They were in the first graduating class from the new facility, and like everyone in their class, they hated it. It didn't help that the principal, Mr. Stall, strode the halls like a Nazi commandant, yelling about PDAs back when it meant "public displays of affection" and making sure no one had any sort of fun.

He had been there with Adam the night they'd backed his truck up to the new school's double doors, intending to leave tire marks on the fresh concrete. Only the combination of alcohol, pot, and nerves made Adam back up just a hair too much, smashing the outer glass. They'd left tire marks, all right, as they tore out of there, giggling in terror and shouting in triumph when it became obvious no one was following. Everyone knew they'd done it, including Mr. Stall, but no one could prove it. So they got away scot-free, and became minor celebrities for a brief time.

Well, "scot-free" wasn't entirely accurate. Nothing happened in Cloud County that old, now-dead Rockhouse Hicks didn't know about, and he definitely knew about this. The Tufa legends began and ended with him, and he wielded a kind of power unlikely ever to be seen in this county again, unless that little Harris girl grew up a lot meaner than she appeared. (Duncan had seen her publicly facedown an enemy, and even offer that enemy a gun to shoot her with, when she'd been only twelve. Rockhouse, on the other hand, would've sent someone to shoot that same enemy from a safe distance.)

So Rockhouse had showed up at his parents' farm at dinnertime a few days later, spewing obscenities about punk kids and their worthless parents. Duncan had never seen his father turn so red before, and yet he'd said nothing back, because you didn't have a smart mouth around that old man. If you did, things would happen to you that could never be traced back, but that Rockhouse was without a doubt responsible for. Duncan had been grounded for two weeks, with no TV and, worse, no music. There was hardly a worse punishment for a Tufa, even one with faint Tufa blood like him.

Now he reflected how glad, how motherfucking *delighted* he was that Rockhouse was no longer around. Junior Damo was nothing compared to the old man.

But beneath these memories, beneath his current thoughts, that song about Handsome Mary continued to run.

I courted her awhile, in hopes her love to gain,
But she proved false to me, which caused me much pain.
She robbed me of my liberty, deprived me of my rest,
They called her Handsome Mary, the Lily of the West. . . .

The WHOMP team moved along the stream. They'd passed through the ravine and were now deep in Half Pea Hollow. The valley had never been logged, burned, or otherwise cleared. Jack had studied satellite pictures, topographical surveys, even Google Maps of the area, but had gotten very little useful information. This was one of those isolated places that could be learned only by walking its trails. If there were trails.

In front of him, Bronwyn faintly hummed a tune that Max couldn't quite catch, despite following her so closely, he could almost whisper in her ear. At last he said quietly, "What's that song?"

"Just something my daddy sings," she said.

"What's it called?"

"We shouldn't be talking, should we? We might scare the hogs."

Max fell silent, but after a few moments added, "You live around here, don't you?"

"I do."

"So you're a Tufa?"

"I am."

"Is it true what they say about you?"

Now she turned and gave him a skeptical glance. "Is this the best place for this conversation?"

"It's not the best place for any conversation," Jack whispered harshly from the lead.

"I didn't mean anything by it," Max said.

"Of course you did," Bronwyn shot back.

"Well . . . I'll admit, I'm curious. So did you learn to shoot in the army?"

"I learned to shoot in my backyard."

"Is that where you learned the bow and arrow?"

"No, I picked that up after my daughter got fascinated with it from catching glimpses of *The Hunger Games* on TV. I figured I should learn my way around so I could teach it to her when she gets old enough, if she's still interested. Turns out I have a real knack for it."

"But how did you—?"

"You know what I did learn in the army, Max?"

"What?"

"Not to talk on patrol."

"Will you two shut up?" Jack said.

Bronwyn had told them that this path was known as the Devil's Courthouse because a dense patch of rhododendron called a "laurel slick" made going slow and miserable, like waiting for a jury to decide your fate. It closed in around the creek once they left the ravine, and the way the light filtered through the trees overhead gave the whole area a strange, underwater vibe. The dense vegetation held the air still, and the late-summer humidity had them all sweaty and damp under their gear.

There was also the very real danger of copperheads and rattlesnakes, and although they all wore snake-proof boots, they wouldn't protect against a stray hand put down for balance or a stumble that sent a whole body sprawling into the undergrowth.

The wild pigs, of course, could navigate this strange, almost tropical plant-sea with ease. And so could the dogs.

"Great gosh a'mighty," Max said. "Smells like a sewer line broke."

"Whoa," Jack said as he stopped. The others fanned out around him.

Ahead the relatively narrow stream had been recently widened. The ground was muddy and torn up, and the previously clean water was opaque with sediment and excrement. This was where the hogs wallowed to cool off in the heat.

"Y'all check that out," Bronwyn said, and indicated an enormous flattened area, bigger than any of them, at the edge of the bank. Something huge had rolled around there.

"That's our boy," Dolph said. He took three long paces to measure the size of the impression. "Seven feet, at least."

Max looked around. "Think he's watching us right now?"

"Hogs don't act like that," Jack said.

"Hogs don't normally shove trees around, either."

"They went up the hill," Dolph said, indicating the trampled vegetation. In one bare patch of mud they saw the tracks of several hogs, with two clear dog prints impressed over the top of them. Dolph swiped at the mosquitoes drawn to their body heat and blood.

They followed Jack uphill out of the slick. About halfway up, they unknowingly crossed the very trail that Duncan had run down just minutes before. The dogs, locked on to the scent of the pigs, paid it no mind.

As the air warmed, more insects emerged and swarmed them. They hadn't wanted to risk any bug spray scent giving them away, and now they paid for it.

Bronwyn continued to hum a tune that Max could not identify, so quietly it blended with the buzzing of the bugs and the birds chirping in the trees.

"Look," Dolph said softly. Jack held up his hand to halt, and they all gathered around the discovery.

Protruding from the leaf litter was the lower jawbone of a hog. The V-shaped bone sported a pair of two-inch tusks and a row of angled, worn incisors at the very front. It was light and dirty-white, the edges worn down by rain, wind, ice, and snow.

Dolph picked it up, examined it, and said, "Been here about two years."

Jack nodded. "So they've been in Half Pea Hollow for a while."

"Long enough for one of 'em to grow to be a monster," Max said. No one argued.

But Jack still couldn't believe a hog had grown that large on what it could find in the wild. He suspected there was something else, a layer of secrets that the hog's presence would reveal once they found it.

He looked around at the heavy forest and changed that last thought. *If* they found it.

Duncan crept slowly along, suddenly unwilling to force the confrontation. It was all up to fate and the night winds now: if he saw Adam first, then it would clearly be their will that he got his revenge. If not, then he'd made a good-faith effort to restore his besmirched honor; he could hold up his head at the old cave, and he could look Junior in the eye.

Thoughts of honor brought that song back to the front of his brain.

One evening as I rambled, down by a shady grove,
I saw a man of low degree conversing with my love.
They were singing songs of melody, while I was sore
distressed,
O faithless, faithless Mary, the Lily of the West.

Something stirred in the undergrowth ahead, and before he could even raise his gun, an emu with two striped chicks stepped out. The birds looked just as surprised to see him.

He'd seen them crossing the road before, and at least one that had lost that race to a barreling semi. But he'd never come across one in the wild, this close.

It stared at him, and he slowly raised the gun. He'd heard they could viciously kick, and he wasn't about to get laid open by one like Panel Barton's award-winning coonhound.

The emu—was he remembering right that it was the fathers who raised the young?—defiantly ruffled its feathers and bobbed its long neck. Duncan took a step back. If he fired, the noise would bring Adam running. Isn't that what he wanted?

The emu grunted repeatedly and kicked detritus and dead leaves at him. Duncan backed up another step and prepared to shoot.

But, apparently satisfied that its point had been made, the emu turned and led its chicks off into the forest. Within moments they were lost to sight.

Duncan's heart thundered so hard, he glanced down to see if the front of his shirt vibrated. He took several deep breaths and wiped sweat from his eyes. Then, moving even more slowly, he continued into the forest.

"Stop," Jack hissed, and held up his hand.

They watched the emu and its two chicks emerge from the forest and move across their path. The adult turned in their direction once, but either didn't see them, or didn't think them a threat. In a few moments they were gone.

"That is one big mama bird," Max said.

"That's actually the daddy," Dolph said. "Mamas lay the eggs; daddies raise the chicks."

"Huh. They're from Australia, right?"

"Yeah."

"They must do everything backwards down there."

"My husband," Bronwyn said with narrowed eyes, "is home watching our girl right now so I can be out here pig hunting with you. Is that backwards?"

"I didn't mean—"

"I think we can have this discussion later," Dolph said.

Jack glared at them. "Is the concept of 'quiet' too complicated for you three? Because if it is—"

"My bad, Jack," Bronwyn said. "Sorry." She looked directly at Max with the intensity that had given her, in her teen years, the nickname "the Bronwynator."

The song grew in Duncan's head. He could hear the plaintive voice of Aoife O'Donovan now, as clear as if he'd worn earbuds.

One evening as I rambled, down by a shady grove,
I saw a man of low degree conversing with my love.
They were singing songs of melody, while I was sore distressed,
O faithless, faithless Kera, the Lily of the West. . . .

He shook his head. It was Mary, or Flora, depending on the version, not "Kera." But he swore that's what the voice sang in his head.

And then he spotted movement ahead. He froze.

At first he thought it was another emu. It was certainly too tall to be a wild pig, even the monster they supposedly sought. But then Adam stepped into a shaft of sunlight.

Now all the questions he'd asked himself roared back. Should he fire from hiding? Or should he confront Adam, so the son of a bitch would know why he was being killed? Did he offer to make it a fair fight, with knives or fists? Or did he just scare his friend, make him think he was about to be killed, and then walk away?

Before he could begin to sort through all these questions, the rage exploded, Hulk-like, and he raised the gun. He knew *exactly* what to do to the backstabbing son of a bitch. Surprisingly, his hands did not shake.

I stepped up to my rival, my rifle in my hand.
I caught him by the collar, and boldly bade him stand;
Being driven to desperation, I shot him in the head,
But was betrayed by Kera, who once shared his bed . . . .

He blinked. In the song, Mary, or Flora, betrayed the singer to the law. But how could Kera do that to him? She was dead, after all. Dead and gone.

Dead and gone. Because of that motherfucker. The rifle was rock-steady as Duncan sighted down the barrel.

And then a rancid, appalling smell washed over him.

They were halfway up the slope of Dunwoody Mountain and had finally emerged from the ankle-snagging undergrowth into a no less overgrown, but easier to navigate, forest of old trees. These were mostly white oak, and the team knew that their mast, consisting of white oak acorns, was a favorite of wild hogs. This might explain why they'd taken up in Half Pea Hollow in the first place. Certainly the ground was bare of any acorns in the immediate vicinity, and there were older piles of scat.

"Hog heaven," Dolph observed.

"And it looks like the angels have been having a high old time," Bronwyn agreed.

"Let's hope we add at least one devil to the choir," Dolph said.

"Hey. Hey!" Max called from back down the trail. He pointed into the dense growth they'd just left. "Look!"

They joined him. In a dozen places, the weeds were pressed down in roughly oval-shaped patches. The hogs had used it for a bedding-down area, and recently, too. The trees showed evidence of rubbing as well, with bare patches of bark. None were so large as the one they'd found at the trap site, though, and none of the beds looked suitable for their monster.

Max slapped at his neck. "Man, *everything* in this hollow bites."

They resumed their climb until Jack once again held up his hand, and the team stopped.

"What?" Max asked. Bronwyn slapped his arm for quiet.

Jack sniffed the air. If there was one odor he recognized, it was the smell of wild hogs. "They're close," he said so softly, he wondered if the others heard him.

Dolph and Max quietly closed the breeches on their guns, and Bronwyn smoothly drew and nocked an arrow.

Dolph shouldered his rifle and pulled the Glock from his belt holster. From the butt hung a small dove feather, and as they watched, the wind moved it, showing that the breeze came from the south. The hogs were that way, farther along the slope, possibly back down in the laurel slick.

"It smells like a pig's ass, all right," Max observed in a whisper. Brownyn rolled her eyes.

Jack knelt and put a hand on the ground. Sometimes he was able to feel the approach of pigs, if there were enough of them, or if they were big enough. It wasn't a rational ability, but it had proved itself. This time, though, he felt nothing.

The team formed a square, each facing a different direction, ensuring nothing would sneak up on them.

Jack wondered, why hadn't the dogs cornered them yet? If they were close enough for a human being to smell, then the dogs should have gotten to them long ago. Unless something had happened to the dogs—

Then the distinctive squealing reached them from down in the valley.

And then they heard a gunshot.

Followed by a scream.

11

"Hey," Janet Harper said as she entered the Pair-A-Dice. This early, the kitchen wasn't up, and except for the coffeepot on the end of the bar, there were no beverages available. Most of the tables were empty as well, with the chairs still stacked upside down from Friday night, and Janet made her way to the little stage in the corner.

Mandalay and her boyfriend, Luke Somerville, sat side by side on the edge of the stage. They were four years younger than Janet, an eon by teenage standards, but Janet had not hesitated when Mandalay asked her to come jam with them. You didn't turn down the leader of the Tufa, no matter how old she appeared to be.

Besides, Mandalay was one of the few Tufa musicians who could really keep up with, and sometimes challenge, Janet. It wasn't bragging to say that Janet Harper was the best musician alive in Cloud County; despite her heavily diluted Tufa blood, thinned by marriages to humans over the past few generations, something in her was true beyond belief. She could play any instrument, learn any song almost at once, and jam with anyone. Some folks could best her on their specialties, like Page Paine on the fiddle, but none approached her versatility.

She put her guitar case down on the stage and said, "Good morning."

"Hey," Mandalay said. "How are you?"

"A little preoccupied," Janet said as she took out her guitar. "I can't get my brain going. Like there's something weird in the air, you know?"

"I know," Mandalay agreed. She turned to Luke. "See? It ain't just me."

He shrugged, unable to look at her. "I guess not."

Janet dragged a chair away from a table and sat down facing them. She picked along with the song Mandalay strummed, even though she didn't quite catch the melody at first. At last she asked, "Hey, what exactly are we playing?"

"You don't know?" Luke said.

"Nope. Sounds familiar, but I can't quite place it."

"But . . . you're playing it."

"I'm just following along."

"It's 'Poor Ellen Smith,' " Mandalay said. "It's been in my head all day."

"Ah-ha!" Janet said. "Now I recognize it. The Neko Case version?"

Mandalay shook her head. "Nope. Mine." When the verse came back around, she sang:

Poor Ellen Smith how she was found
Shot through the heart lying cold on the ground
Her clothes were all scattered and thrown on the ground
And blood marks the spot where poor Ellen was found.

Luke strummed rhythm, simply trying to keep up. Mandalay played broad, open lead, which Janet filled with soft picking like the sound of tears hitting the concrete floor. Janet nodded to Mandalay, and she sang:

They picked up their rifles and hunted me down
And found me a-loafing in Mount Airy town
They picked up the body and carried it away
And now she is sleeping in some lonesome old grave.

Mandalay slowly stopped playing and stared off into the distance, as if receiving some message that only she could hear. Janet picked a harmony rhythm with Luke, waiting, but eventually even the two of them stopped. They sat in silence, waiting for Mandalay to speak.

Finally Luke said, "You all right?"

Mandalay blinked, then gave him a luminous smile. His genuine concern for her always made her feel warm and special. "Yeah, I'm all right. It's just . . ."

"Something in the air," Janet said.

"Yeah, exactly."

"Think it has anything to do with Kera Rogers's getting killed?"

Mandalay chewed her lip. "Maybe."

"I'm covering it for the school paper. Care to give me a comment?"

Mandalay grinned. "No, ma'am, I would not."

"You believe she was killed by a wild hog?"

"I believe it until somebody proves different."

"And you think that's why you're all twitchy today?"

Mandalay thought that over. "No. That's something that already happened. This feels . . . impending."

"Should we tell somebody?" Luke asked.

"It's all too vague," Mandalay said. "I wouldn't know who to tell." She began to strum again, going back into the song. Luke kept watching her, concerned, while Janet immediately picked back up where they'd left off.

Then, with no warning, Mandalay set her guitar aside and said, "Sorry. I have to go." And she did.

Two things happened at once, and even after the panic had burned off, Duncan couldn't quite believe it.

He raised his gun and put the bead at the end of the barrel right over Adam's face. He deliberately filled his mind with the selfie from the phone, of the two of them snuggled together in Adam's bed. He let the rage come, the stinking jealousy that enveloped him so strongly, he really could smell it. He waited for Adam to look his way; he wanted the smug bastard to know who'd blown his head off. As the rage increased his heart rate, the end of the barrel trembled, and he gritted his teeth as he fought to hold it steady.

But then he realized he really *did* smell something vile and rank. He had a moment to puzzle over it.

Then a shadow drifted out of the forest behind Adam. Because it came down the slope toward him, it appeared to loom over him, squat and huge, almost elephantine.

Adam froze, aware that something was wrong. His face wrinkled at the odor.

He turned and saw the giant wild hog bearing down on him. He screamed and tried to bring his gun around to fire in time, but in his panic, he pulled the trigger too early, and didn't have time to jack another shell into the chamber. The hog mowed him down, stood over him, and dug into his belly with its enormous tusks. As it tossed its head, chunks of bloody meat and innards flew through the air.

Duncan froze, looking down the barrel at this scene. He could fire, and maybe hit the animal in the sweet spot behind the shoulder blade, where it would tear through lungs and heart and drop the beast in its tracks. But he didn't. He just watched. He couldn't see exactly what was happening, but Adam never made another sound. The only noises were the monster's grunting and the wet, cracking sound of snapping bones.

Then the others emerged, smaller hogs, even piglets, who tore into Adam. Many were black, some mottled, and two had white Hampshire stripes. At first Duncan wondered if some of the squeals came from Adam, but he realized that by this point, Adam was long past making any noise.

It was like a scene from a horror movie, and even from this distance, Duncan could see the dark red on the animals' snouts as they rose to catch a breath before diving back in. The gigantic leader moved away, his tusks also stained with red. He had one of Adam's arms in his mouth, and dragged the dead man's shredded body after him. The corpse was missing one entire leg and part of the dangling arm; luckily mud covered his friend's face. Again the monster presented the perfect side shot, and again Duncan didn't take it.

And then two silent dogs burst into the clearing.

The WHOMP team clearly heard the pig squealing in unmistakable terror, but there had been no subsequent human scream. Jack led the sprint through the forest toward the sound. The team moved with surprising stealth for all their speed, with Bronwyn Chess making the least amount of noise. They reached the overgrown stone foundations of an ancient cabin, and Jack hopped up on the remains of the chimney, trying to sense the direction.

There were no more gunshots, either, just the sound of porcine panic. But all the birds and insects in the immediate woods around them fell silent, the way they always did when something was afoot that could kill anything that drew its attention.

He jumped down and motioned for them to continue on

toward the bayed pig. They burst into a smaller clearing just in time to witness the chaos.

Random and Hobo had been as silent as possible, but the monster had nonetheless fled before they arrived. They fixated on the first hog they saw, a big sow with brown patches. Growling low in their throats, they circled it closer and closer, until they could dash in for quick bites.

Usually when dogs settled on one hog, the others would vanish. But the rest of the herd seemed like hairy pinballs, bouncing off each other and trees in a desperate bid to escape, and thus failing.

"Hobo! Random!" Dolph yelled. "Back! *Now!*"

The dogs obeyed and backed away from their quarry, whose flanks now bled from dozens of nips.

"Take 'em down," Jack said, and immediately drew a bead on one. He fired, dropping it where it stood. Max and Dolph did the same. The noise was sudden and the sharp cracks made everyone's ears ring.

Only Bronwyn worked silently, drawing back her bowstring and letting fly with the aid of a wrist-mounted caliper release. Each arrow struck exactly where it needed to, dropping its target where it stood. And before that arrow even reached its target, she'd drawn another, nocked it and clamped the caliper around the string in the same motion, and taken aim at the next one.

Max, as he fired, caught a tiny snippet of the song Bronwyn softly hummed. He couldn't believe he heard it correctly:

And another one's gone, and another one's gone,
Another one bites the dust. . . .

Seven pigs lay dead by the time the others had scattered into the woods, including the one bayed by the dogs. But none of them was the monster.

"Go," Dolph said to the dogs, and they scurried off after the escapees.

Jack looked around. "Everyone all right?"

After the acknowledgments, Bronwyn said, "So who screamed?"

"I don't know," Max said, "but look at all the blood."

The ground was spattered with it, far more than the dead pigs could've lost.

"Where did that shot come from?" Max asked.

"From this," Dolph said, and picked up Adam's gun. The stock bore marks from hog teeth. "And now I think I know where the blood came from, too."

"Who was it?" Jack said.

Bronwyn delicately held a ragged, blood-soaked piece of denim. "Whoever wore these."

"Jesus," Max said. "Where's the rest of him?"

"They ate him," Dolph said.

"No, there wasn't time," Jack said. "We got here too fast. The big one must've dragged him off."

"Pigs don't do that," Max said. "Besides, there's no sign the big one was even here."

"Oh, yes, there is," Jack said, and pointed to the clear track of the monster in the churned-up earth. There was also the smudged line of something heavy that had, in fact, been dragged away. "Let's go. Fan out and be careful. He can't be too far ahead."

Duncan stood absolutely still and watched the hunting party head off into the woods after the monster. He felt nauseated, and cold, and as if he might both throw up and wet his pants simultaneously. At last his legs gave out, and he sat down hard on the ground, the rifle sliding from his hands.

What had he done?

He began to cry then, hard tears that made his face ache with the effort of producing them.

He didn't know how long he'd been crying, but when he looked up, he let out a shriek that echoed through the forest.

Bronwyn Chess stood over him, her bow in her hands, an arrow nocked. From his huddled perspective, she looked like some dark-haired primal deity against the treetops and blue sky beyond, a grim Artemis in a baseball cap. Even the gnats and mosquitoes swarming in the cool air stayed away from her, as if intimidated. He expected her to point the arrow at him and declaim a stray line that had stuck with him since school: "Every man is guilty of all the good he did not do."

Instead she said, "Duncan? What are you doing here?"

He stared up at her. Despite her slender and feminine appearance, everyone knew she was Mandalay Harris's enforcer, the woman who meted out justice in the Tufa community. To run afoul of her was to risk being dropped from the sky, as had happened to Dwayne Gitterman when he killed her brother. If she knew what Duncan had just done . . .

He choked out the word, "Adam."

"Adam? Adam Procure?"

Duncan nodded. Then he pointed toward the site of the attack.

"Adam Procure was killed by the pig?"

He nodded again.

She grabbed him by the front of the shirt and hauled him to his feet. "What the *hell,* Duncan? What were you two doing out here?"

"W-we were hunting it," he choked out. "It killed Kera."

"The hog? You and Adam were hunting the hog?"

He nodded.

"Are you out of your mind? That thing is a *monster.* Adam didn't have a chance."

"I didn't—"

"Come on," she said, picked up his gun, and pressed it into his hands. As she strode away, he realized he had a perfect shot at her back, just as he'd had at the pig. He could put a bullet right through her heart.

He shook off the thought. What was *wrong* with him? Then he rushed to catch up.

They reached the site of Adam's death. He stared at the ground, churned and ripped by the herd of pigs, and then he spotted a hiking boot that was stuck ankle-first in the fresh mud. He knew without checking that Adam's foot was still inside it.

"Just stay here," she said, and took out a walkie-talkie. "Chess for Cates. I found someone else here. He and a friend were hunting the damn hog. Come back."

After a second, Jack Cates's voice came over the radio. "He knows who the victim was?"

"He does."

"Great," he almost growled. "Well, the son of a bitch is gone for now. None of us could find the trail, including the dogs. They got spooked and wouldn't keep going. Stay there, we're on our way." Then he summoned the others to meet back at the site of Adam's death.

Bronwyn said nothing else, and instead retrieved her arrows from the dead hogs while also watching the woods around them for any sign the monster might return. Duncan stood with his gun in his slack hands, mouth open, staying on his feet just because it was easier than falling down.

When the others returned, Jack said to Duncan, "So tell me, in great detail, what the hell you thought you were doing?"

Duncan gulped before he spoke. "That thing killed my girlfriend. I deserve to be the one to kill it back."

Jack looked at Bronwyn. She shrugged.

"Do you know anything about wild hogs?" he asked Duncan.

He shook his head. He felt like a child before the grade-school principal.

"They are faster than you can imagine, and more ruthless than you'd believe. Your friend didn't have a chance, even with a gun, once it got up close to him."

Duncan fought to suppress the image of the pig knocking

Adam to the ground, then swinging its big head as its tusks tore into his flesh. "We didn't—"

"Think?" Jack roared. Startled birds lifted off from the trees overhead.

"Well, if it was coming back, that sure scared it off," Dolph said dryly.

"We have to call regular law enforcement again," Jack said. "Someone will have to stay here with the . . . remains." He looked down at the boot still stuck in the mud. Flies now congregated around it and the surrounding blood.

"I will," Dolph said. "My knees could use the rest anyway."

Bronwyn handed him Duncan's gun. "Keep this. He's not up to carrying it, and you might need it."

"Thank you, ma'am," Dolph said, and touched the brim of his cap in salute.

They left the veteran outdoorsman leaning against a tree, watching the shadowy forest around him with the nervousness of a man wearing steak underwear in a piranha pool.

12

When the WHOMP team and Duncan walked out of the forest behind the Rogers house, both Mandalay Harris and Junior Damo waited for them. Sam Rogers and his two older children, Spook and his sister, Harley, stood nearby, shifting nervously on their feet. Bliss Overbay followed Brenda Rogers out of the house.

"We heard shots," Sam said when they were close enough.

"We fired them," Bronwyn said. "We got several of the herd, but we missed the big one."

"How do you hit the little ones and miss the big one?" Junior asked, grinning his typical snide grin.

"Shut up, Junior," Mandalay said. She looked at Duncan, whose face was bone-white. "So where did you find him?"

"He and Adam Procure decided to go hunt it down themselves without telling anyone," Bronwyn said. "Personal revenge or honor or something. The big hog killed Adam."

There was a moment of silence; then Brenda let out a wail and threw her arms around Sam. Her husband, surprised by the sudden dead weight around his neck, stumbled and nearly fell. Spook helped him regain his footing. Quigley the dog came from the porch and stood beside them, whining and looking up at Brenda.

"Are you sure?" Mandalay whispered.

"Duncan saw it," Bronwyn said. "And we saw what was left."

"It wasn't much," Max interjected, and set Brenda wailing again.

Jack glared at Max, then said, "Dolph Pettit is staying on-site until we can get the state police out there. I suppose that'll be that Tufa trooper again?" He said this with a significant look at Bliss.

"Yes. Call him," Mandalay said to Bliss.

Jack couldn't believe just one state trooper could handle the investigation into two deaths. There would be all sorts of law enforcement involved now, and once word got out, the media would descend. After all, a genuine, real-life monster story was irresistible. And all those people meant even more chances for someone to get hurt.

To Jack, Mandalay said, "And so what happens now?"

"The alpha hog is too big for any pen trap I have access to. We'll have to go back out and keep hunting it."

"Will it come around here?" Sam asked, still holding his wife. His children had one hand each on his shoulders.

"I don't think so. They tend to stay away from places once they've been spooked, and I'm pretty sure we've spooked it, if nothing else."

"Who's going to tell Adam's family?" Bronwyn asked.

"I will," Bliss said.

Bronwyn helped Duncan to the porch, where he sat numbly in a canvas chair. Not two days earlier, he'd been on the front porch of this very house, feeling almost exactly as he did right now. He stared down at his hands, which shook like they were palsied. Suddenly long, delicate feminine fingers encircled his wrist, and he looked up with a start, expecting despite everything to see Kera beside him. But it was only Bliss, checking his pulse.

"You're in shock again," she said. "Can someone give him a jacket, or a blanket?"

Max draped his orange vest across Duncan's shoulders. "Sorry, guy," he said uncomfortably, and patted Duncan's shoulder.

After the older man walked away, Duncan asked hoarsely, "Who was that?"

"Apparently one of the four best hog hunters in Tennessee," Bliss said. "Part of a special team the game warden put together."

Duncan blinked a few times before saying, "Everyone should be good at something, I guess."

Bliss knelt and looked into his eyes. "Duncan, are you hurt? Do you need to go to the hospital?"

"No. I'm not hurt."

"If you change your mind, just holler. Not every injury bleeds, you know."

"I'll be fine."

Bliss left Duncan on the porch huddled beneath the orange vest. Quigley left the Rogerses and stopped in front of him. This time, instead of coming to comfort him, the dog just stared.

"Get the fuck out of here," Duncan muttered, and waved a hand at the dog. Quigley turned and walked away around the house.

Bliss went over to Jack, who was looking at his phone. "Are you all right?" she asked softly.

"What?" he said sharply as he looked up.

She gave him a little smile. "Well, that answers that."

"I'm sorry, I was just checking with some sources." He put away his phone. "I've never seen anything like this, Bliss. It's like something out of *Moby-Dick,* except it's a hog instead of a whale."

"And you're Ahab?"

"No, I think Ahab is sitting on the porch over there with the shakes," he said dryly. "If they hadn't been there, we might've—"

"You'd have gotten away with it if it weren't for those darn kids?"

"Very funny. But yeah." He looked at Sam and Brenda, still holding each other while their children stood near. "And at least I get to walk away when that monster is dead. Those poor people will have nightmares for years."

"Come on and have some coffee," Bliss said, and took his arm. "You can't do anything else about it now."

He started to protest, then realized she was right. He followed her into the Rogerses' kitchen and took the cup she offered. As he sipped, he looked around at the signs of the life that filled the place. Photographs on the refrigerator showed a young woman with Tufa-black hair grinning and making faces at various ages. "Is that Kera?" he asked softly.

"No, that's her older sister, Harley. That one's Kera."

The indicated photograph showed her standing in a field of alfalfa, slightly turned away and looking back over her shoulder at the camera. She held a sunflower that covered the lower part of her face, leaving only her eyes showing. It was a professional-quality shot, and radiated that mix of innocence and sensuality that was almost irresistible.

Jack looked out the window. The Rogerses still stood in the yard, the children now huddling close. "Must be incredibly hard for them. I can't imagine."

"You have kids?"

"One. A son. He lives with his mother in Bowling Green. I get him every summer and Christmas. He just went back home two weeks ago, in fact, to get ready for school. You?"

"No. At least," she added with another little smile, "none that I know about."

"That's terrible," he said, unable to hide his own grin. "You make terrible jokes at the worst possible times, don't you?"

"I know. But sometimes all you can do is joke."

"Do you know Adam's family very well?"

"We all know each other well around here."

"Please pass on my regrets to them, too."

Bliss looked out through the kitchen window at Duncan, seated on the picnic table. "You know . . . ," she began, but then trailed off.

"Know what?"

She looked around the little kitchen and into the dining room to make sure they were alone. "Jack, I've known these kids all their lives. I can't imagine them doing this. It's just way out of character for them."

"How so?"

"They're not outdoorsy types. Duncan works at a convenience store, and Adam installs cable TV. Why would they be out hunting?"

"He said it was a personal vendetta."

"Maybe. It just sounds wrong to me, like we don't have the whole story. I'll have to talk to Duncan when he's in better shape."

"So will the police. Well, that is, if you people allow them in. Two deaths in three days—"

She put her hand on his shoulder and stepped close. "Listen, Jack, I know you think more police have to be involved, but that just won't happen here. Alvin Darwin will take care of it, just like he did for Kera. And we're not hiding anything; you know that, right?"

"You wouldn't tell me if you were, would you?"

"Jack, please—"

"And who's going to prepare a coroner's report, and a cause of death, and—?"

"That's all on me. I'm the coroner for Cloud County."

He looked at her dubiously. "Really?"

"Really. Unofficially, of course. But it's never been an issue before. And it won't be now."

"Then why didn't you people just handle the hog yourselves? Why involve me?"

"Because I knew from Bronwyn Chess that you were in a better position to do it than anyone here."

He shook his head. "Not so you could tell it from last night and this morning. You know, eventually somebody official is liable to notice all this."

"Somebody official like you?"

"My job's just to catch and kill that pig before he hurts somebody else. And make sure all the wildlife laws are followed. I don't mean me. But I have superiors, and so does your Trooper Darwin. All the dotted *i*'s and crossed *t*'s in the world won't help if the story they're telling draws the wrong sort of attention."

"So you won't be making any phone calls, maybe leaving any anonymous tips? . . ."

There was an edge to her questions that Jack finally noticed. He put down the coffee cup and looked at her steadily. "A paranoid man could hear a threat in that line of questioning."

"A paranoid man hears a threat in everything."

"But like they say, just 'cause you're paranoid doesn't mean they're *not* out to get you."

"You think I'm out to get you?" she said, and leaned close. "If I am, I promise you, it has nothing to do with work."

He laughed. It was the first time he remembered doing that without irony in what felt like days. "Look, Bliss, like I said, I have my job to do, and that's all. I don't want to alienate people around here, because if I do, they won't help me. There's an animal out there that's killed two people, and it's my job to both stop it before it does any more damage, and make sure nobody else gets hurt going after it. I have no interest in causing trouble for your folks."

"I believe you. And I'll try to help. It'll be hard to keep more people from going after it, though. We're a pretty do-it-yourself bunch."

"That's just how that boy Adam died: trying to do it himself." He thought this over. "Is there a town hall in Needsville?"

"It's in the back of the post office building. Why?"

"That's not big enough. I want to have a community meeting to talk about the situation, answer questions, and explain what I'm doing. The sooner, the better."

"There's the Pair-A-Dice. It's an old roadhouse. It's as close to a community center as we've got."

"That'll do, as long as we can shut off the beer taps for an hour."

"You ask so much," she deadpanned.

"Who's the mayor now? I'll talk to him—"

"I'll get it set up," she interjected. "When do you want to do it?"

"This evening. Tonight. Late enough so the people at work can come."

"I'll get the word out."

"Where is the Pair-A-Dice?"

"Out on the old highway toward Randy's Gap."

He frowned. "Really? I've driven that a bunch of times, and never seen it."

"Well, it's there. I'll give you directions. And I'll get the word out."

He heard a fresh wail from Kera's mother outside, and suddenly all the weariness of the morning caught up with him. He pulled out a chair and sat down. "All right. We'll have to go back up and try to find the hog again this afternoon, although it's probably pointless. Is there anyplace in town I can clean up before tonight, so I don't have to go all the way back home? I need to check for ticks, too."

"The fire station's got a shower," Bliss said.

"Thanks." He drank some coffee. "Some days are just harder than others, you know that?"

"I do," she said.

13

Duncan had no idea why he was here, but Bliss had insisted. She said it was important to everyone, and he was too numb to argue with her. But as he looked around at the packed room, he realized he didn't belong. They were all going to be told to leave the hog hunting to the professionals; for him, that was closing the barn door after the horse has come home.

The Pair-A-Dice roadhouse, an old concrete building that sported a bar, stage, dance floor, and minimal kitchen, was the one neutral spot in Cloud County where the Tufa from both sides could hang out in nominal civility. Here their music could blend and their harmonies soar, despite their otherwise mutual antagonism. There were rare breaches of the peace—Dwayne Gitterman had stabbed Kell Hyatt a few years ago, for example, and little Mandalay Harris had pulled a gun on Bo-Kate Wisby—but for the most part, everyone got along. The stage was wide open to anyone who wanted to play, and if you chose to take that stage, you'd better bring your A-game.

Now that stage was empty except for the game warden he'd seen up on Dunwoody Mountain, a portable movie screen borrowed from the high school, and a projector on a table. The warden fiddled with his laptop, and a blue square of light appeared on the screen.

If he starts showing us a presentation about hog farming, Duncan thought, *I'm out of here.*

Jack Cates said loudly, "Can everyone hear me okay? Bliss, do you think I can get a microphone?"

Duncan sipped his beer. The bar was closed, but Bliss had brought him one anyway. No one disputed her medical opinion.

Duncan's day had only gotten worse. He'd had the awful experience of seeing Kera's mother wrenched with new agony. He never wanted to hurt Brenda deliberately, and he felt awful that he'd done so inadvertently . . . well, sort of inadvertently. He knew she was mainly crying for her daughter, but everyone had known Adam, and some of that grief had to be for his parents.

Yeah, and how well did *she know Adam?* that awful voice in his head asked snidely. *Did she know her daughter was fucking around with him behind your back? Is that why she's bawling like a toddler?*

Then his own parents, and his big brother, Poole, had shown up. His mom had gone into hyper mode, wanting to tend to his imaginary injuries, bring him a fresh change of clothes, and even bathe him herself. Poole was both annoyed that his little brother was getting so much attention, and genuinely sympathetic at the loss of yet another friend to the monster. Duncan remembered he and Adam tagging along after Poole when they were all much younger, and far more innocent.

And then came the worst thing his mother could have said. "I'd heard Kera was also seeing Adam. I was proud of you two boys for not letting it come between you. A girl has the right to see anyone she wants, anytime she wants, as long as she's not breaking her word, and you two took it like grown Tufa men. I just wish you hadn't gone out there together to try to avenge her."

So his mother knew. And never said anything. And thought *he* knew, and that he was okay with it.

Fucking hell.

The wildlife man, Jack Cates, had questioned him for an hour, politely but insistently getting detail after detail from him. For his part, Duncan told the truth, except that he left out the bit about raising his rifle, and having a chance to save Adam. There was no sign Cates suspected anything, but it still made Duncan nervous. But fuck, what was there to suspect? He hadn't done anything wrong.

And that, he knew full well, was the problem. He hadn't *done* anything. He'd just watched the pig slaughter his rival, and done nothing.

He got a sudden rush of both horror and fury. Goddammit, this was something else Adam and Kera had in common: Both were killed by the same wild hog. And Duncan was left out completely. They'd be cemented together in the common memory now, and before long, someone would write a song about them. A song, Duncan suspected, that would paint the two of them as tragic lovers, and Duncan as merely the hapless witness.

Is that why I'm here? Duncan thought. *To witness the start of this new legend?*

Janet Harper knew exactly why she was there. She settled into her chair, checked the recording app on her phone, and picked up her reporter's spiral notebook, the kind that flipped open like a *Star Trek* communicator.

"Why do you need both of those?" Ginny asked.

"I take the notes on stuff I think is important right now," Janet said. "The recording is to CMA."

"CMA?"

"Cover my ass. Make sure I get the quotes right."

"You write for a high school newspaper, Janet."

She indicated a dark-haired man with an identical notebook leaning against the wall. "See that guy? He's a real reporter, from the *Weekly Horn.* He's got one of these, too."

"So what does that mean? Are you role-playing?"

"It means that there's a right way and a wrong way to do things, Ginny. Just because I'm writing for a school paper doesn't give me an excuse to do the wrong thing."

Ginny waved a hand dismissively. She looked around the room; she knew everyone, some better than others, but it reminded her again how small and tightly knit the Tufa community was.

She touched Janet's arm. "Look. There's Duncan Gowen. I can't believe he's here."

"Where do you think he would be? This is all about what's happened to him."

"I thought it was about what happened to Kera and Adam."

"Kera and Adam are gone. He lost his girlfriend, and then saw his best friend killed. He's the center of attention now. Shit, I've got to talk to him, too." She scribbled a note on the pad.

"Not now," Ginny said, a hand on Janet's arm.

"No, not now. But maybe I can catch him when this is over, get his reactions to the game warden's comments."

Ginny looked again, more closely. She could only partially see his face, but Duncan appeared suitably sad and morose, and his body language—slumped in his chair, one hand dangling limp, his feet splayed out as if to keep him from sliding to the floor—only reinforced that. "I dunno, Jan. I don't think he's up to it tonight."

Before Janet could respond, the lights overhead went out, leaving only the ones over the stage. She snapped a quick photo of the game warden, catching him in profile with his visage set in grim determination.

Oh, that's good, she thought. She quickly wrote in her notebook, *His visage set in grim determination.*

Jack tapped the microphone to check if it was on. After the echoing thump faded, he said, "Thank y'all for coming out tonight. I'll make this as brief as I can, so we have plenty of time for questions. I'm Jack Cates, from the state wildlife agency. You may know me from other presentations such as, 'Can I See Your Fishing License?' or 'It's Not Deer Season Yet.' "

There were a few laughs, but not many. He wasn't sure if it was because the jokes were old, or that he'd read the crowd wrong.

"As many of you know," Cates continued, "we had a fatal encounter with a wild hog two days ago. A local girl was killed. Well, today we had another one, and this time a young man lost his life. We're almost certain it involves the same animal. And it's my job to make sure no one else dies."

Murmurs went through the crowd. Everyone knew about Kera, but the word hadn't finished spreading about Adam.

"Here's the culprit," he said, and pushed a button on the remote in his hand. The screen came to life with an image of a giant hog, with long yellowed tusks, standing in the midst of some greenery. There was nothing in the picture to give it explicit scale, but it definitely looked big, and mean.

"This isn't the actual hog we're after," Cates continued, "but it's a good representation." He then gave a quick rundown of the history of feral hogs, and their increasing presence in Tennessee. When he finished, he said, "How many of you have heard of Hogzilla?"

A few hands went up.

He clicked through to another picture, of a huge mud-covered hog hanging by its hind legs over a gravelike hole. A man in a white T-shirt stood beside it, providing scale. "This animal was killed in Georgia in 2004. It was eight feet long and weighed at least eight hundred pounds. And since then, even larger wild pigs have been killed. The one roaming your forests is, I think, a good two hundred pounds heavier than this one."

The murmurs grew louder, and people began discussing it among themselves. Someone reached up and patted Duncan on the shoulder, as if reassuring him that no one faulted him for not slaughtering such a behemoth. He didn't look back to see who it was.

"We got this image of it last night," Cates continued. "It's not the clearest, but I think it gives you a sense of how dangerous it is."

Now the screen showed a capture from the night-vision video. There was the monster, broadside, with both the corral and the other pigs for scale. The air pressure in the room dropped as almost everyone gasped at once.

"I know what a lot of you are thinking right now," Cates said. "You've got guns, you know the terrain, so you think you can go out and put this animal down. I should remind you, that's what the young man who died this morning thought.

"I can't stop you from doing this. There's too many of you, and too few of me. There's also no season or limit on wild hogs in Tennessee. I can only ask you to please, *please* leave it to me, and the professionals I bring in. We want this animal stopped as badly as you do, and we will waste no time getting it done. We were out this morning, and we'll be back out there tonight. So please: stay out of our way. Keep your friends out of our way. We were only a few minutes too late to save that boy this morning, and if he hadn't been there, we might've gotten the animal already. I don't want any more deaths on my conscience, or yours."

After letting that sink in, he added, "Are there any questions?"

The man leaning on the wall raised his hand. "Don Swayback from the *Weekly Horn,* Mr. Cates. Are you certain only one pig is involved?"

"There's a herd of normal-sized ones that accompany the big

one, but we're pretty sure it made the actual attack. Smaller pigs just don't behave that way."

A teenage girl in the middle of the crowd raised her hand. He nodded at her, and she stood up.

"Janet Harper, from the *Raven's Caw,*" the girl said, mimicking the other reporter's tone. "Is it safe to say that this pig is more dangerous than ever, now that it's developed a taste for human flesh?"

The crowd buzzed at that thought. Jack, taking note of her age, asked, "Miss Harper, just where is this paper you represent?"

"Cloud County High."

He felt a surge of relief. At least it wasn't some outside media organization that had gotten wind of this. "Miss Harper, this is an animal. It's an opportunistic feeder, and in both cases, the victims were alone, and the encounter appears to have been completely random. The animal certainly wasn't hunting human beings; that just wouldn't happen."

"Unless it's out for revenge. Like the Tsavo lions."

Jack was surprised she knew that story. "That's not really a valid comparison, Miss Harper."

"Well, what should we do to stay safe, *Mr.* Cates?" She said this with the cocky attitude so many teens had toward adults, and Jack felt a bit of admiration for her nerve. But she'd asked a valid question, and he took it seriously.

"Don't go into the woods alone is the most important thing. And don't go searching for this animal, either by actively hunting or putting out bait. I have trained hunters preparing to find it and finish it off. It's not a job for amateurs, as I said. Now—" He looked out at the crowd. "—are there any other questions?"

The teenage girl immediately raised her hand again, but he looked past her, for anyone else. All he saw were worried faces, though. With no choice, he said, "Yes, Miss Harper?"

"Just one more question, Mr. Cates. Has anyone posted a reward for this animal?"

"No, there is no reward that I'm aware of. It would be very unwise for someone to offer one, because it could lead to more people getting injured, and that might lead to lawsuits."

"So what should people do if they see it?"

"*That* is a very sensible question, Miss Harper, and the answer is, call me. I have a stack of business cards up here with my name, number, and e-mail address."

The girl nodded, said, "Thank you, Mr. Cates," and sat back down. He thought, *If she's that serious as a teenager, what will she be like when she's grown?* And he spared a kind thought for any unfortunate husband she might acquire.

As people left the Pair-A-Dice, Bliss joined Jack at the stage. She'd watched from the back of the room, with Bronwyn Chess, and Dolph Pettit.

He looked up from powering down the projector, saw her, and smiled. "How do you think that went?"

"They heard you. The sensible ones listened."

"Like that girl reporter?"

"Janet? She is sensible, believe it or not. She's just young."

"And the ones who aren't sensible?"

"They wouldn't listen if you shot fire from your eyes."

He laughed. "I'll have to see about that next time, after the way my *Simpsons* joke went over. My job doesn't usually require a lot of showmanship."

"Are you really going back out tonight?"

"Dolph and I are. Maybe we'll get lucky."

She touched his arm. "I'll be at the fire station all night. When you get done, come by. I'll make you both breakfast."

He met her steady blue eyes, and for a moment they communicated without speaking. At last he said, "We might just do that. If we're not too beat."

"It's an open invitation."

"Thank you."

Again they looked at each other, until Bliss nodded and walked away. Jack watched after her long after she'd gone through the door with Bronwyn.

"Pretty thing," Dolph said.

"Which one?" he asked, trying to appear casual.

"Well, both of 'em. But that Bliss, she's got that thing that makes you keep looking at the door after she leaves the room. Doesn't she?"

Jack realized he was doing exactly that, and he felt his cheeks burn. "You caught me, old man."

"Not me. But I do believe *she* just set the hook."

Duncan hunched in his chair, staring down the neck of his beer at the liquid inside, as the rest of the Tufa filed out. How many, he wondered, would now try to go after that damn pig? And who else might die because he failed to take the shot when he had it? When he'd let the animal do the very thing *he* lacked the balls to do?

He closed his eyes against the vision of those yellow tusks dripping red. He only wished he could close his ears against the memory of Adam's final scream.

"Mr. Gowen?"

He looked up. Two teenage girls stood over him. Their body language was tense and uncertain, as if they worried he might collapse, or attack them. "Yeah?"

One said, "I'm Janet Harper, from the *Raven's Caw*."

"Yeah." He remembered the paper from high school; he and his friends used to mock it for its amateurishness. And now that he heard her voice, he realized she'd asked questions earlier.

"I'm very sorry for your loss," she continued. "Your loss*es*. I wondered if I might ask you a couple of questions?"

"I don't think so," he said.

The other girl, Ginny Vipperman, grabbed Janet's arm. He knew Ginny from coed softball. "See? Now, come on."

Janet pulled away. "I understand you and the late Adam Procure were out hunting the pig this morning. What happened?"

"Janet!" Ginny whisper-yelled.

He looked up at her. She was so young, and so sincere. He couldn't decide if it made him sad, or furious. "No comment. I ain't answering questions. Not right now."

"Can I call you tomorrow?"

"Won't you be in school tomorrow?"

"Tomorrow's Sunday. And they canceled school on Monday because of the funerals."

Of course they did, Duncan thought. Two funerals he'd be expected to attend. Just dandy. "I won't be available tomorrow either. Sorry."

Ginny tugged on her arm again, and this time Janet gave in and let her friend pull her away. Duncan closed his eyes and took another long drink of his beer.

He felt a slender, feminine hand on his shoulder. His first thought was that the girl reporter had returned, but it wasn't her, or Bliss. It was Renny Procure, Adam's sister. She wore a battered straw cowboy hat and a black tank top, the very image of the girl in a "bro-country" music video. "All hips and lips," the boys used to say about her, but right now her bleary eyes canceled out any overt sexiness. "Can I talk to you for a minute?" she asked softly, her voice ragged from recent sobs.

He nodded. She pulled a chair up closer to him and sat so that she was almost in his face. He could smell something harder than beer on her breath, but she didn't seem drunk.

"I can't imagine how you must feel," she said. "Losing your girlfriend and your best friend so close together, and in such horrible ways. I don't have the words, or the songs. It's been a nightmare for me, watching Mom and Dad fall apart, and me having to suck it up and handle things."

"I'm sorry," was all he could croak out.

"No, that's not what I'm here to tell you," she said, and touched his face lightly with her fingertips. "I've known you all my life, Duncan. We rode the bus together all through junior high, remember? I'm here if you need to talk about this to somebody who knows a little of how you feel. And I hope you'll be here for me."

"I will," he managed.

She smiled, sad and tender, then kissed him on the cheek and left. He didn't watch her walk away the way he normally would.

Now Bliss Overbay did appear beside him. Never in his life had so many attractive, powerful women been so interested in him. "Hey," she said gently. "You ready to go home? I've got the truck warmed up. It's getting late, and it's been a long day."

He held up the beer. "I need about ten thousand more of these if I'm planning to get any sleep tonight."

"I have a trazodone you can borrow."

"If I borrow it, you won't get it back."

"Consider it a permanent loan, then."

He stood up and followed her outside. The parking lot was nearly empty, except for Jack Cates loading the projector screen into his truck. He waved at them, but said nothing.

On the drive home, Duncan looked out at the forest, already growing indistinct as dusk turned to night. Were any of those shadows the monster, passing through the woods on its way to do whatever mischief it had planned for the night? Or was it in fact long gone, chased out of its safe little hollow by the morning's chaos?

"I think," he said quietly, "I need to throw up."

Without a word, Bliss pulled over, and Duncan got out. He vomited up the beer he'd drunk, and the water, but since he hadn't eaten all day, that was all. It didn't stop his body from trying to expel something that no mere physical process could eliminate, though. The guilt he felt, the certainty that Adam's death today—and hell, maybe even Kera's death, too—was his fault choked him like a rotted chicken bone crossways in his throat. No matter how his body tried, it couldn't puke *that* out.

Finally he stopped, sputtered, and got back to his feet. He leaned against the truck's fender for a long moment. The insect noises were as loud as a tropical jungle in his ears, almost drowning out the truck's idling motor.

Bliss said softly, "You think you're done?"

"Yeah. Got nothing left to puke out."

"Come on, then."

For the rest of the ride home he huddled against the passenger door, wondering how he could face . . . well, *anyone* tomorrow. Surely someone, whether it was Kera's siblings, or Adam's sister, or Bliss, or Junior, or Mandalay, would see through him to the truth. He could have saved Adam. He could have avenged Kera. But instead he just stood there and watched.

For the first time since he'd heard about Kera, he began to cry.

14

The night was officially cold by the time Jack and Dolph gave up. It was after midnight, and their reconnaissance of Half Pea Hollow following the community meeting had been fruitless. No sign of the monster, or anything other than some deer and one sleepy emu.

Dolph breathed heavily as he shortened the leads on the dogs. Jack, concerned, said, "You seen a doctor about that wheezing?"

"Sure have," Dolph said as he led the two dogs to the tailgate. "You know what he said? 'You're an old man. Things shrivel up.' "

Jack smiled as he unloaded his M220. "We've got to come up with a different approach."

Dolph unsnapped their leashes, and the dogs jumped up onto the open tailgate and went obediently into their crates. "Not that many ways to hunt pigs. You either go after them, or find a way to bring them to you."

"Which would you suggest?"

He chuckled. "Neither one has worked out too well so far."

Jack secured his rifle behind the seat in the cab.

"They're down in that valley, I know it. With four of us, we ought to be able to root 'em out."

"True enough."

"And really, the one we're looking for is as big as the bed of this damn truck. How does something like that hide so well?" But even as he asked, he knew the answer. Hogs were shy, and easily spooked. If they heard or smelled you before you saw them, they'd vanish, and you'd never even know you'd been close.

"We got it to the trap that first night with no trouble," Dolph said. "I suppose we can try baiting it without a pen. Get it used to coming up to eat."

Jack looked up. "Wonder if we could get an infrared camera on a drone to help us find it?"

"Whoo-ee, listen to you," Dolph teased. "I guess they must've tripled your damn budget since my day."

Jack laughed. "Well, that is a point. I don't really have that extra thousand or so lying around in petty cash. I suppose we'll just have to keep spending the only things we've got: time, expertise, and boot leather."

Dolph closed the tailgate. "You know you can count on me, son. I still feel kind of responsible for this area."

Jack looked around. "I still feel confused by it. I mean . . . how can they live like this in the modern world? No law enforcement, no civil authority, barely any schools. How has nobody noticed?"

Dolph leaned against the truck's fender. "You want to know what I think?"

"You think we need a drink?"

"My God, you're a mind reader."

Jack laughed and got the hidden bottle of Jim Beam he kept under the floorboard mat, in a little recessed area he'd installed just for this purpose. Dolph opened the bottle, wiped the mouth with his sleeve and took a swallow. Then he said, "What do you think'll happen if the Tufa decide we're causing more trouble than we're fixing?"

"I don't know. They'll stop talking to us?"

"Let me tell you a little story, son. Back around 1986 or so, during those glorious Reagan years, I got a call about some fellas out spotlighting deer over on the other side of Needsville. I drove out and, sure enough, caught 'em at it. They took off, and I followed 'em. We were on a stretch of road that was dead straight for a good two miles, and while I was looking right at 'em, they turned off onto a side road. Keep in mind I wasn't a minute behind 'em, and I had my eyes on them the whole time."

He took another drink before continuing. "When I got to the spot they turned, the road wasn't there. There was nothing, just shoulder, and ditch, and field. Not a sign of them, no dust in the air, no headlights in the distance. Just nothing."

"What did you do?"

"I drove up and down that stretch of road for half an hour. They hadn't reached the curve ahead, which went the other direction anyway, and they sure hadn't doubled back. They'd turned onto a road that just flat-out disappeared."

"That's not possible."

"Of course it's not. That's why I came back when the sun came up. What you reckon I found?"

Jack shrugged.

"A road, just as pretty as you please. Wide enough for two cars to pass. Led up into the hills, past a whole bunch of old houses. Finally found the truck I'd seen parked in front of one of 'em. Rousted 'em out of bed, made 'em show me their firearms, and walked around their property. But of course, I didn't find any proof of anything."

"Of course."

"Now, I grant you, the first thing anybody would say is, 'You must've just missed the turn in the dark.' You've known me for a long time, Jack. You think that's what happened?"

"No," he said honestly.

"Then how would you explain it?"

"I can't."

"I can. The Tufa have their own ways here. They don't bother nobody, and more importantly, they don't tolerate nobody bothering them. As long as you remember that, you'll get along with 'em fine."

"So you never did catch them poachers?"

Jack chuckled. "Never had to. Stopped in at the Catamount Corner—this was back when Mr. and Mrs. Goins ran it, before that gay fella and his New York boyfriend took it over—and just let 'em know that this sort of hunting was bad for everybody. About two weeks later, I heard from a friend at the hospital in Unicorn that a Tufa fella had been brought in, one who lived in that house where I found the truck I was chasing. Seems a buck deer just crashed right through the front window and gored him in the nuts while he was sitting on the couch."

"That's poetic."

"Ain't it? So see? Things do get handled here. It's just . . . different."

"I'll keep that in mind. You about ready to go home?"

"I'm so tired, I might fall into bed and miss."

Jack thought about Bliss's offer at the fire station, but like Dolph, he was beat. And he had to come back tomorrow. "All right. I'll pick you up in the morning and we'll see what we can find during the day."

He drove the old man home, but kept thinking about the look in Bliss's eyes.

Duncan was back at the roadhouse on Monday for the first of the two funerals. He doubted he could survive it, but he had no choice. He was both the grieving boyfriend of one victim, and the lamenting best friend of the other.

These weren't funerals in the traditional sense, of course. They were memorial services, or wakes, since neither had any body to display. And except for the crumbling remains of an old chapel of ease that nobody in their right mind ever visited, there were no churches in Cloud County. Brownyn Chess was married to a Methodist minister, and he'd spoken at funeral services in the past. But Duncan doubted Junior Damo would ever ask him to speak for any of his people. And both Kera and Adam were his.

Adam's service was first, and was held at the Pair-A-Dice. There was some talk of holding it at the old Shine Cave, but past attempts at similar events had not gone well. Now the roadhouse's tables had been pushed to the wall, and a dozen rows of mismatched chairs set out. Only about two dozen people attended, every one of them family except Duncan and his brother, Poole. Junior Damo didn't even put in an appearance, which was pretty much the way old Rockhouse Hicks would've behaved.

Renny arranged a display with Adam's old banjo, baseball cap, and favorite cowboy boots, a sort of stand-in for the coffin. And she stood in her black dress, playing long mournful notes on her fiddle, sliding in and out of every sad song she knew. And she knew a lot.

At last Adam's father, Porter, stood up and walked to the microphone. He spoke about his son in flat, nonspecific terms, and then his mother, Vandeline, played and sang an acoustic version of Adam's favorite song, Nickelback's "Photograph."

Duncan fought down the memories of all the times he'd teased Adam about this song, and his liking for Nickelback in general. "They sound like every band from the early 2000s got put into a blender, and this is what came out," he'd told him. But Adam's fandom was unwavering.

Then Duncan was asked to speak, but he demurred. *Let them think I'm overcome with grief,* he thought. *I'm sure as fuck overcome.*

When the ordeal was finished, lunch began. It was a typical Southern add-a-dish affair, with far more food than any gathering this size could eat. The idea was to have enough leftovers to tide the grieving family over for a few days.

Each dish had been sung over as it was prepared, soaking up the music of grief and loss, until some swore they could taste those very emotions in the glazed ham and mashed potatoes. Duncan couldn't taste anything; he had no appetite, and couldn't imagine ever having one again.

He was the unmoving center of the room, staring into space as people pulled out tables and set them up all around him. He didn't even look up when they sat directly behind him, bearing mountainous plates of food.

"Hey," his brother, Poole, said. He still didn't look up. "You want something?"

"Nothing they've got here."

Poole patted him on the shoulder and went to get in line for the food.

Duncan recognized the voice of Adam's mother, Vandeline, from somewhere close behind him, and tried not to listen, but he couldn't help it once he realized she was talking about him.

"I remember when Adam and Duncan here were little boys," she said. She tousled the back of Duncan's hair. "They used to run up and down the creek, seeing who could cram the most crawdads into an old mason jar."

She kept rubbing his hair, and every muscle in his body tightened. He knew people watched him, the grieving best friend, in the same way they watched NASCAR, and for the same secret reason: They hoped to see a crash, and blood, and horror.

"They'd sleep over at each other's house on the weekends," she continued. "I'd have to make them go to sleep, and even then, they'd stay up all night whispering."

Her fingertips tickled the hair at the back of his neck. His jaw muscles almost spasmed as he clamped his teeth shut against any reaction.

"Some nights they'd stay up playing music together, especially when they got electric guitars. They'd get the most god-awful howling noises out of those things."

Now she ran her fingertips along his ears. He kept his eyes focused straight ahead, not wanting to see if anyone was watching. His entire field of vision was the painted cinder blocks of the walls across the room, where the layers almost, but not quite, hid the texture of the concrete.

"They were such good friends," one of the other women with her said. "They didn't even fight over Kera."

"They surely were," Vandeline agreed, finally taking her hand away. "They surely were."

"This is turning into a snipe hunt, not a pig hunt," Dolph said through a yawn as he climbed into Jack's truck.

"Yeah," Jack muttered. After less than four hours' sleep, they'd gone as deep into Half Pea Hollow as they could, following tracks and looking for sign. They'd glimpsed some normal-sized wild pigs but found no evidence of their monster. The dogs had done no better.

"How 'bout the elk we saw?" Jack said, searching for a bright side. Elk had been reintroduced in 2000, but they were still rare. "When I was training, I had to help put collars on some of the bucks. Did you know that in rutting season, elk breed eight to twelve times a night?"

"That's why you hardly ever see them," Dolph said dryly. "They're exhausted." He buckled himself into Jack's truck. "You know, maybe that big pig has moved on out of your jurisdiction."

"I should be so lucky," Jack said, starting the engine.

"There's always the chance that Max's shot did get through, and it just took a while for it to finally die."

"It killed somebody else. Not bad for a zombie."

"You and I both know how dumb some animals are. You can

shoot 'em through the heart, and they'll run a mile before they realize they should fall over. I wouldn't rule it out."

"I'm not. But I can't operate on that idea, either." The truck bounced as they went over a ditch, and the dogs in their crates barked their disapproval.

"So what's your plan, then?" Dolph said.

"I'll just keep my eyes and ears open, and keep checking for sign."

Dolph gave him a sideways, knowing smile. "Does that include sign from a certain dark-eyed young lady? I think you're already making plenty of headway with her."

Ginny Vipperman sat on the edge of Janet's bed, softly playing a slow, methodical version of "Dizzi Jig" on a hammered dulcimer. They were aware of the funerals, and of course had known both Kera and Adam, but they were from the other group, and so they knew they wouldn't be welcome. Besides, Janet was obsessed with getting her story on their deaths just right, so she'd gone over and over it.

Ginny stopped and said, "You ever thought about redoing this like Constance Denby? With some low bass strings so it sounds like it's got some balls?"

Janet took a drag off the joint they shared and passed it to her friend. This dope was known locally as Gitterman's Gold, since it was harvested from some plants left to grow wild and unattended since Dwayne Gitterman's death some years earlier. Only a handful of people knew where it was, and they made their money selling it down in Knoxville, or at truck stops along the interstate. Those in Needsville and Cloud County got the "Tufa discount."

"I don't need my dulcimer to have balls," Janet said. "That's what an autoharp's for."

She turned back and stared at her laptop screen, her nose wrinkled in thought until Ginny said, "You're making that face again."

"What face?"

"The one that either says, 'I'm thinking real hard,' or 'I smell something real bad.' "

"I'm thinking."

"About what?"

"What I need to call that giant hog in my story. I mean, 'Hogzilla' is taken."

" 'Hog Kong'?"

"Too obvious."

Ginny put the dulcimer aside, handed the joint back to Janet, and tapped the handle of one of the dulcimer hammers against her lips as she slowly exhaled smoke. "How about 'the Baconator'?"

"No, that's a sandwich."

" 'Snuffles'?"

Janet turned and looked at her. "Seriously?"

"Fine, smart gal. You come up with something."

Janet pondered for a moment. " 'Uberhog.' "

"Does it wear a cape and threaten a superhero?"

Janet giggled. " 'The Evil Dr. Porkchop.' "

Ginny snorted. " 'Truffles the Mighty.' "

Now they both laughed. There was a knock at the door, and Janet's father called, "Y'all getting high in there?"

"You bet!" Janet answered. They giggled some more. Her dad always asked that when they made too much noise, but he had no idea how often he was right. Then again, they had no idea how often they failed to fool him. He'd just rather have them stoned in Janet's bedroom than somewhere else.

"Does he really think you burn that much sage?" Ginny asked Janet after they heard his footsteps fade.

"I do burn a lot of sage," Janet said. "That way he doesn't notice the weed."

"How about 'Hogwild'?" Ginny suggested.

"Sounds like he should be judging a wet T-shirt contest."

" 'Bighoof'?" When Janet looked blank, Ginny added, "You know, like Bigfoot?"

"Oh, I got it. But no." Janet picked up her guitar and began to noodle on it. Ginny knew it always helped her friend think, so she lay back on the bed, put one arm behind her head, and drew long and hard on the joint. "Maybe," Ginny said at last, "we should just give it a person's name."

"What, like 'Steven'?" Janet said.

"Yeah. Maybe something from politics. Like 'Trump,' or 'Hilary.' "

" 'Nixon'?" Janet suggested, and they both giggled again. Then she said, "How about a diminutive? You know, a cutesy name, something to make it seem less dangerous?"

" 'Porky'?"

" 'Muffin.' "

" 'Tiny.' "

" 'Li'l Bit.' "

" 'Bacon Bit.' "

" 'Hamdinger.' "

Ginny suddenly sat up and snapped her fingers. *" 'Piggly-Wiggly'!"*

"Perfect!" Janet cried, and quickly typed the words into her laptop. Her story for the *Raven's Caw* was finished, and she added the old-fashioned "*30*" at the end.

15

Kera's funeral was held later that day, at the Rogerses' house. Unlike the event for Adam, this one drew people from both sides of the Tufa. Nothing brought people together like the death of a beautiful girl, and Kera was well liked by everyone.

Cars and trucks lined the gravel road leading up to the Rogers farm, and four picnic tables had been strung together in the front yard to hold all the food. Cyrus Crow catered it for free, standing behind the steam tables and ladling massive portions of barbecue, mashed potatoes, and other Southern dishes onto plastic plates.

An ad hoc band of elderly fiddlers, banjo pickers, and guitarists sat in the shade of a huge maple tree, playing lively instrumentals. There would be no sad songs here; dying dirges served an entirely different purpose.

Duncan arrived in his family's ancient LTD. He rode in the passenger seat, the air conditioner blasting full into his face. He wore a suit that he'd borrowed from a cousin, one that was too big for him and smelled of weed and some kind of chemical solvent. At least he'd managed to wear his own tennis shoes, despite the shiny black hard-sole ones left for him. He dared someone to criticize him.

His father, Saggory, a.k.a. "Sag," drove resentfully, his shirt collar and tie so tight around his baggy neck that it looked like it was pinching off his head. His mother, Bobbie, wore her black funeral dress, and his big brother, Poole, wore just a polo shirt and jeans.

"Look at all these dumb rednecks," Sag muttered as he sought a closer place to park. "Half of 'em barely knew that girl. The other half just wanted to see her nekkid."

"Hush, Sag," Bobbie said.

"It's true. Ain't it, Poole?"

"Maybe you should listen to your wife," Poole said flatly. He and Sag had never really gotten along, and the tension only grew stronger now that Poole was out on his own. He was here not for Sag, or even for Duncan, but for their mom. Poole was the kind of man who, if he got called a son of a bitch, got into a fight because you'd insulted his mother.

Duncan snapped, "Why don't every last one of you shut the fuck up, okay?"

They did, until Sag said, "There we go," and pulled into a space behind a mud-spattered Jeep.

Duncan got out of the car and strode toward the house. He felt every eye on him, the mourning boyfriend who'd lost not just his girl, but also his best friend. Two funerals in one day was rare in Cloud County; the last time it had happened, it was the memorial service for Bo-Kate Wisby and Jefferson Powell, and that had been as much a celebration of their demise as a wake.

He couldn't look at any of them. How many, he wondered, knew about Kera and Adam, and thought he was just being a "good Tufa man" for sharing his girl with his best friend? No, he and Kera didn't have any exclusive arrangement, but at the same time, wasn't it just polite to let him in on it? She had no obligation, true . . . but why didn't she?

Because he would have resented it and broken things off with her. She had to know that.

The crowd seemed enormous, all with Tufa-black hair except for the elderly whites and grays. Many were children, who played both games and instruments as if they were at a park. Duncan understood that services like this were as much a celebration of life as they were a marker of death, but that made it no easier to endure. In a way, he preferred the tight, grim send-off Adam had received that morning.

He went into the house without speaking to anyone. Inside, the furniture was pushed back against the walls to make room. People milled about in small groups and spoke in low tones, and although some turned to look at him, none stopped talking as he passed.

He went to the refrigerator and took out a beer. When he closed the door, Mandalay Harris stood right there. He almost yelled in surprise.

"Sorry," the girl said. She was clad in a simple black dress, with her black hair pulled up into a severe bun. "Didn't mean to startle you."

"You didn't, I'm just a little tense," he said. He twisted off the cap, turned up the bottle, and drank a long draft.

"Two funerals in one day would make anyone tense. How are you making it otherwise?"

He shrugged without meeting her eyes. "All right, I guess."

"Is there anything I can do?"

Before he could answer, Junior Damo popped up next to them. He wore a pin-striped suit, and his hair was slicked back from his forehead. He resembled nothing so much as a public-access evangelist. "What are you two talking about?"

"I'm expressing my condolences," Mandalay said.

"He's one of mine," Junior said.

"I think he belongs to himself," Mandalay said firmly. "And he's a Tufa, just like the rest of us. He's suffered a loss, and I'm giving him my sympathies."

"Yeah, well, you should check with me before you . . ."

His voice trailed off as she fixed him with a withering look.

"You're just a kid," he managed to croak out.

"Then challenge me."

When he realized neither one was going to back down, Duncan said, "Uh, guys? This may not be the place for this."

"You're exactly right," Mandalay agreed. "This is not." She turned away from Junior, who let out an audible gasp of relief. She asked Duncan, "Has there been any word about the animal that did this? Has it been dealt with?"

"Not that I know of," Duncan said. "Nobody's told me anything, at any rate."

"Well, let's hope they find it soon, before anyone else suffers." With a final look at Junior, she turned and went to speak with a group of women in black. Junior stayed, sweat trickling down from his Brylcreemed hairline.

Junior scanned the room and said, "Lordy, there's Deedee Pillow. This must be the first party she's been to where she didn't jump out of a cake." Then he turned to Duncan with a little conspiratorial smile. "So you took my advice, I see."

"I don't know what you mean," Duncan said hollowly.

"Sure you do. You and Adam were close, right? And you always want what your friend has. Especially when it looks that good in blue jeans."

"I didn't do anything," Duncan mumbled, unable to meet his eyes. "The pig did it. Besides, Kera could see whoever she wanted."

"Of course," Junior said with a wink. "Well, don't worry, it's safe with me."

Like Mandalay, Junior sauntered away to mingle with the others. Duncan looked down at the beer in his hand, which trembled like a can in a paint mixer. Foam sloshed out onto the floor.

A big hand settled on his shoulder. He looked up sharply to see Doyle Collins, who ran the gas station where Kera worked. "Hey, Duncan."

Beside him, his wife, Berklee, stood in a black dress. Her eyes were red from crying. She said, "I am so sorry to hear about Kera, and then Adam. You must feel awful."

"Yeah."

"Listen, if there's anything we can do—"

"Thank you."

Berklee looked up at Doyle, who was probably the tallest man in the room, and one of the few without jet-black hair. His Tufa blood was faint, but he was a good man and most everyone trusted him.

Doyle leaned close to Duncan. "Kera left some odds and ends at the shop. I thought I'd give you first crack at them before I tell her parents. Just come by when you have a moment."

"Sure," Duncan said, knowing he'd never do it. He had enough of Kera's odds and ends bouncing around in his head.

Eventually everyone took seats in the folding chairs borrowed from the high school. They made four short rows in the living room. Duncan, Renny, and Kera's parents took the front row. Her brother and sister sat right behind them.

Azure Kirby, a folklore professor and a respected "granny-woman" in the community, stood before them. She had taught Kera how to read the clouds and predict the weather when she was a little girl. With great dignity, she said, "I'd like to tell you a little bit about Kera Rogers."

While she spoke, Duncan stared past her at a stain on the wallpaper, just as he'd done at Adam's service. His suit, previously too large, now felt tight and uncomfortable, like too-small armor.

"Y'all know when Kera was born, where she went to school,

and when and how she died," Azure said. "I'm not going to dwell on that. What I'm going to tell you is some things you maybe didn't know.

"She was a hell of a mechanic, as Doyle Collins will back up. She learned to change oil before she was six, and brake pads by the time she was ten. These newfangled computer-controlled engines didn't throw her off, either. She could run down an electrical problem faster than you could tell it. In fact, one reason she always painted her nails black was because that way she didn't have to dig the grease out from under them all the time."

Some people chuckled at this. Duncan did not. He had no idea; she'd never mentioned it.

"She also knew her way around a song," Azure continued. "When she was a little girl, I'd hear her squawking on a penny-whistle, trying to force the notes into the right shape. You couldn't show her anything; she had to figure it out for herself. It was the exact opposite of the way she learned about cars, and just goes to show that people are more complicated than you might know."

Duncan slid down in his seat.

"We should be proud of Kera, for being true to herself. So many young women of her age are defined by their husbands, boyfriends, or even children. They never learned to be true to themselves, because the world never let them. The folks of this community, we pride ourselves on that, and that pride let Kera live a life, short as it was, that was nevertheless a true one."

Azure nodded, and three older people, all with instruments, came to the front of the room. They began to play, softly, Enya's "On My Way Home." Duncan heard sniffling around him, but he had nothing left.

In his dreams that night, Duncan relived the moment over and over. There was Adam, the wild hog—having grown to the size of a bus in his subconscious—looming out of the forest behind him. There was even a red circle on the animal's fur, a literal target showing where Duncan should shoot.

Adam stood there oblivious. And then Kera walked out of the woods and into his arms. They kissed, and his hands roamed all over her. Then the hog opened its mouth, revealing yard-long tusks in rows all the way back to its cavernous throat. It swallowed them whole, and as its maw closed, blood squirted out.

He woke up sweating, and wondered if he'd actually screamed. But since no one came running, he assumed he hadn't.

He was in his old bedroom at home. The family's two dogs lay on the floor beside it, and neither had awoken with him. He scooted back to sit against the headboard, and ran a hand through his tangled hair. There would be no sleeping for the rest of the night, he knew from the pounding in his chest.

He quietly dressed, put on a Jack Daniel's baseball cap over his sleep-matted hair, and slipped out of the house. He started his car and drove into town, where he knew the Fast Grab would be open. Old Mr. Tirrell was working the late shift, reading a book about a cemetery by someone with the last name of Eco. He looked up as Duncan entered, but didn't seem surprised.

"Can't sleep?" he said as he tucked a lottery ticket into the book to mark his place.

"No," Duncan said.

"Heard what happened. Not sure I could sleep, either. Want to buy a lottery ticket? Powerball's up to ninety million."

Duncan ignored him and walked to the beer cooler. He normally drank Budweiser, but tonight he grabbed a quart bottle of Colt 45.

As he took it to the counter, the door jingled again. Renny Procure entered, in cutoffs and a T-shirt, her hair spilling haphazardly from beneath her cowboy hat. She stopped dead when she saw Duncan.

She nodded at the malt liquor bottle. "That looks serious."

"Serious as I can get without breaking into the liquor store in

Unicorn," Duncan said. He was struck by how beautiful she looked in her fresh-from-sleep state. How had he never noticed this before? And what was wrong with him that he noticed it now?

"Well, then, we're here for the same reason," she said. "Want some help finishing that off?"

"Decide soon," Tirrell said. "I have to stop selling in three minutes."

"Ring it up twice," Renny said, and strode back to the cooler. "And add an iced coffee." She grabbed her own bottle of malt liquor and followed him out to his car with the two drinks. She'd driven Adam's truck, and the sight of it made Duncan catch his breath.

"Come with me," she said, and grabbed his arm. "Adam would want us to tell him good-bye in his truck. He loved that thing more than anything."

Almost anything, Duncan thought, but he climbed into the passenger seat as he'd done so many times. She started the engine and floored it, slinging gravel out of the parking lot.

They tore through the night, and Duncan held tightly to the oh-shit handle above the door. Renny drained the iced coffee, then pulled off the lid with her teeth and began chewing on the ice. She hit a bump, and ice flew into her face.

"Dammit!" she said in mock outrage. "I eat ice all the time without spilling it, and now look at me. I blame you."

Reflexively, Duncan shot back, "Hey, if you can't hit your own ice hole, it's not *my* fault."

She barked out a surprised laugh. Duncan couldn't help but smile. After all the heaviness, it felt almost supernaturally good to be amused again.

Secure that no police would stop them, he opened one of the bottles. She grabbed it before he could drink and turned it up for a long chugging swallow. Then she handed it back to him and belched.

"I had the worst fucking nightmare," she said, her eyes straight ahead. "Adam was in the woods, and there was that monster pig behind him. I kept yelling at him to turn around, or run, or do something other than stand there. But he didn't. And the thing . . ." She suddenly choked up.

Duncan said slowly, "I had the same dream."

"Your girlfriend and my baby brother," she said, shaking her head. "Killed by a motherfucking pig. We raise pigs, you know that? And it was all I could do not to go out there and shoot every single one of 'em."

"That wouldn't have accomplished anything."

"It would've made me feel better."

"Not for long."

She sighed. "That's true. I bottle-fed some of them, when they were piglets." She took back the bottle and drank again. "I can't wait until they kill that thing and bring its worthless carcass through town."

"Why would they do that?"

"Oh, come on. If you and Adam had killed it, you mean you wouldn't have showed it off?"

"I suppose so."

"My parents are both passed out drunk," she said. "That's why they didn't come to Kera's wake today. My big brother is stoned out of his mind. He kept blowing shotguns for the dog, so even the dog's high as a kite. I'm the only one sober, and I don't like that at all."

"Maybe I should drive, then."

"Nothing's going to happen to us." She made an elaborate hand gesture, one that appealed to the night winds to watch over and protect them. Every Tufa learned it as a child, and Duncan mimicked it halfheartedly.

"Where are we going?" he asked after a long stretch of silence, the only noise being the tires on the highway.

"I have no idea," she said.

"Well, at least we'll get there on time."

She laughed, took another drink, and belched again. "You're a funny guy, Duncan. I didn't used to think so. The whole time we were growing up, I thought you were just another punk who'd end up never amounting to anything."

"Not far off," he muttered.

"But not many guys would get off their ass and go after the monster that killed their girlfriend like you did."

He was glad it was so dark that she couldn't see him blush from shame.

"Okay, to be honest, I *do* wish you hadn't gotten Adam to help you," she continued. "But he was basically a dumb-ass, and he probably would've insisted on coming along anyway. So I don't blame you for that."

"Thanks," he said, and drained the first bottle. He put it on the floorboard and opened the second one.

She slowed and turned off the highway onto a gravel road. He knew it, of course: it led up the mountainside to a scenic overlook that took in the whole valley. He'd last been there for a school picnic his junior year of high school, which now seemed decades ago. He and Kera had just been flirting then, catching each other's eye and quickly looking away, trading insults and completely denying that either had any interest in the other. What had Adam been doing that day? He couldn't remember.

The truck's gears struggled in a couple of places, and Renny shifted expertly. He was struck by the family resemblance in the way she drove, her body moving in the same way he'd seen Adam's do so many times. It sent a weird jolt through him, because even though her feminine presence was almost overwhelming, he couldn't shake the idea that Adam was there, too.

At last they reached the spot. A picnic table and garbage can occupied a clearing, and on the other side, the open ground ended at a sloping cliff that gave them a spectacular view of the night sky, the mountains, and the cluster of lights that marked Needsville.

Every surface was damp with dew, and she slipped as she stepped on the bench, and then up on the table.

He stayed by the truck, uncertain what he should do.

She threw back her head and let out a long, loud undulating cry, a combination of war cry and grief-stricken sob. In the night's stillness, it rang through the air, silencing all the insects and disturbing sleeping birds. The only direct response was a distant owl cry.

"Well, that figures," she said. "You know, some Indians believe owls are the spirits of the dead who ain't quite ready to move on?"

"Didn't know that," Duncan said. The malt liquor had begun to seriously fuzz his thoughts.

"Think that was Adam?"

He shook his head. "No. I don't think he'd have any reason to hang around."

She stepped down off the table, strode over to him, pushed him against the truck and kissed him hard, her tongue forcing its way past his lips. She was only a little shorter than he was, and when she broke the kiss, she kept him hemmed in by bracing her arms on either side of him.

"What was that?" he asked. He couldn't look her in the eye.

"A kiss, stupid."

"Why would you . . . ?"

"Because I am tired to death of death, and there's only one way I know to feel alive at a time like this."

"I'm not sure I'm the right guy to—"

"I don't *care* if you're the right guy. You're the guy who's here. Pretend I'm Kera if you want, I don't care."

He looked up sharply, and his anger rose. "Don't you *ever* say that, you fucking bitch."

She smiled. "Now, that's more like it. Fuck me angry, because that's how I intend to fuck you. Let's show the night winds how we feel about what they've done to us."

The sudden rage had burned through a lot of his buzz. He

grabbed her by the waist, spun her around, and slammed her back against the car. She laughed into his mouth as he kissed her with as much fury as he could, and she pulled his hands to her breasts, braless beneath her T-shirt.

16

Janet's cell phone buzzed. She lay on her bed, eyes closed, listening to the music running through her head. It never went away, but not all of it was worthy of her concentration.

Beside her, Ginny lightly snored. Ginny and Janet had been having sleepovers since they were five, and although they still shared the same bed, there had never been anything erotic between them. Ginny liked boys, and Janet liked music, or at least she hadn't yet met a boy she liked as much as, let alone more than, music. Still, people talked about the two girls, even if for the most part they didn't judge. Luckily, neither girl cared.

Janet picked the phone up from her nightstand. It vibrated in her hand. "Hello?" she said softly.

"Janet, this is Mandalay. I need a favor."

She sat up straight. "Hi."

"Hi. Can you take me somewhere?"

Janet looked at Ginny, who continued to sleep. She crossed to the closet, stepped inside, and closed the door. "I beg your pardon?"

"I need a ride somewhere, and you have a license."

"Oh! I mean . . . sure. Where do you want to go?"

"Out to see Miss Azure."

"When?"

"Now."

Janet glanced at the clock. It was just before midnight. "Okay. I mean . . . I guess."

"Good. I'll expect you in a few minutes."

She hung up, and Janet stared at the phone. She quickly added the number as a contact. Then she quietly pulled on her pants and ran a brush through her hair.

She started to wake Ginny—it was often easier to include her than to spend the time explaining things later—but Mandalay hadn't mentioned her. And Ginny showed no sign of waking.

Why the hell did Mandalay need a chauffeur? If anyone could ride the night winds, it was one of the Tufa leaders. And Azure's cabin was neither hard to find nor dangerous to visit.

But it wasn't the kind of summons Janet could turn down. And with her insatiable curiosity, she wouldn't have even if she could.

"Well, that was a surprise," Bliss Overbay said breathlessly.

"A pleasant one, I hope," Jack Cates said. He looked down at the way her hair spread over the pillow, and bent to kiss her. It started as a simple touch of lips, but then her arms slid around his neck, as tightly as her legs around his waist, and in moments, they kissed as passionately as they had earlier. They were naked beneath a scratchy blanket on a cot at the fire station, and what had just transpired between them would have seemed unlikely, if not impossible, mere hours earlier.

When it broke, she said, "They say a kiss steals a minute off your life."

"It seems like a fair trade."

"You're a good half hour closer to the grave, if I'm counting right."

"What about you?"

She nipped at his chin. "Luckily, time doesn't work the same for everybody."

They both laughed, the kind of intimate, exhausted laugh that comes after realizing just how compatible you are. Jack tried to slide off her, but she tightened her legs and kept him in position. He didn't struggle.

"Are you sure," he said after another kiss, "that this is a good idea?"

"Why wouldn't it be? You're not married, I'm not married. We don't work together— "

"But that's how we met."

"Okay, we work *near* each other. And we don't have families that are feuding. So why not?" She ran her hand through his hair. "Why the hell not?"

He laughed. "I just can't believe I'm this lucky."

"Maybe I feel the same way," she said, and kissed him again.

He truly couldn't believe it. In her work clothes, Bliss had looked lean and angular, like so many mountain women. But naked, she'd proved to be exactly the kind of woman he'd always fantasized about. He kept expecting to wake up back home, but no, this had really happened.

He and Dolph had spent the day looking for more signs of the killer hog, to no avail. It was as if the beast had simply vanished or, worse, moved on to another area, and more unsuspecting people. Disheartened, he'd dropped his friend at his truck, then called Bliss to take her up on her offer to shower at the fire station.

She met him there after Kera Rogers's memorial service, showed him the shower, and then surprised him mightily by slipping into the water with him. He started to protest, but she gave him no opportunity.

After their first kiss, she held up his right hand. "Do this," she said, and made a particular gesture with her own fingers.

He repeated it, then said, "Why?"

"Always pay the insurance," she replied, and pulled him into another kiss.

When the hot water ran out, they scurried together under the blanket on the cot, where they'd gotten to know each other even more.

Now he looked down at her in wonder. "Tell me now if this is a onetime thing."

"Do you want it to be?"

"A question with a question. That's your standard response, is it?"

She smiled. He'd never seen anything so beautiful. Her face was free of makeup, her skin flushed, her lips swollen ever so slightly. "No, I'm just teasing. It can be a onetime thing if that's what you need. But I'd like it not to be."

He kissed her neck. "I would, too."

He thought back to recent events. The day after Adam Procure's death, he'd accompanied Bliss and the inscrutable Trooper Darwin up to the site of the second killing in Half Pea Valley, where Dolph stood watch over the remains. Darwin took his time examining the site, something Jack ordinarily would have respected. But he seemed to be putting on an act for Jack and Dolph's benefit.

"Any questions about anything?" Jack had finally asked.

"Hm? No, I figure I got all I need. I'll need statements from everyone who was here—you two, Bronwyn, and the other guy, the one who was hunting with you. But I don't think there's any hurry for that."

"No hurry?" Jack said. "Two people have died."

"And the paperwork won't bring 'em back. You got the word out about how dangerous this critter is, right? And I'll sure keep repeating it. That's really all we can do until somebody finally kills it."

"You with the Criminal Investigation Division, then?"

"Not so's you could tell it."

"But you're out of District Five in Fall Creek?"

"You bet. Troop E."

"Who's your superior?" Jack asked suddenly.

"Corporal Tom Hancock," Darwin replied without missing a beat. "Junior, not senior. Senior retired last year. You know him?"

"Yeah," Jack said. "I might give him a call."

"You do that. Tell him I said howdy."

"You think he'll approve of you handling a murder investigation all by yourself?"

Darwin laughed. "This ain't murder. This is an accident. And I do those by myself all the time."

"Really?"

"Here in Cloud County . . . really."

And that had been that. The whole area was photographed. The one bit of human remains they'd found was bagged and tagged. These, along with the statements, would fill all the crucial spaces in the official files, and unless someone was driven to look into why all these pieces of evidence were collected by the same guy, it would never even be noticed. The right song, sung in the right way, would effectively hide them in plain sight.

The bodies of the dead pigs were left for coyotes, other scavengers, and their own kind to dispose of. On the long hike back to the Rogers farm, Darwin said nothing, and in fact appeared almost jauntily preoccupied. Dolph and Jack exchanged looks of disbelief. Bliss brought up the rear, silent and inscrutable.

When they reached their vehicles, Bliss said, "I'm going to see about the Rogerses. They'll be having the funeral day after tomorrow."

"Give them my best," Darwin said before he climbed into his Ford Explorer with blue lights on top.

So Jack and Dolph had once again hunted without success. And this time, since Dolph brought his own ride, Jack had called Bliss to take her up on the shower offer. And now here they were.

He propped up on one elbow and looked down at her. Her

black hair was spread around her, and he was fascinated by the snake tattoo on her arm. It curled around her biceps and up onto her shoulder, where acorns fell from its mouth down onto her breast. He traced the path lightly with his finger, and leaned down to kiss the lowest acorn. "What's the significance of this?"

"It's personal."

"I didn't mean to be rude."

"No, that's not what I meant. It's just . . . it would be difficult to explain. Maybe, if this develops into something, then I can tell you."

"I don't have a lot of free time for dating," he said honestly.

"Neither do I."

"It might end up being a whole relationship of things like this, where we just find out we've got a moment and grab it. Hard to plan around that kind of thing."

"What makes you think I need to plan?"

He kissed her, and she ran her fingertips along his stubbly chin. He'd heard stories about men who trifled with Tufa girls to their peril, but at the moment, any such worries were far from his mind.

"We're bound to cross paths professionally, too," he said. "Would that be a problem for you?"

"No."

He grinned again, and somehow all the anger and frustration, for this moment at least, dissolved away. "Well, then, Bliss Overbay . . . do you want to go steady?"

"I believe I do, Jack Cates. I believe I do."

Janet glanced at Mandalay in the passenger seat. The younger girl wore a UT Vols hoodie and blue jeans. She had one foot propped up on the dashboard.

"So," Janet asked, "what are we doing?"

"We're driving down Max Welton Road."

"Ha. No, seriously. Why didn't you just—" She made a fluttering motion with her hand, then finished, "—out to Azure's place?"

"Because I wanted to talk to you as well."

"Me?"

"Janet, you may not believe it, but in a lot of ways, you're more important to the Tufa than I am."

Janet snorted. "You're right, I don't believe that."

"You're the one who's going to leave here someday and take the Tufa into the world."

"People don't leave, Mandalay. Look at Rockhouse Hicks, or Bronwyn Hyatt. Sure, they left. But then the night winds blew 'em right back. And what about Rayford Parrish? He didn't even get the *chance* to come back."

"That was then. This is now. Things change."

"Not for the Tufa."

"Even for us," Mandalay said with a heaviness that made them both ride silently for a while. Then she asked, "You have a boyfriend, Janet?"

"Not currently."

"You're not dating Amos Collins?"

Janet snort-laughed. "Good Lord, no. Who says I am?"

"Just heard it around school."

"He has a crush on me, but I promise you, it ain't mutual. I mean, he once failed a spelling test because he spelled 'farm' *E-I-E-I-O.*"

Mandalay laughed. "I see what you mean." Then, more seriously, she said, "I have a boyfriend."

"I know, I met him."

"You could tell?"

"Well, I mean . . . like you, I heard about it around school. People tend to notice things about you, you being so important and all."

"You ever had a boyfriend?"

"Sure. But they didn't appreciate that I spent so much time

playing music. You'd think a Tufa would understand that, but nope. They just wanted to make out and stuff."

"And you didn't like that?"

"Oh, sure, I liked it. I mean, who doesn't? But if I have to choose between dick and guitar, then—" She caught herself. She'd relaxed so much, she'd forgotten whom she was talking to. She quickly made the hand sign for respect. "I'm sorry, I didn't mean to speak out of line."

Mandalay smiled at her discomfort. "Relax. I brought it up, remember?"

They rode in silence some more. At last Janet said, "You still haven't explained why we're going where we're going."

"Miss Azure is in touch with some things I'm not. I want to ask her about them."

"Does this have anything to do with Kera and Adam?"

"It does."

"What about them?"

But Mandalay said nothing else. She remained silent until they pulled up the rutted gravel drive and parked behind Azure's ancient Jeep. The little cottage's lights were on, and smoke rose from the chimney.

As they got out of the car, Azure opened the door and stood silhouetted by the light from inside. "Must be important to come visiting this late."

"It is," Mandalay said with a hand gesture of respect.

Azure responded in kind. "Then come on in. It gets cold out here this time of year. Who's with you?"

"Janet Harper, ma'am," Janet said, and made a similar gesture. Azure simply nodded, though, and did not return it.

The little cabin was warm and cozy. Azure went to the stove and poured them tea that was already brewed. As she handed them cups, she said, "I assume this has to do with those poor unfortunates who died."

"Yes, ma'am," Mandalay said. Although in the Tufa world,

Mandalay had authority over Azure, she was also sensible enough to know she'd get more flies with honey than with vinegar. So she remained deferential.

"Terrible thing, just terrible."

"I'm wondering about the animal that did it."

"What about it?"

"Well, first of all . . . were they really killed by an animal?"

"Yes," Azure said with no hesitation.

Mandalay waited until Azure had returned the teapot to the stove so she could look the other woman in the eye. Grimly she asked, "And is there anything about this animal that I should know, and don't?"

Azure considered the question. "You want to know if it's real, or a haint?"

"Or a manifestation of something else."

"Like what?"

"If I knew, I wouldn't need your help."

Azure visibly puffed up at this. *Nothing like having your leader needing your counsel,* Janet thought as she watched. Azure said, "If you've got time, then, let's ask the leaves."

"I've got time," Mandalay assured her.

Azure again looked at Janet. "And what purpose do you serve?"

"She's here because I asked her," Mandalay said before Janet could reply.

"And why would you do that?"

Mandalay spoke with the voice of her authority, no louder than before but with an intensity that vibrated the air. "Because I wanted her here."

Azure stepped back and lowered her eyes. She made a contrite hand gesture to the girl. "My apologies. Finish your tea and let's take a look."

They sat silently, the only sound the muted sipping of tea. Janet was the first one finished.

"Give me your cup," Azure said.

"Me?" Janet said in surprise. "Why?"

"Because you're the first one done. Come on."

Janet handed over her cup, but looked at Mandalay for some support or context. The younger girl just shrugged.

Azure put on her glasses and studied the tea leaves. After a long silence, during which the only noise was the distant hoot of an owl and the crackling of fire in the cast-iron stove, she said, "Your monster resides in Half Pea Hollow."

"That makes sense," Mandalay said. "It's just over the ridge from Dunwoody Mountain."

"They say pigs can see the wind," Azure went on. "Did you know that?"

"I'd heard it," Mandalay said.

"I wonder what they see when the night winds blow," Azure mused.

"Is it real?" Mandalay asked.

"You mean a real animal?"

"Yes."

She looked back into the tea leaves. "Mostly."

"How can something be 'mostly' real?" Janet asked, then slapped her hand over her mouth. "Sorry."

"No worries," Mandalay reassured her. "That was my next question, too."

"When things are born, they come into this world all of a piece, all connected and joined up," Azure said. "But sometimes, things kind of . . . leak over. Or drain. Or are called. So they join this world piece by piece, moment by moment."

"So it's not a haint," Mandalay said.

"No, it's not the spirit or trace of something once dead. It's a whole different thing."

"Who would've called it?" Janet asked softly.

Azure shrugged. "Someone with a need for it."

Mandalay and Janet exchanged a look. "Somebody who needed a giant killer pig?" Janet said.

"The way some men need a gun, or some women their cell phones," Azure said.

"That's a little offensive," Mandalay said with a tiny smile.

"Or," Azure said as she leaned back from the cup, "it was called up by its brethren."

It took a moment for that to register. "What, the other pigs?" Janet said.

"Pigs aren't stupid," Azure said. "They're smart enough to get by just eating and rolling in the mud. Not many people can manage that."

"Yeah, but still," Janet said. "Calling up their own . . ." She trailed off, unsure of the word to use.

"God?" Mandalay finished for her.

"They say everything creates God in its own image," Azure said. "If you want to know more about that, though, you'll have to drive over and ask Bronwyn's husband, the minister."

"No, that's all I need to know," Mandalay said. She made a quick but elaborate gesture. "Thank you."

"There's one other possibility," Azure said. "That maybe it just happened. Maybe it's just one of those things."

Mandalay thought this over, then nodded. "I'll think on it. You ready, Janet?"

Janet stood, almost knocking the chair over. "You bet. Thanks, Miss Azure."

In the car on the way back to town, Janet asked, "So, seriously, Mandalay: Why was I there?"

"This may sound strange to you, Janet," the girl said, "but I value your cynicism."

"I'm a cynic?"

"You are. You question everything, especially motives. You always assume the basest reasons for people doing things. I'm not saying you're always right, but a lot of times I'm too sympathetic for my own good, and I tend to give folks the benefit of the doubt.

So it's nice to have the other side of the argument sitting right next to me."

"Thanks," Janet said dubiously. "So what happens now?"

"We leave things to the professionals. Let that wildlife guy and his people deal with it."

"Do you really think the other pigs conjured it up?"

"Maybe. Or maybe someone else did, to use it for their own ends."

"Who would want to do that?"

"You're the cynic, you tell me."

"No one's really benefited from it." She paused, and her eyes opened wide with realization. "No, wait: no one's really *acted* like they've benefited from it."

In the dark, Mandalay smiled.

"Duncan Gowen," she said with a gasp of insight. "If his girlfriend and Adam Procure were sneaking around . . ."

"Which they were," Mandalay said.

Janet shook her head. "I'm not sure he's that good an actor."

"Maybe he didn't do it on purpose."

Janet snorted. "And I'm *definitely* not sure he's that good a Tufa."

"He probably has as much Tufa blood as you. He just doesn't express it." After a long silence, she said, "This is all just conjecture, anyway. We need something concrete to tell us what's going on."

"Like what?"

Mandalay looked out at the night. "Like a bone song," she muttered, but didn't explain. And after all the evening's weirdness, for once Janet Harper didn't ask any more questions.

"Oh, for God's sake," Ginny asked. "What's wrong now?"

Janet stood at the window in her T-shirt and underwear, staring out at the cold darkness. Ginny sat up and repeated her question. She'd just gotten back to sleep after Janet returned home and told her what happened, and was a little annoyed at being awakened again.

"Why would Mandalay Harris invite me to drive her to see old Miss Azure, Ginny?"

"She told you why," Ginny said, and yawned. "You're important."

"She told me something. But I'm not sure I believe it."

"Oh, come on, Janet. You've heard that shit your whole life." In a singsong mockery of an adult voice, she said, "Law, that Harper girl, she's done gone and got the magic, don't she? I ain't never heard nothing like it.' "

Janet couldn't help but smile. "It wasn't like that, though. I mean, I didn't *do* anything, I just carried her back and forth."

"Why don't you ask her, then?"

"Because it's three A.M."

"Oh, so you'll wake me up, but not her?"

Janet sat back down on the bed. "I didn't mean to wake you up, dumb-ass. You sleep so lightly, a moth can flap once and wake you up."

"You don't mind that when we're camping and a bear comes around."

Janet playfully yanked her hair, and they both laughed with practiced quiet. Then they stretched out beside each other again.

"I wonder why," Janet asked, "no one's been able to kill that pig yet?"

"Maybe it's not of this earth," Ginny said through a yawn.

Janet nodded her agreement on the pillow. "That's exactly what Miss Azure told us." But Ginny was already asleep again.

17

"So now we're going to skip ahead a few months," Janet said to the crowd at the storytelling festival. The sweaty, rapt faces gazed up at her with wide eyes, hanging on her every word. She loved this aspect of performing here, and was grateful that there were no drunken boors determined to break the spell. At this festival, unlike her arena concerts, no one would dream of interrupting her with a request or a sexual remark.

She strummed a gentle refrain of "Handsome Mary" as she continued. "After all, the winter shuts everything down. We get ten inches of snow on the ground, and it gets colder than your boyfriend Tom when you accidentally call him Harry. So nobody does much of anything. Well, except for what I told you that troubled boy and his best friend's sister were doing just now."

She chuckled along with the audience's laugh.

"But I'll get back to them. The game warden and the paramedic settled into a relationship that fit them both like an old comfortable hand-me-down quilt you snuggle under when the wind's howling against the windows. They saw each other when they could, talked on the phone and texted when they couldn't. They didn't make a big show of it, but pretty soon everyone knew about it, and they were happy for them. The paramedic had spent her whole life caring about other people, making sure they were safe and happy, fighting the fights the girl with the secrets in her head wasn't yet ready to handle, and she'd earned this. The warden was a decent guy, not too imaginative, but far from stupid. If he noticed strange things about the paramedic or the other Tufa, he kept it to himself, content to enjoy what he had. If only more people could do that."

Then she changed to a more chopping melody, one of her own tunes, "The I-40 Reel." In concert she played it on a fiddle, but now she got the same feeling from her electric guitar. "The troubled boy and his best friend's sister, though . . . they were different. They were young, and filled up with feelings they couldn't put into words, or even songs."

She segued into a "wacka-wacka" riff, mocking the cliché music found in old porn movies. The audience laughed.

"So they went at it almost every night after that first time: at her place, at his place, and at any place they could find. They discovered that they were a perfect match that way, and since they were young, and hurting, and this made them feel better, they took refuge in it. Everyone in town thought it was a fine thing. It had that symmetry about it, you know? Dead man's sister and dead man's best friend. There was a song in that somewhere, everyone knew, and it was just a matter of time before someone sang it at their wedding."

She segued into the *Peter Gunn* theme; only a few people in the audience recognized it. "But not everyone felt that way. Since the game warden spent a lot of time with the paramedic, going to Tufa barn dances and shindigs at the Pair-A-Dice, he also had a chance to watch the troubled boy and his best friend's sister. He still had a sneaking suspicion about the boy, something he couldn't put into words. And so did the girl with the secrets.

It wasn't that she thought the troubled boy had killed his old girlfriend, or his best friend; there was absolutely no evidence of that. But something important hadn't come out in the open yet, and the night winds weren't telling, neither. So both the warden and the girl with the secrets watched, and waited, to see what it might be."

She slowed to a steadier, even darker rhythm. "And while this was going on, the monster slept. There was a big mass hunt, with over three hundred people marching through Half Pea Hollow and over the slopes of Dunwoody Mountain, but it was all for nothing. No one saw it, no one heard it, certainly no one found it. It, too, had its mysteries, but no one had begun to discover them.

"But that didn't keep the warden's old friend from looking. He had no dog in this hunt, as they say around here, but that didn't mean he was ready to walk away. He was an old man, and he felt like this was his last chance to do something that mattered. And if that monster got him in the process, then he'd go out standing up, with his boots on. So he spent every spare moment of those short winter days traipsing through Half Pea Hollow, looking for pig tracks in the snow, poking into every hole and cave, looking for the monster's den."

She abruptly stopped and gave the audience a sly smile. "Oh, but y'all don't care about that pig, do you? You care about the troubled boy and his best friend's sister, and what's gonna happen to them, right?"

The crowd murmured its assent.

She grinned and returned to the melody of "Handsome Mary." "Well, let me tell you. If you thought that things weighed heavily on the warden, or the girl with the secrets, you can *imagine* how they pressed down on that poor troubled boy. From the knowledge that he'd deliberately caused his friend's death came the absolute certainty that he had to watch everything he said and did, to make sure he didn't give that away. And you know what? It wears on you to live like that. It plumb grinds you down. It makes you short-tempered, and makes you seek out things to take your mind off stuff. And that's what that boy did, even as something else he didn't expect was just about to change his life all over again."

18

"Dude, I'm pregnant."

Duncan looked up from his coffee. Renny sat on the other side of the bistro table in his apartment, looking as she always did in the morning: disheveled, intimidating, and adorable. In only blue panties and a man's undershirt, with thick wool socks on her feet, she watched him with the same scrutiny she applied to NASCAR and *Halo.*

He stopped in mid-sip. The coffee jammed in his throat as he choked out, "What did you say?"

"Pregnant. Knocked up. A defective typewriter. Robin is in the Batcave. Pea in the pod. Eating possum for two. You know."

Duncan coughed the coffee down, sat silently for a long moment, then said, "A defective typewriter?"

"I skipped a period. It's from *Grease.*"

"Okay. I mean, though . . . are you sure?"

"I've got a little forest of blue sticks with my pee all over 'em on the bathroom counter if you want to double-check. I'm pretty sure."

He very carefully put down his cup. Outside, the wind blew hard and made the little window over the sink rattle. In the winter it was always a little chilly in the apartment, but now Duncan began to sweat. He glanced up, but couldn't meet her eyes. "So . . . what do you want to do?"

"Do? I'm gonna finish my coffee, wash out my cup, maybe watch some *Stranger Things* on Netflix—"

"About the baby."

"I imagine I'll be changing a bunch of diapers about seven months from now. Used to babysit for Idgie Mulligan when her twins were little, and if I could keep up with them, I ought to be able to keep up with one of ours. Oh shit, though, what if *we* have twins?"

She said this so calmly, with so little overt emotion, that he laughed.

"And this is funny how?" she snapped back.

"It's not funny. You are. This is huge, and you're just . . ."

"Not freaking out?"

"Well . . . yeah."

She tucked her hair behind her ears. He'd learned the hard way that this gesture meant she was not in the mood for nonsense. "Duncan, if you want me to laugh, or cry, or do a crazy dance around the room, you've got the wrong girl. You ought to know that by now. I only freak out if you hit the right spot. Otherwise . . . this is me."

He took another sip of coffee, wishing it were something much stronger. "Do you want to get married?"

"Because I got pregnant? No. Absolutely not. I've seen how that sort of thing turns out."

"What if it's because I love you?"

"What if I don't love *you*?"

"You've said you did."

"Oh, sure, when you're slamming me against the headboard or you've got me bent over the kitchen counter. I ain't exactly thinking critically then."

"And the rest of the time?"

A very small smile touched the corners of her lips. "Don't worry, hotshot. I love you the rest of the time, too."

"So *will* you marry me?"

"Because you feel like we should, because I got pregnant?"

And then the fog that he perpetually lived in cleared. He felt a certainty that he hadn't experienced in months. "No. You should marry me because we love each other. You should marry me *soon* because we're going to have a baby."

Her smile grew. "I used to think you weren't that bright, did you know that?"

"Yeah, you've mentioned that before. You mention it a lot, actually."

"But I think I might've misjudged you." She stood and slid onto his lap. She kissed him, ignoring his coffee breath, and the fact that he wore only boxers. In fact, she shifted to straddle him, arching her back so that she pressed against his chest.

"Do you know," she said as she broke the kiss, "what happens to a woman when she gets pregnant?"

"I know the basics. Is there something in particular—?"

"Mm. Well, one of the side effects is that she gets really, really horny a *lot.*"

"A lot as in right now?"

"A lot as in I don't care if we make it to the bedroom."

"I don't think this table would hold us both. Remember the last time."

"The floor is just fine with me."

"Aren't you worried about linoleum burns?"

"Who said you were going to be on top?" Again she kissed him, and he forgot all about his coffee. He also, for a few brief blissful minutes, forgot that he'd watched her brother die and done nothing to help.

Dolph moved as silently through the cold forest as he could, his rifle across his right shoulder. It was below freezing, and his old bones felt the temperature more vividly than he ever remembered. The wind found all the little gaps in his layered clothing, biting at him like frozen mosquitoes. Once he'd bounded through forests like this even in the winter, up and down slopes, across frozen streams and ponds, with the agility of a deer leaping fences. Now his joints popped so audibly, it surprised him when he saw any animal he *hadn't* spooked.

The only human tracks he'd seen in Half Pea Hollow were his own. The rest belonged to deer, raccoon, rabbit, and the occasional hungry squirrel. And, of course, the pigs. But they were rare in this season, and tended to be old and half-covered by the time he found them.

He moved a few yards at a time, watching the ground and carefully placing each step. He stopped and listened, then moved again. He'd seem some of the animals that left their sign. A few times he'd even spotted some coyotes before they spotted him, a rarity in any season. If he stayed out late enough, he heard owls.

But the animals he sought, the *animal* he sought, remained frustratingly out of sight except for those scarce, half-hidden tracks.

Dolph had been that bounding young man when he first took over this region in the late '70s. There hadn't been much poaching then, and the concept of canned hunts had been unknown. He encountered a few hunters who resented him because of his race, but not many.

He hated to be one of those guys lamenting the "good old days," but truthfully, he missed them. For the most part, people got in trouble because they didn't know the rules, not because they deliberately set out to break them. He handed out far more warnings than he did tickets, and people understood and respected guns. Anyone who stockpiled weapons was looked down on by true hunters as a weirdo; now the weirdos ran the asylum.

He didn't envy Jack having the job now. People were just *meaner:* better armed, more dishonest, and *much* more trigger-happy. A gun was no longer a tool; it was a political statement. And that meant it was inevitable that a warden would eventually get shot down in the line of duty here.

He recalled one of his last professional encounters, with a fat redneck and his equally obnoxious wife, who'd been shooting deer from their truck. Despite Dolph catching them in the act, they refused to accept their summons, and Dolph was afraid to even try wrestling their bulks from their vehicle to arrest them. "There ain't no sign saying we cain't do that!" the woman kept mewling. "There ain't no sign!" The man muttered about "nigras not knowing their place."

It had been the final straw. The next day he put in for his retirement.

Now he sat on a rock, cold against his butt even through his hunting coveralls, and thought about the first fatality he'd ever investigated, on an equally cold day. A young man had waded into a pond to collect duck decoys after a fruitless morning, and had left his shotgun propped against a tree on shore. His retriever, also tied to the tree, managed to knock the gun over, and when it hit the ground, it discharged, killing the man instantly.

He'd heard the dog barking as he patrolled the shore, his truck window down despite the chill. When he pulled the body from the water, he saw that the blast had struck the man in the back of his head, and the impact distorted his features in a way Dolph still had nightmares about.

But even that hadn't been as bad as a young man and woman eaten by hogs.

He'd studied the video from the night in the fall, looking for more clues about the animal. It wasn't black, so it wasn't a true wild boar, descended from the Eurasian ones released here long ago. It had a docked tail and blunt snout, which meant it was probably born on a farm and escaped. Based on comparisons against the size of the trap, it was easily nine feet long, if not larger, and probably weighed close to a thousand pounds. Most wild hogs topped out at two hundred.

His slow personal patrols came after many other attempts at trapping. He'd modified the drop doors so they were big enough to catch the leader, but had snared only a few stray domestic pigs that had gotten loose and not yet turned feral. The big one, and his herd, were now trap-shy.

Jack didn't want to have the WHOMP team in the field through the winter, and Dolph didn't blame him. It was a slim chance at best that he might find the herd, let alone the monster. Pigs didn't hibernate, but they did hide in their dens, and if they heard the WHOMPers traipsing about, they certainly wouldn't emerge.

Not that Jack wasn't spending a lot of time in Needsville. He was certainly allowed to date whomever he wanted, but there were so many rumors about Tufa girls. They were attractive, yes, but also dangerous; more than one young man, the stories said, was led to his ruin by the love of one of those enigmatic dark-haired beauties. He seemed to recall a tune by R. C. Bailey from the earliest days of country music that mentioned the Tufa, but he couldn't quite bring it to the front of his brain.

But Jack didn't seem under any sort of duress, or spell. He still met Dolph for coffee on Wednesday at the Iron Kettle diner on Cane Valley Road, still laughed at the raunchy jokes the waitress shared with them, and seemed no different from before. Except, that is, for being happier. So Dolph reserved judgment.

At their last kaffeeklatsch, though, Jack had brought up another relationship, one that had him thinking. "So that Duncan Gowen has been keeping company with the sister of that boy who died, did you know that?"

"No. Why should I care? And why should you?"

"There's something that's not quite right about all this, Dolph. No one's seen that pig since that night we saw it on the monitor. It's like it vanished."

"It could've died."

"And that's not the only thing. I mean, I don't think the Gowen boy had anything to do with that girl being killed. His alibi checked out, he was nowhere around, and God knows he sure looked tore up about it that day. But he was right there when that boy died. And really, all we know for sure is that the pigs tore up the body. We've only got his word for them actually doing the killing. And we all heard that gunshot."

"But he hadn't fired his gun," Dolph said. "I checked it myself. The dead boy must've tried to shoot the hog. Unless you think there was a second gunman on the grassy knoll?"

"Don't be a smart-ass, old man. And I also hear that the dead girl and the dead boy were sneaking around together behind that Gowen boy's back."

"So what do we do?" Dolph said. "What's the crime here?"

"Ah, I don't know. We need some proof of something. And by now, the proof's done been chewed up and shat out."

"Well, I hope you're wrong. For everybody's sake. There's a couple of families that have gone through enough."

"Yeah," Jack agreed. "But I'm going to keep my eyes and ears open. If I'm right, there's always the chance that he'll slip up."

But so far, at least according to what Jack had told Dolph, that hadn't happened. And now all these thoughts went around and around the old man's mind, in the embracing silence of the winter woods.

He got up and hiked to the top of a ridge, then leaned against a tree to rest. He kept his rifle in his hands, though, and slipped the shooting glove's little cap off his trigger finger so it would be ready.

He'd learned this little valley almost as well as he knew his own backyard garden, but he also knew that despite the undergrowth's winter die-off, animals could hide in the shadows of a bare branch if they had to. In places the ground cover still had thick tangles of many seasons'-worth of dead weeds, under and through which the pigs had made clear trails. He couldn't possibly crawl into them, but at the same time, neither could that monster. But Dolph could use them to verify when the pigs were actually on the move.

And they were. In places, the snowy ground was churned by a multitude of small hooves. But where were they going, and where had they come from?

In a way, the pigs were like the Tufa: He knew they were there, but they came and went in their own mysterious ways.

He laughed out loud, breaking the cold silence. He'd have to be sure not to share that observation with Jack.

He finally caught his breath and began his descent, his rifle loose in his hands, his thumb over the safety, ready to take it off and raise the weapon in one well-practiced motion. But nothing moved.

Then he paused. What was that smell?

19

Junior Damo opened the door of his trailer. He squinted out at Duncan and Renny. It was nearly noon, but he looked like he'd just woken up. "What do you two want?"

"We'd like to talk to you," Duncan said, and made the deferential hand sign acknowledging Junior's position.

"We can come back," Renny said quickly. She was nervous, and tightly gripped Duncan's other hand. If Duncan hadn't been so nervous himself, he would've been astounded that anything could rattle her like this.

A little boy of around two, wearing a winter coat and a diaper with no pants or shoes, tried to push past Junior and go outside. He nudged the boy back with his leg and said with surprising gentleness, "You just stay inside, Trey." Then, loud and harsh, he said, "Loretta! Put some goddamn clothes on this kid!"

"We'll come back," Duncan said.

"No, fuck it, y'all come on in," Junior said, and stepped aside. They entered.

The trailer was too small for a family of three, with baby items like a high chair, playpen, and various toys jammed into every available space. It smelled of stale garbage and cigarettes. By the time the door closed, the baby Trey was gone, and Junior indicated two empty chairs at the tiny table.

Duncan held one chair for Renny, then sat. "We'd like your blessing on our marriage," Duncan said.

Junior looked at him dubiously. "That a fact. You're Adam Procure's sister, ain't you?"

"Yes, sir. Renata."

"And you want to marry him?"

"Yes, sir, I do."

"You knocked up?"

Renny turned red. "Yes, sir, I am."

Junior laughed, a mean little chuckle that would have done his predecessor Rockhouse proud. "Well, ain't that something? You didn't waste no time, did you, son?"

"It ain't like that," Duncan mumbled, but couldn't look at Junior.

"No, I'm sure it ain't. But you both want it, right?"

"Yes, sir," they said deferentially, a beat apart.

"Well, then, go for it. No skin off me either way."

Duncan and Renny looked at each other, then stood. "Thank you," Renny said, and shook Junior's hand.

"Tell you what," Junior said. "Renata Procure, you wait outside. I want a word in private with loverboy here."

She left, and when the door was shut behind her, Junior slapped Duncan on the back and said, "Ain't that a kick in the head?"

"I don't know what you mean . . . sir," Duncan said.

"Oh, come on. Her brother was shim-shallying around with your girl, then met with that little 'accident.' Now you done planted yourself in the belly of his sister. Boy, when you get back at somebody, you don't fuck around." He snorted. "Or I reckon you *do* fuck around."

"That ain't what happened. I didn't do anything to Adam."

"Course not. That pig ate him, I heard all about it. But somebody must've called 'sooey,' right?" He winked.

"Look, please, believe me. I didn't do anything to Adam."

"That ain't what you said that night at the moonshine cave."

"I was . . . My feelings were hurt."

"Aw," Junior said mockingly. "I bet I can get Trey to loan you his pacifier, if you want."

Duncan clenched his fists. "And I was drunk."

"Right. Well, you're a grown-up, just like she is. Y'all got a song yet?"

" 'Could I Have This Dance.' "

Junior burst out laughing. "What, that fucking old Anne Murray song?"

"Yeah." Duncan was growing tired of Junior's snideness. "What's wrong with it?"

Junior threw up his hands. "Hey, whatever floats your boat. Ain't a jury in the world would convict you anyway. So go marry that girl, raise that baby, and"—his voice dropped—"pray to God she don't put on fifty pounds and the worst attitude this side of a damn bull with his nuts caught in a barbed-wire fence."

"I heard that, you bastard!" Loretta yelled from somewhere down the short hallway.

"You got clothes on that baby yet?" he yelled back.

"Fuck you!" she screamed.

Junior shook his head. "That, my friend, is fucking marriage."

When he rejoined Renny in his car, she asked, "So what did he say?"

"Nothing." He turned the key and put the car in reverse.

"No, seriously, what did he want to tell you?"

As he pulled onto the blacktop, he yelled "Nothing!" It was the first time he'd ever raised his voice at her.

She reached down and slammed the gear lever into park. The vehicle jerked to a halt in the middle of the road. Then she grabbed him by the face and snarled, "Yell at me like that again, Duncan Gowen, and you won't be fathering any more children, you understand that?"

He slapped her hand away. "You ain't the boss of me, Renny. I don't have to tell you every damn thing that goes on in my life."

Renny glared at him. Then her eyes grew wet and poured swollen, sudden tears down her face. She turned away and said with a shaking voice, "Don't you think you made me cry, Duncan. This is just pregnancy hormones fucking with me."

He sat still, the tension in his body so strong that he was afraid any move would snap him like a rubber band. He breathed in long and slow, while Renny sniffled and quietly sobbed. She looked out the passenger window, her breath steaming the glass.

"I'm sorry I grabbed you," she said at last, in a small voice he'd never heard before. "I have a terrible temper. I need to learn to control it before . . ." She patted her stomach.

"Junior was making jokes," Duncan said. His head had begun to pound, and he had no juice left for more fighting. "Stupid jokes about me and you and . . . how I was marrying Adam's sister."

"Jokes?"

"Jokes. He thought it was funny."

"God, he's the right man to follow Rockhouse, all right."

"But he did still give us permission."

She nodded, wiped her nose with the heel of her hand and said, "Hope I didn't fuck up your transmission."

"Me, too," he said honestly. Gingerly he put the car into drive and pulled back onto the road. As he listened for any change in the engine's noise, inwardly he sighed with relief. He hadn't lied to her: he'd picked his way through the minefield of the truth without blowing off a limb. Maybe it *was* possible that this would all work out.

As they drove, Renny reached over and took his hand. He could feel the warm snot on her palm.

Dolph moved even more slowly as he searched for the origin of the unmistakable smell. He tried not to visualize what he might find. The hillside was studded with large boulders, remnants of the ancient sedimentary rock that formed the mountains. Erosion from rain and snowmelts had exposed them, and now they were covered with brown, winter-dead moss, except for the tops, which were bare.

He didn't recall ever seeing these rocks before, but he recognized that odor. Rotted meat.

It couldn't be an animal's carcass dead on the ground: it would be frozen, and thus wouldn't smell. He'd come across the remains of a deer and a coyote already, and there was no odor from either.

Ahead, two car-sized boulders protruded from the ground. They leaned against each other and formed a triangular cavity between them that led back into the hillside. The snow and ground outside it was well worn and trampled flat, and even at this distance, he could tell it was from the passage of wild pigs.

He'd found a den. Was it *the* den?

The opening was big enough for the monster to use, and if it was in there right now, this might be the perfect chance to kill it. His heart pounded and everything grew clear and sharp as adrenaline coursed through him. His knees quit hurting, his back loosened up, and he felt as young and agile as a thirty-year-old.

He did not approach the entrance, but instead very quietly climbed the slope and crawled out to sit atop the rock, where he had a clear view straight down. There was no response from the cave; either they hadn't smelled him, or they weren't in there.

The rotting-flesh smell now mixed with the odor of manure. This was the source, all right. Once he was in position, his rifle ready, he took a deep breath and let out a loud, ululating hog call: "Sooooo-*eeee*! Soo-*ee* soo-*ee* soo-*ee*!" He hadn't done that in a long time, and he was surprised his gravelly old voice would still go that high. Perhaps it was the adrenaline, too.

His cry echoed off the sides of the hollow, then faded. For a long moment nothing happened. Crows cawed in the trees and launched their black forms into the sky, but otherwise, there was no sound, or no movement.

Then, like someone had turned on a spigot, pigs poured from the cave. Their hooves rumbled against the frozen ground, and a few squealed in confusion.

Before he'd even thought about it, Dolph had the rifle at his shoulder, the bead trained on the stream of porkers. He fired as quickly as he could, and his targets squealed as they went down and their compatriots trampled them. But there was no way he could keep up, and when the last pig had disappeared, there were only six dead ones left behind. At least twenty had escaped.

And there had been no sign of the monster. It either hadn't been there in the first place, or it was still in there. Or, in a best-case scenario, it was the source of the rotting smell. And there was only one way to find out.

He dug out his cell phone and propped it atop the rock. If anything happened to him, this way the GPS would lead Jack and the search party right to him.

He climbed down, his rifle ready, and stood to one side of the entrance. Again he cried out, *"Soooo-eeeee!"* but nothing else emerged, and nothing moved inside.

He took out his small halogen flashlight and shone it into the cave.

The cavity went back farther than he expected, and dropped down about six feet from the entrance. He moved into the darkness, and the intense odors made him gag. As he descended the ramplike path, he started to kick things with his boots. When he shone the light on them, he saw they were bones.

He knelt and picked one up. It was a pig's rib.

He realized then the source of the rotting smell. Crammed into this hole, with so little to eat available outside, they'd begun cannibalizing the weak and helpless members of their own herd, including newborn piglets.

At the bottom of the slope was a chamber with a five-foot ceiling, about fifteen feet across. The remains of other hogs were here as well, some fresher than he liked to imagine. But there was no sign of the monster, either in the bones or in the mess of tracks on the floor.

He went back outside, retrieved his phone, and took pictures of the remains. It was only when the flash went off for the sixth one that he spotted the skull.

The upper part sat upright, and he found the lower jaw nearby. A portion of the spine and two ribs were still attached. The bones were brown with time and exposure. He'd seen enough skeletal remains to tell from the overall bulk that this had been a man, and he knew of no other possible victim than Adam Procure.

He turned his phone over in his hand and checked for a signal. He got nothing. He immediately took more pictures of the human remains and left the cave, careful to watch for ambush as he emerged into the light. When he checked again atop the rocks, he got three bars and quickly dialed Jack.

"Hey," he said, his voice surprisingly steady. "Anybody else turned up missing in Cloud County this winter?"

"Not that I know of," Jack said. "Why?"

"In that case, I think the skunk's off our hunt. I found what's left of that Procure boy."

20

She'd been silent for so long that Duncan jumped in his seat when Renny said, "I guess we need to go into town and get a marriage license. How long are they good for, anyway?"

"I don't know," Duncan said. His hands were sweaty on the steering wheel.

"Do you still have to do blood tests to make sure you ain't got syphilis?"

"I don't think so. Never heard of anybody doing it."

"Think we should, just to be on the safe side?"

"I don't think so."

"Wonder if they check for AIDS, too?"

"Can we not talk about this?" he snapped.

"Sure," she said in a small voice.

"Ah, I'm sorry. I'm just tense."

"Second thoughts?"

"What? No." He looked over and saw that Renny was crying again. Before today, she'd never done that not in all the time they'd known each other, certainly not since they'd begun dating. For a moment, he couldn't respond. At last he managed, "Wow, honey, I'm sorry. I didn't mean to upset you."

She wiped her eyes. "For fuck's sake, I told you, it's just hormones, Duncan, don't worry. Apparently I'll be crying at every sunset and ASPCA commercial until the baby comes."

"And you're not upset?"

"Why should I be? I mean, you don't have syphilis or AIDS, do you?"

"No."

"And you love me, right?"

"Of course," he said, and suddenly realized it was true.

"And I love you. So there's nothing wrong."

Before he could say anything else, she turned on the radio and cranked the volume. Of all things, "Achy Breaky Heart" blared out. He repressed a shudder and resumed staring out at the passing trees.

Jack used a pen to lift the skull from its place on the den floor. He examined it carefully, especially the teeth. Like those of all Tufa, they were white and perfect, even when the rest of the skull was discolored. So even in death, even in decomposition, Adam still "grinned like a Tufa."

"It's him," Bliss said flatly, holding the plastic bag as he lowered the skull into it. She sealed it with a practiced zip.

Jack nodded. "Have to use dental records to confirm that. Or do you Tufa not have dentists?"

"We do all have pretty good teeth," Bliss said, not rising to his sarcasm. "But that's because we *do* go to the dentist when we need to."

Dolph, covering the entrance in the unlikely case the monster appeared, called back, "That state trooper's here."

Darwin ducked down as he entered, and stopped to take in the carnage. "Jesus Christ," he whispered. "They even kill their own."

Bliss held up the skull. "This is Adam Procure."

"Poor bastard." He looked at the other bones. "Hard to tell which ones are the rest of him."

"I can tell," Jack assured him. He wore blue latex gloves, and his boots were protected by white sterile shoe covers. He lifted a single human rib up into the light.

"Good thing you're here, then. I reckon I'll let you and Miss Bliss gather up the remains, then. I'll be outside with Dolph, seeing if ol' Piggly-Wiggly is around."

"Who?" Bliss said.

He laughed. "That's what the kids at the high school call it. Somebody named it that in their school paper, and it caught on."

Jack shook his head. "That girl from the community meeting. The one who acted like she was Woodward and Bernstein."

"She's like a snapping turtle, all right; she don't let go until it thunders," Darwin said, then left.

Jack looked at Bliss. He held up a few still-connected vertebrae. "This is no joke. 'Piggly-Wiggly'? People aren't going to take it seriously."

"That's how kids are," Bliss said as she opened the next plastic bag. "They don't have the emotional context for this yet."

"I hope they never do," Jack muttered, and collected some more bones. He looked around and said, "We should call the TBI. Get them out here with a real forensics team. What if we don't find all the remains?"

"We'd be wasting their time. We'll find what there is to find." She put the bag in the cooler with the others.

"You sound awfully certain of that."

She looked at him seriously. For a moment, her eyes reflected light the same way an animal's might. "I am," she said.

At the fire station that afternoon, Bliss looked down at the bones arranged on the long table. They made an almost complete skeleton, missing only some of the finger, toe, and rib bones. "There he is," she said as she stepped back.

Jack and Darwin stood with her. Dolph, exhausted, had been sent home, despite his insistence. Jack had also discovered Adam's mud- and shit-soaked wallet in the cave, which pretty much settled the identification, although dental records would still be checked to confirm it.

Darwin sighed and said, "I'm not looking forward to telling the family. I hear tell that even after the funeral, they convinced themselves that he just ran off to work on the oil rigs in the Gulf."

"I'll tell them," Bliss said.

"No, not this time. It's my job. You can come with me, though. Give me a minute to check in with my dispatcher." He put on his hat, touched the brim in salute, then left them alone.

Bliss turned to Jack. "I didn't know wild pigs kept a larder."

"I didn't, either," he said. "It's the first time I've ever seen anything like this. Obviously the smaller pigs couldn't have done it, so it must have been the big one. Or . . ." He trailed off.

Bliss prompted. "Or?"

He looked up at her. "Or the body was placed there by person or persons unknown, so we'd *think* the pigs took him."

Bliss said nothing, but she knew his suspicions. The only eyewitness report of the fatal encounter came from Duncan Gowen. And if Duncan was lying, then they might not be able to trust any of their conclusions.

Darwin returned, and watched silently as Jack inspected the bones. "You see any sign of foul play?" Darwin asked.

"I didn't," Jack said, and gestured at Bliss. "Ask the coroner."

"Nothing overt," Bliss said. "But I'll take a closer look in more detail."

Jack stood up and looked at them both. "*I* think we should bring in a real coroner now."

"Let's see what Bliss finds first," Darwin said. As Jack started to protest, he added, "But you may be right."

Jack was about to snap a reply, when Darwin continued, “Mr. Cates, why don’t we get out of Bliss’s way? Ride with me down to the Pair-A-Dice, and the first round’s on me.”

“I thought you were going to give the Procures the bad news.”

“Nobody wants to hear bad news over lunch. We’ll go see them later this afternoon.”

“I’m not hungry,” Jack said honestly.

“I think this might be a day for a liquid lunch.”

Before he could protest more, Bliss said, “Go on. I’ll call if there’s anything.”

Jack looked at her. She was serious, and although he resented it, he had to trust her judgment. She gave his hand a little squeeze, then got back to work.

“All right,” Jack said.

Bliss waited until the sound of Darwin’s big Ford Explorer faded. Then she sat down, folded her arms, and rested her chin on them. She looked at the skull, trying to put the flesh back on it in her mind. *Adam, if you’ve got any secrets, now’s the time,* she thought. *If only you could sing us a song about what happened.*

Everyone knew the song “Knoxville Girl,” recorded by so many country and folk stars. It had come over from England as “The Wexford Girl,” and even that had been a version handed down. What no one knew was that it had been sung originally to force a confession, by someone who suspected the murder but had been unable to prove it. Should Bliss write a song like it? “The Boy of Half Pea Hollow”?

“Is that him?” Mandalay said behind her.

“It is,” she said. She was so used to these sudden appearances that she didn’t even jump. Instead, she stood so that Mandalay could get a good look.

The girl took it all in. “Not all of him, though.”

"The hogs ate some of the bones. Or they were too small, we missed them."

"Any sign of the monster?"

"No."

Mandalay sat in Bliss's chair and leaned her chin on her hands, just as Bliss had done moments before. "I went to see Miss Azure back in the fall, did I ever tell you?"

"No."

"She read the leaves for me. She said the hog that did this is mostly real."

" 'Mostly'?"

"Yeah. Which means it's partly not."

"That explains some things. If she's right in what the tea leaves said."

"She's seldom wrong."

"But you said it was months ago. Maybe it wasn't strong enough for her to read then?"

Mandalay and Bliss held each other's gaze. They both knew what she meant by "it"—or rather, *whom* she meant. So far, no one had reported any visits by his haint, and the night winds had not mentioned his name. But a man so powerful in life might not fade away so easily. She reached out and touched the skull with one fingertip. "Can you leave me and this young man alone for a bit? Junior should be along shortly, but I'd like a little time first."

Bliss nodded. "I'll be outside."

When the door closed behind her, Mandalay laid her head directly on the table, her right cheek flat against the surface. It was cold against her ear, but it put her on eye level with the skull.

"Adam," she said, "I'm sorry you're having to go through all this. I know you were running around with Kera behind Duncan's back, and I know love can make people do things they'd never do otherwise. You should have been honest with him from the start. If he killed you . . . show me. Let me see it. He's about to marry your sister. You can't rest until the truth gets out."

She closed her eyes and began to sing.

There was a man who lived in the West,
And of all the pickers he was the best,
The man he has a-hunting gone
And left his lady all alone. . . .

The song, similar to the ancient story of Orpheus, hung in the air over the bones. She waited to see if it called anything up from this particular Underworld.

The Pair-A-Dice was sparsely attended that afternoon, with only a half-dozen black-haired, sullen men seated by themselves. There was no sound other than the whir of the big heater in the corner. No one took the stage, not even to start a jam.

Darwin brought two beers from the bar, where the bartender Rachel watched him with the suspicion all bartenders had for cops, even Tufa cops. He handed one to Jack as he sat down.

"Thanks," Jack said.

"You don't like me much, do you?" Darwin said.

Jack was a bit taken aback by the forthrightness. "I . . ." He paused as he mustered the word. "I don't understand your approach to your job."

"Really?"

"I've worked with the highway patrol before. They've always been cooperative and by the book. I mean, we're all on the same side, and we should enforce the same laws."

"And you think I don't?"

"You haven't even called in the county sheriff, let alone a real coroner. And since this animal could very easily be across county lines, calling the TBI seems like common sense."

He chuckled. "There ain't no county sheriff, Mr. Cates. The last time they had a real election in Cloud County was nearly twenty years ago. A write-in candidate won. Know what his name was? 'None of the Above.'"

"I don't follow."

"Nobody in this county *wants* a sheriff."

"I imagine that's true of most counties around here." With no jobs, no education, and no hope, a thriving criminal community had sprung up in the mountains, not just moonshiners and bootleggers but also meth dealers, painkiller merchants, and marijuana farmers. "But what if something happens? What if somebody kills somebody?"

Darwin kicked back in his chair, one boot on the edge of the table. He radiated redneck cockiness, something Jack couldn't stand. He said, "You've been keeping company with Bliss Overbay of late, haven't you?"

Jack was instantly on his guard. "We've hung out a little, yes."

"She ain't told you about the First Daughters or the Silent Sons, has she?"

"No. What are they?"

Darwin took a drink and looked around, like a man who didn't want to be overheard. When he spoke again, his voice was pitched so low that Jack had to lean forward to hear.

"Let's just say that they're the ones who step in when things need to get taken care of. There's no one in Cloud County but the Tufa, and the Tufa look out for their own."

"So they have a private security force? Like the Klan?"

Darwin looked at him with narrowed eyes. "That's kind of harsh. Did you know a hundred years ago, the Klan might've lynched people all over this county? The Tufa were considered more black than white, even though the blacks didn't claim 'em, and neither did the Indians. I sure wouldn't have been hired to enforce the law."

Jack was too tired to continue being polite. "What are you trying to get me to do or say here, Officer?"

"Please, call me Alvin. I just want you to accept that things are being handled in the best and most efficient way, even though it may not look like it. Bringing in outside people won't make things better, and might make things worse."

"Worse than two kids dying?"

"Yeah. Look, what's really happened here? A wild animal killed a girl. That's not unheard of, anywhere. Then that boy goes looking for that animal, finds it, and gets killed. The first one is totally random, the second one is the result of that boy deliberately seeking out trouble. It's not the start of a pattern."

"You hope. I've seen animals on a rampage like this before. I helped track down a mountain lion that was eating nothing but family dogs."

"This is a little different."

"Only in scale."

Now it was Darwin's turn to let the amusement fade from his expression. "You're a stubborn fella, ain't you?"

"It's been said."

"Look, Jack—may I call you Jack?—we're both paid by the state. Like you said, we're on the same side of this. I don't want anyone else to die. I want that hog dead. So do you. Why are we acting like enemies?"

Jack thought for a moment, then decided on total honesty. "Because you seem to want other things more than you do those two. Like keeping things quiet and not attracting attention."

Darwin spread his hands and grinned. "That's just the Tufa way."

"So you're a Tufa first and a law enforcement officer second?"

"That's kind of an insult."

"But you didn't say no."

The two men looked at each other for a long moment. Jack finally said, "I don't think we have much else to talk about. Except I should ask: Will I start getting tickets every time I leave my driveway? I'll need to budget for that."

"Not as long as you obey the rules of the highway," Darwin said flatly.

He stood. "Thank you for the beer."

As he walked away, Jack realized every eye, not just Darwin's, followed him. He was ridiculously glad when the door closed behind him.

Then he remembered that Darwin was his ride.

21

Mandalay watched Junior look down at the bones of Adam Procure. The battery-operated clock hummed in the silence, punctuated by soft measured clicks as the minute hand moved. Bliss stood back, letting the two Tufa leaders have their privacy.

At last, Mandalay said, "It's him, for certain."

"Yep," Junior agreed. "Is that why you called me here?"

"I called you here out of respect for your position," Mandalay said. If Junior noticed her annoyance, he gave no sign. "This is one of your people. You should feel his loss as much as anyone."

"Can you tell what happened to him?" Bliss asked Junior.

"A pig ate him," he said with a chuckle.

"But is that what killed him?" Bliss pressed.

"How should I know? You're the damn paramedic."

"Come on, Junior," Mandalay said. "Here's his bones. What song do they sing to you?"

Junior swallowed hard, but tried to hide it. He'd grown to rely on the messages in his head, the ones that whispered in Rockhouse Hicks's voice and hinted at what he should do or say. But it always fell silent around Mandalay, and now was no exception.

"You don't hear a bone song?" Mandalay said.

"Look, don't fuck around with me," Junior snapped.

Mandalay did not respond, but just looked at him until he had to turn away and step around the table.

"This isn't helping," Bliss said.

"No," Mandalay agreed. She picked up one of the long finger bones from the table and turned it over in her hands. It was coated with mud, pig manure, and the dregs of flesh and blood. She rubbed a spot clean down to the white. Then she picked up another one. "I'm taking these," she said.

"Why?" Junior said.

"If you have to ask," she said as she tossed one up and casually caught it like a toy, "then you're not at all what you claim to be."

Junior's face darkened, and he said, "Well, I'll just leave y'all to your pile of singing bones, then." He left, slamming the windowless firehouse door behind him.

Bliss said, "That was—"

Mandalay put a finger to her lips. She tiptoed to the door and yanked it open. Junior nearly fell inside.

"Go home, Junior," Mandalay said. He didn't look at her as he scurried to his truck. Not for the first time did he remind Bliss of a rat.

When they were certain he'd driven off, Mandalay turned back to Bliss. "What were you about to say?"

"That you seem to be poking him with a stick a lot lately."

"I know. I can't explain it, but he irks me. He doesn't scare me, like Rockhouse used to; he just disgusts and annoys me. I hate that I have to deal with him."

"You had the chance to take over. You chose not to."

That moment of choice, in the chaos following Bo-Kate Wisby's defeat, came back to her. *Shit or get off the pot,* she'd told Junior; take over for Rockhouse, or stop acting like you're going to. She didn't have to give him that choice; she could've moved to lead all the Tufa, and healed the breach between the two groups once and for all. But she *had* given him the choice, and now she was stuck with him. "I know."

"Second thoughts?"

"As soon as the words left my mouth that night. I knew damn well you can't make a heel toe the mark."

Bliss didn't push the issue. Instead, she indicated the bones in the girl's hand. "What do you plan to do with them?"

"We have to know what really happened to Adam. And Kera, for that matter. We can't face the danger if we can't see it."

"And?"

"And how do the Tufa face anything?" Again she tossed the finger and caught it. "With a song." Then she sang, "Old Bangum, blew both loud an' shrill, and the wild boar heard on top of the hill, drum-down-drum-down."

Poole Gowen shook his head and said to his little brother, "Never figured you'd get hitched before me. Son, don't you know what causes that? You gots to wear a raincoat if you're gonna dance in the storm." He laughed and patted Duncan on the back.

They sat on the same picnic table, at the same scenic overlook, that Duncan and Renny had visited the night they both couldn't sleep. This night was clear, and in the west there was still a hint of sunset along the edges of the mountains.

"It wasn't like that," Duncan muttered. He'd told Poole first, before his parents, because he needed to know he'd done the right thing offering to marry Renny.

"Hell, Dunk, I'm just messing with you. Renny's a hell of a girl. Do you know what she's having yet?"

Duncan shook his head.

"Have you at least set a date?"

"We're bouncing some around."

"Well, Mom and Dad'll be tickled to death. They've been itching to be grandparents ever since I got outta high school."

"You think?"

"Oh, shit yeah." He looked more seriously at his brother. "What's wrong with you? You feeling shotgunned?"

"No, I want to marry her. I love her. It's just . . . Adam."

"Ah."

"What does that mean?"

"Just means it makes total sense that he'd pop up between you two."

"Not the image I was after."

"You know what I mean. Hell, I can't imagine."

Duncan fought down the image of that day, of the last look on Adam's face. He took a long drink. "Do you think it'll ever pass?"

"Hell, man, I don't know. I guess eventually it'll fade into the background. Most tragedies do."

They sat silently after that. Poole stared out at the valley below, the lights of Needsville small pinpoints, like the stars above. Duncan gazed into his beer.

"Ah, well," Poole said at last. He sang softly:

Now my trial has come on, and sentenced soon I'll be.

Duncan froze. It was another lyric from "Handsome Mary," his earworm that horrible day when Adam had died. He turned to Poole. "What the hell you singing that for?"

"It's just a joke. You've been tried and sentenced to the life of a married man. Wow, Dunk, you're really taking this seriously."

"Sorry," Duncan said. He managed a little grin and clinked bottles with Poole. He wanted to join in, but this was more weight than he'd ever experienced in his life, and he just didn't know how to handle it. And the secret, the truth of what had happened between Adam and Kera, and between him and Adam that day in the woods, bore down on him like a concrete slab.

"You guys talked about names?" Poole asked.

Duncan shook his head.

"Poole's a good name. Helluva name for a boy."

"What if it's a girl?"

"Poola," he deadpanned.

That made Duncan laugh, and momentarily the ghosts of Adam and Kera faded from his mind. But they never went far, and by the time he opened his next beer, they were back, hovering just out of sight.

"And, one, two, three, four . . ."

Ginny hit the bass note, and Caledonia Wentworth eased into the surging chord that began the song. Mary Elizabeth "Mazzy" Gentry did a light roll on the drums, and Hiley Paxton strummed the rhythm. Ginny, her own guitar slung behind her, stepped to the microphone and began to sing the aching first verse of Peter Gabriel's "In Your Eyes."

Little Trouble Girls practiced a lot. A *lot.* To Janet, there was no higher calling than getting good at your musical instrument, and she drove the other four hard, and often to distraction. None of them shared her prowess or her determination. But once they started, once the band found its pocket as it did on this song, none of them would rather be anywhere else than in the old garage beside Janet's house.

This was their traditional way to warm up. They did covers only in rehearsal, except for rare requests at the shows they played. Janet was a prolific songwriter, and she always had new songs for them to learn. They had a slot at this weekend's barn dance, and everyone was always curious to hear what new tunes they'd come up with.

At the chorus, Ginny stepped close to sing into Janet's mike, and Caledonia harmonized. All of them could sing, but Janet was careful about who sang when: the blend of voices was as much an instrument as anything else. As they finished, she said, "Nice. Very nice."

"Can we play it for live people sometime?" Mazzy asked. "You sound so great. Maybe we should make a video of it, and try to get Peter Gabriel to see it."

"Peter Gabriel doesn't do covers," Janet said, "and neither do we. Did you get the new songs I e-mailed you?" They all nodded. "Then let's—"

A cell phone rang. It was the generic, faux-jaunty tune that came built in.

"Who is that?" Janet asked, annoyed.

"Not me," Mazzy said, holding up her drumsticks in deference.

"Not me," Ginny echoed.

"Shit," Janet muttered. "It's mine. Hold on."

As Janet stepped out of the garage to take the call, Caledonia said, "Why does a woman so obsessed with music not use different ringtones?"

Ginny shrugged, but she'd watched Janet drive herself to distraction trying to decide what song fit which person, before finally giving up.

Janet went cold when she saw the name on the screen. The wind blew the still-bare trees around her, and the soft rustle reminded her of distant soldiers rattling their swords. "Hey, Mandalay," she said, trying to sound blasé.

"I'm sorry to interrupt your rehearsal, but I need your help again."

"Sure." Her throat seemed to tighten around the words. "What can I do for you?"

"I need a ride somewhere, and a hand doing something . . . questionable. But necessary."

"Of course."

"Good. Pick me up as soon as it's dark, and dress to get dirty."

"I beg your pardon?"

"We'll be getting dirty, so don't wear anything you're too fond of."

"Okay."

"And bring a shovel if you've got one. See you then."

The call ended. Janet stared down at it, wanting to scream. What had she just agreed to?

Ginny stepped outside, arms crossed against the chill. "Everything okay?"

"That was Mandalay Harris. She wants me to take her somewhere again. She said, 'dress to get dirty.'"

"Dirty how? Like mud, or . . ." And here Ginny raised her eyebrows.

"I assume the muddy kind, because she said bring a shovel."

"What are you going to dig up?"

"She didn't say."

"And you didn't ask?"

"I didn't think!" Janet said almost defensively.

Mazzy joined them. "What's up? We get a record deal or something?"

"No," Janet said. "Sorry, it was something personal. Let's get back to work."

She led the two girls back in, and they continued rehearsing, although all of them could sense that Janet was preoccupied. It didn't affect her playing, but they didn't try to learn anything new. Instead, they played covers all afternoon, and it was the most fun they'd had in weeks.

Except, of course, for Janet.

This time they didn't drive in silence. Mandalay brought along a mix CD, and they listened to the Avett Brothers, Alison Krauss, and the Steep Canyon Rangers. And then, from nowhere, came Bill Withers singing "Ain't No Sunshine."

"That's out of left field," Janet said.

"He's from West Virginia," Mandalay said. The mountains the Tufa called home encompassed all of that tiny state. "He's more genuine than Steve Martin."

"Steve Martin's great!"

"Steve Martin *plays* great. But there's no soul in it. No spirit."

"Well, I disagree." She risked a glance at the girl, but could not see her face in the dark. "Where are we going?"

"Just turn left when this road dead-ends."

"That heads up to the Rogers place." Janet had attended the funeral, including the graveside service where she'd heard the most moving version of the Doors' "The End," suitably revised for the occasion to leave out the oedipal section. "Do they know we're coming?"

"They do not."

"Why are we going there?"

Mandalay said simply, "We're going to dig up what was left of Kera."

Janet said nothing for a long moment. Then she said, "We're going grave-robbing?"

"Yes."

Chills ran up Janet's arms, and the hair on the back of her neck stood up. "I can't do that, Mandalay."

"Aren't you curious why?"

"Of course, but—"

"I can't tell you yet."

Janet said nothing. She wasn't scared; she was just totally overwhelmed. Nothing in her brief life had prepared her for being faced with this. How do you turn down the basically immortal leader of your people when she asks you to help her rob a grave?

They reached the intersection, but Janet didn't turn. The car sat there idling, the turn signal softly clicking, until Mandalay turned off the music and said, "I know it sounds crazy."

"I'm glad you know," Janet said honestly, staring straight ahead.

"I wouldn't ask you if it wasn't important. Usually for these things I ask Bliss Overbay to do it, but I have to start taking responsibility for things myself. If I want something done, I should do it, or at least organize it."

"Sounds sensible," Janet said to fill the silence.

"I already have some of Adam's bones. I need at least one of Kera's. With them, I think I can help them rest in peace."

"I didn't know they were restless."

"They're not. Yet. They're waiting to see if justice is done."

"And what would justice be for them? They were killed by a wild animal."

"That doesn't mean there wasn't a human hand in there somewhere."

Janet took a deep breath. "I'm pretty scared right now, Mandalay."

"I'm a little nervous, too."

"You? You know everything."

Mandalay chuckled. In the darkness, it sounded like the cackle of an old woman. Janet's head snapped around, but only the thirteen-year-old girl sat beside her.

"Imagine," Mandalay said, "that all the knowledge in the world was printed on a single sheet of paper, but you could only read the parts that were under your magnifying glass. That's how it is for me."

"So you know everything, but not all at once?"

"Exactly."

Janet smiled in the darkness. Then she put the car in gear and turned. As they neared the Rogers farm, Mandalay said softly, "Kill the lights."

22

It didn't take long, which was good, because the work was horrendously hard. Janet had been smart enough to bring gloves and a flashlight, but hadn't thought of water, so by the time they'd opened the grave—really, a hole about three feet across but the standard six feet down—she was exhausted.

"I don't think . . . I can lift any more dirt," she said as she climbed out of the grave and lay on her back on the ground.

The Rogers ancestral graveyard was up the hill from their farm, and held seven generations of their family. A few hadn't made it—Casper Rogers died on the fields of France, blown apart in a trench in 1917, and Old Roy Castellaw, who'd married a Rogers girl, had been buried at sea—but the rest were here. Some of the graves had little houses built over them, an affectation that had perplexed anthropologists and sociologists. Most of the headstones were worn and faded, their inscriptions visible only to those who could see through the glamour's patina.

"It's okay, I think we found it," Mandalay said. She'd shoveled as much as a thirteen-year-old could, but sounded like she hadn't exerted herself at all. She lifted a two-foot wooden casket from the hole, put it on the edge.

Janet offered her a hand up. "This is hard work."

"Desecration shouldn't be easy," Mandalay said as she climbed out.

"Did you have to use that word? Now I feel terrible."

"Don't worry, any divine retribution's on my head."

Janet fell back onto the ground, and Mandalay sat on the edge of the hole, both breathing heavily. Then suddenly Mandalay grabbed Janet's leg.

"Ow!" Janet said. "What are you—?"

The flashlight went out, and Janet felt one of Mandalay's small, dirty fingers across her lips. She tasted dirt and wanted to spit, but froze when she heard voices.

Two figures approached from down the hill, silhouetted against the glow from the Rogers house. It was a man and woman, and they walked unsteadily.

Janet looked around. There was no place to really hide, except behind a tombstone, and there was no way these folks approaching could miss the fresh hole.

Mandalay pulled her hand away, stood in plain sight, and made a series of gestures. Janet had never seen them before, and in the darkness she couldn't follow them. But she realized who the two approaching figures were: Spook Rogers, Kera's brother, and her sister Harley. Both were older, but like a lot of young adults Janet knew, had never truly separated from their childhood: they still spent most weekends at home, and thought nothing of bringing loads of laundry for their mother to do. They were harmless, but they were also doomed; until something traumatized them, they'd stay half-children.

They were also drunk.

". . . so I finally said I'd meet him at the coffee shop in the Walmart over in Unicorn," Harley was saying. "We're talking, everything's going fine, and then he gets this weird look on his face. 'What's wrong?' I ask him. 'Nothing,' he says, 'I just have to fart.' And he does! I heard it, right there in the Walmart!"

They were now a dozen yards away. Spook switched on a flashlight and shone it ahead of them. The circle of light caught Mandalay where she stood.

"I hope there weren't no second date," Spook said as if he didn't see the girl at all.

"There wasn't even the end of a first one. I swear, Spook, dating is the hardest damn thing in the world."

With no warning at all, Spook burst into tears. The flashlight shook in his hand.

"Goddammit, Spook," Harley said.

"I just cain't believe she's gone," he said, drawing each word out in a series of stuttering sobs.

"I came up here because you promised you wouldn't do this."

"I cain't help it!" He threw his arms around his sister, who was a full foot and a half shorter. She staggered back under the sudden weight.

"Look, what's done is done," Harley said. "Get yourself together and grow a pair."

Janet started to stand up, but Mandalay gestured sharply for her to stay still. The brother and sister remained in place, the flashlight swinging wildly as Spook adjusted his hug.

"I was going to write a song for her wedding someday," Spook said. "I'd even started it. 'My baby sister—' "

"Stop it!" Harley snapped, and pushed him to arm's length. "This ain't helping you, or me, or her."

"But I just don't understand it! Why would that monster kill her? She was an angel—" And again he dissolved into sobs.

Harley slapped him. It made no difference. Then she drew back and drove her knee into his groin.

His sobs cut off at once, he let out a soft squeak, and fell to the ground. The flashlight rolled away back toward the house.

"Now, stop that," she said.

"Owwww . . ."

"I'm sorry, but you needed it."

He got slowly to his knees. She helped him up the rest of the way, and the two walked back down the hill to the house, picking up the flashlight when they reached it.

When she was certain they were too far to hear, Janet said softly, "Why didn't they see us?"

"I hid us."

"You've got to show me how to do that sometime."

"If I showed you," Mandalay said sadly, "you'd have to carry all I carry."

Janet brushed dirt off her jeans and said nothing. Mandalay knelt and opened the small coffin, with the remains of Kera's hand in it. Janet couldn't see what the girl was doing, and truthfully didn't want to. In a moment, Mandalay closed the box and said, "All right, let's put it back."

Although she was exhausted, Janet worked diligently, because the sooner the hole was filled in, the sooner they could get the hell out of there.

As the pearl gray light of dawn peeked in around the curtains, Duncan watched Renny sleep. She lay on her stomach, her black hair covering her face. He wondered if that position would hurt the baby, but decided he or she was so young, it probably didn't matter.

She'd essentially moved into his place, although they agreed they would soon have to look for someplace larger. There was no room for a baby in this bachelor-sized pad.

He brushed the hair back from her face. Her mouth was open, half-scrunched on the side pressed into the pillow. In the dimness, her expression looked a bit like Sylvester Stallone. That made him smile.

Then her eyes opened. "Stop staring at me," she said sleepily.

"I'm not staring, I'm looking."

"Why?"

"Wondering how I got so lucky."

She rolled onto her back and smiled up at him. "Maybe I'm the one who got lucky."

"Maybe we both did."

"That still don't explain why you're not sleeping."

"I have a lot on my mind. I mean, I don't know anything about being a daddy."

"You think I know what it's like to be a mother? Have you *met* my mother? Hell, when the Ekvails moved in down the road, Mama had to warn 'em that despite what they might hear, my middle name wasn't 'Goddammit.' "

"Well, you won't be like that as a mama."

"I'll try. Except, to tell you the truth, I don't even like kids."

He put his hand on her still-flat stomach. "I bet you'll like this one. I hope he or she likes us."

Renny put her hand over his. "Dude, what's really bugging you?"

Duncan glanced at the clock. It was a little after five-thirty. It seemed like the time of day when honesty was demanded. He said, "All my life, I've been trying to be right about everything. It was important to me to be right. I used to get into fights about it as a kid."

"I know. I remember watching a couple at school."

"Did I win?"

"It was a split decision both times. Coach Leckie came out and broke them up."

"Well, I feel different now."

"You don't want to be right all the time?"

"No. I just want to be . . ."

"What?"

"Better. Better each day than I was yesterday."

She took her hand from her stomach and touched it to her face. "Oh, honey," she said, all her usual sarcasm absent.

He kissed her. "I love you, Renny."

"I love you, too, hotshot."

Ginny opened the back screen door of her family's porch. She yawned, still in her sleep shirt, and turned on the porch light. When she saw it was Janet who'd rung the doorbell, she said, "It's five in the morning and it's a school day. What are you doing here?"

"Get dressed," Janet said, and pushed her back inside. She kept shoving all the way into Ginny's bedroom.

Ginny's family lived in a one-story house that had seen better days, but was still comfortable and homey enough. Ginny's room was a mess, cluttered with books, clothes, and pieces of artwork that depicted mythological creatures. She'd even painted an enormous unicorn on her closet door. She cast around for something to wear in the discards.

"Do you ever do laundry?" Janet asked.

"Look, you come banging around here at sunrise, waking everybody up—"

"Oh, I didn't wake anybody but you."

"The hell you didn't!" Ginny's father yelled from their bedroom. Janet always forgot how thin the walls were in this old house.

"Anyway, come on. I have got to talk to you."

Minutes later they were back in Janet's car. "Where are we going?" Ginny asked.

"I don't know. I just . . . I can't . . . it's like . . ."

"Wow, calm down." She dug a roach from her pocket and took the lighter from its place in the ashtray. After she lit it, she said, "It's too small to pass. Lean over."

She took a drag, then blew a stream of smoke into Janet's face.

Janet sucked in as much as she could. Ginny did it twice more before saying, "Now: what happened?"

"Mandalay wanted me to drive her somewhere, right? Just like when we went to see Miss Azure. Only we went to where Kera Rogers was buried and . . . and . . ."

Ginny had never seen Janet so distraught. "What?"

"We fucking *dug her up.*"

"What, you mean like you dug up her grave?"

"Yes."

Ginny was speechless for a moment. Then she asked, "Is that why you smell like that?"

"What, do I smell like the dead?"

"No, you smell like dirt."

"Then yes."

"Why did she want to do that?"

"I don't know! She took something out of the coffin, and then we buried it back."

"What did she take?"

"I don't know. I couldn't see." She shuddered. "The coffin wasn't any bigger than a damn shoe box, Ginny. I don't even know what was in it. I'd heard that hog ate some of her, but if that's all that was left . . ."

Ginny shook her head and pulled the last bit from the roach. "That's crazy."

"I know! I know it's crazy! That's why I'm freaking out!" She took several deep breaths to calm down. "Ginny, I don't know what to do here. I mean . . . what if she really *is* crazy? We always knew Rockhouse was mean, and capable of some bad shit, but there was, like, clear cause and effect with him: You piss him off, he fucks with you. But he wasn't *crazy.*"

"Have you talked to Bliss Overbay?"

"No, because what would I say?"

"You can tell her what happened. There has to be a reason why Mandalay is dragging you into this instead of her. Bliss is supposed to be her second-in-command, red right hand, or whatever you want to call it." Ginny sat up straight. "Shit. What if Bliss doesn't even *know*?"

Janet drove in silence, mulling this over. "Maybe you're right. But keep this between us, okay?"

"Who the hell am I going to tell?"

"I know, but just keep this extra between."

Ginny made a motion like she was zipping her lips shut.

"Thanks." She turned to begin the long swing back to Ginny's, since they had school later that morning.

23

The next night, after it was full dark, Mandalay left her trailer, stepped into the backyard, and abandoned her glamour. She knew her father and stepmother watched, but also knew they wouldn't interfere. They knew who and what she was.

Within moments her wings spread wide and carried her easily up into the sky. She rode the night winds high above the mountains, where the air was cold, thin, and filled with the things the Tufa worshipped. But she had more to do than simply commune.

The previous afternoon, she'd left the fire station with Junior at her heels, insisting in his whiny way that she tell him what she knew. She finally ordered him to leave her alone, and enforced it with a hand gesture that she'd used only three times in all her incarnations. It was one of the signs that asserted her full authority, and the fact that Junior could aggravate her to the point that she used it was something she'd have to seriously ponder.

Then she'd drafted Janet Harper into helping her exhume Kera's remains. The night winds had been whispering about Janet for years now, and Mandalay figured it was time to get to know her. Their apparent age difference meant they'd never cross paths socially, so Mandalay had taken the initiative. Now she wondered if she'd actually frightened Janet away from the destiny the winds had for her. Only time, that most malleable of things for the Tufa, would tell.

But Janet had done her part, and it was now up to Mandalay.

In less time than it took to think it, she stood atop Esketole Mountain at the southwestern edge of Cloud County. The view was spectacular, and depressing: from here she could see the scars, white in the moonlight, of mountaintop-removal mining in other counties. It was a terrifying thing to witness, and its economic worth never seemed to trickle down to those who saw their world ravaged. As always, the money that was put into Appalachia pretty much left the same way it came.

But no one would ever touch Esketole, or any other mountain in the Tufa domain. There were countless riches to be found there, but they were as hidden as the Tufa's true nature from those who would claim them. Not since Sadieville had anyone tried to mine in Cloud County, and that town had been wiped from memory by time, and magic.

Atop Esketole there was a small clearing, unreachable to most without a day's arduous hike through bear- and bobcat-infested woods. Every landmark on its slope bore an intimidating name: Copperhead Pass, Thunder Rocks, the Devil's Steps, Spider's Way. Rumor said that the bones of the first man to climb it, Merle Elswick, lay in a deep crevice and would never be recovered. So no one would just idly visit Esketole, which was the whole point, given what waited at the top.

She stood barefoot at the edge of a little spring-fed pool that formed the head of a trickling stream. The grass was stiff with frost, and crinkled when she stepped on it. The pool's water wound its way down the mountain, becoming an underground river that actually traveled deeper than the artesian aquifer that formed it.

This was the singularity, the point where tradition held that the Tufa arrived in the New World. Custom said that the Fairy Feller, the woodsman whose hubris caused them to be exiled from their home far across the sea, first drank the water of the New World from this spring. Ever since, all Tufa kept a jar of this water somewhere in their house, so that new children could also have their first drink from this spring, a sort of Tufa baptism. Some, such as Mandalay herself, were actually dunked in this spring as a newborn, to awaken the Tufa within. Legend held that once you drank from the Esketole spring, you were bound to this spot, this valley, these mountains. It was more a tradition than actual magic; that came, she knew, from a completely different source. The wind tousled her hair, as if punctuating that thought.

She knelt and unfolded the square of soft linen, revealing the four finger bones. As she washed them in the icy water, rubbing the residue off until they shone pure white in the moonlight, she sang "The Two Sisters" just loud enough to be heard over the gurgling.

There were two sisters, they went playing,
To see their father's ships come sailing.

And when they came unto the sea-brim,
The elder did push the younger in.

"O sister, O sister, take me by the gown,
And draw me up upon the dry ground."

"O sister, O sister, that may not be,
'Til salt and oatmeal grow both of a tree."

And so she sank, she never swam,
Until she came unto the mill-dam. . . .

As she sang, she was careful not to let the finger bones drop into the pool. Its depth, like its mystical waters, was a thing of legend, and she didn't want to test it. When she was done, she took each one and polished it clean with a chamois cloth. Then she rolled them in her palm, where they clacked like dice.

What did he do with her breastbone?
He made him a lute to play thereupon.

What did he do with her fingers so small?
He made him pegs to his lute withall.

What did he do with her nose-ridge?
Unto his lute he made him a bridge. . . .

The wind stirred the trees, and something moved behind her. She turned. A shadowy figure stood in the deeper shadows between the trunks, visible only when she didn't look directly at it.

"Kera?" she said, hoping like hell it wasn't the *other* ghost she knew prowled these woods, the one with six fingers on each hand and a meanness that held on far past the grave. "Kera Rogers, are you unable to rest?"

Nothing happened. The wind rustled the trees, but the shape did not respond. Wherever she was, Kera had no unfinished business. That was a relief.

But there was the other. "Adam?"

"Yes," came the voice, just barely over the wind. Then the shape dissolved into the other shadows.

Mandalay waited to see if Adam's shade would return. Adam hadn't manifested at the fire station when she first tried, so she'd known that only here might he be summoned. Ghosts were not uncommon in Cloud County, or probably anywhere; most people didn't sense them, very few saw them, and only the rarest spoke with them. Mandalay had ghosts inside her head as well, so they were just part of her world. But that didn't make them any less unsettling.

Still, she held the dead man's finger bone in her hand, and had sung up his ghost with it. Unlike Kera, he wasn't resting. He must have more to say than just hello.

"Adam Procure," Mandalay said loudly. "If you have a tale to tell, come out here and speak with me. You know who I am. Don't be afraid."

There was no movement, but again the figure seemed to coalesce out of the shadows. "I'm here," he said, a voice made out of the sound of wind-rattled leaves.

Mandalay clenched the bones tight in her hand, willing the connection to grow stronger. "Did you deserve to die, Adam Procure?"

The figure's voice was as faint as a birdcall from the valley below. "I was tricked."

Mandalay sighed. Was it too much to ask for a straight answer to a yes-or-no question? But she knew it was. Ghosts were often only partial revenants of the dead, and their minds didn't always fully comprehend the cause-and-effect of questions. She tried again.

"Adam Procure: Were you murdered?"

"No."

Then what the hell are you so upset about? she thought. "But you were wronged."

"Yes."

A light went on in her head. "Could you have been saved by another?"

"Yes." And then he faded again, and Mandalay knew she was alone on the mountaintop.

She considered calling him back up, or trying again to summon Kera, but she'd heard enough. The girl's nonappearance spoke to the accidental nature of her death; there was no one to avenge. But whatever had happened subsequently in Half Pea

Hollow was different. If not a murder, then at least a killing that could've been avoided and wasn't.

She carefully folded the cloth around the now-clean bones and tucked them back in her pocket. Again she looked out at the mountains, from the scarred ones in the distance to the safe ones that she, and the night winds, protected. She was truly, deeply tired, but there was one more stop before she could rest. She looked up into the starry sky, where the night winds crossed and danced in their eternal flights. And a moment later, the mountaintop was deserted.

Jack stood on the short dock, watching the stars, the bright moonlight shining down. There was no light pollution here, and even with the moon, he made out the belt of the Milky Way across the sky. He was restless, but he couldn't pin down the reason. Certainly the last hour or so with Bliss should have taken his mind off anything and everything. The woman's energy and imagination seemed inexhaustible.

He wore his khaki uniform pants and leather jacket, but he was shoeless and bare-chested. Mist rose from the water, curling in little tendrils, and something large sloshed out of sight. That got his attention—what could live in this pond that was large enough to make a sound like that? It was no bass or bluegill surfacing, and if it was a catfish, it was gigantic. He'd have to ask Bliss if she'd stocked something unusual in it.

Behind him, Bliss's house, rebuilt since it burned down two years earlier, loomed over him like a great protective beast. The community had pitched in and reconstructed it as close to the original design as they could. Still, there were modern amenities: central heat and air, wireless Internet, and satellite television. Not everything about the ole days was good.

Somewhere a door opened and closed, and the dock's wood shifted as Bliss walked out to join him. She was wrapped in a thick robe and wore only knee-high snow boots. "Hey, you," she said through a yawn.

"Hey."

A little fringe of ice decorated the edge of the lake. A month ago it had been frozen solid. Jack imagined the bite of that cold water on his skin. Bliss asked, "What's up?"

"That boy's bones."

Bliss suspected that was what had roused him. "What about them?"

Jack turned to her. "He's spread out on a table in the fire station. He deserves better."

"His people will take care of him." She put her arms around him. "You're still angry about that animal, aren't you?"

"Wouldn't you be? *Aren't* you?"

"I'm upset, yes. And wary. But anger doesn't help."

He turned and put his arms around her. "You're a much better adult than I am, Bliss."

"I know. And I understand." Then she kissed him.

"Dolph probably got up early and is out there hunting it right now," he said. "I know he said he wouldn't, but he also told me he'd wait until spring to go looking for it, and it turns out he's been going through that valley all winter."

"He's a good man."

"He's an *old* man. And it should be me, not him."

"You have a job with a lot of other responsibilities. He doesn't. He's trying to help you, not embarrass you."

"I know."

They stood silently until Jack finally said, "Bliss, I know you people know more than you're telling me. You always have. I hate to do this, but it's my last resort. Either you tell me what you know, what the Tufa know, or I can't see you anymore. And I don't want that any more than I hope you don't."

"What do you think the Tufa are, Jack?"

"Some little isolated ethnic group. Part black, part white, part

Indian. It's not that unusual; there are pockets of similar people all over the Southeast."

"So you read up on us."

"Yeah." He couldn't interpret her expression. "Am I wrong?"

"That's what most people think. 'Triracial isolates' is the technical term. They call 'em 'Brass Ankles' in South Carolina, 'Redbones' in Louisiana. And we won't even get started on the Blue Fugates in Kentucky. DNA tests have pretty much established that there's nothing really special about any of them."

"You've done some reading, too."

"I have. It helps to give people an answer when they ask awkward questions, even if that answer isn't true."

"You're saying it's not true about the Tufa?"

"It's *so* not true, Jack, you won't believe it."

"What about the DNA tests?"

She smiled a little and shook her head.

"So where does that leave us?"

Bliss looked up at him, her expression still complex and maddeningly indecipherable.

"Are you going to say anything?" he asked after a moment.

"I'm thinking," she said. "This isn't the first time I've been given that sort of ultimatum."

"This happens a lot?"

"Not a lot. But it has happened. Not long ago, a young man came here and wanted to know about the Tufa. So I showed him."

"What happened?"

She smiled at some inner irony. "He ran off with my sister."

"That must've hurt."

"Not really. It was the right ending for that story. And after all my sister had been through, she deserved a little happiness."

"And how does that apply to me?"

"I showed that young man because he needed to know. I'm trying to decide if you do."

"I'll make it easy for you: I don't. I'll go right on doing what I do, whether you tell me or not."

"I see. I guess I have a different decision to make this time, then."

"Which is?"

"Whether or not *I* need you to know. I can tell you the real truth about the Tufa, Jack. And I can convince you. But that kind of knowledge can't be unlearned. And it might alter things between us."

"You're freaking me out a little, Bliss."

"Good," she said seriously. "You should be freaked out. I want to stay with you, Jack, until one or both of us decide we don't want it anymore, and I want that bad enough to share things with you that don't get shared with outsiders very much."

"Will you get in trouble if you do?"

"Maybe. It wouldn't be the first time I've crossed arbitrary lines. And I've already shown you some of it. Remember that hand gesture I had you make in the shower?"

"Yeah . . ."

"It's actually a form of protection. It keeps mortals from falling under a Tufa's charms. All the smart non-Tufa parents around here include it in 'the talk' they give their teenagers."

"What happens if they don't use it?"

"Usually they die of broken hearts."

She said it with such simple finality that he didn't doubt that she, at least, believed it.

"I don't plan to die, Bliss," he said carefully. "I like you a lot, but not that much."

She stepped back a few feet. Again the dock creaked under her weight. "What you're about to see, Jack, isn't a trick, or a hallucination, or a dream. Well, maybe a dream, although this kind of dream usually happens at midsummer." She chuckled at her own in-joke. "I'm asking you one last time: Are you ready?"

He nodded and crossed his arms. Although the rational part

of his brain said this was all some elaborate put-on, he couldn't ignore the dead-serious way she spoke, and the utter grim purpose with which she stepped out of her boots and then let her robe drop to the dock. Her pale skin shone blue-white in the moonlight, and the snake-and-acorn tattoo stood out in sharp relief.

"Honey," he began, "you don't have to—"

"Close your eyes."

He did. He sensed no change from her, no movement, nothing.

"Now. Look at me."

He opened his eyes. And gasped. And was speechless.

Because what stood before him was beautiful, and magical, and transcendent.

But it wasn't human.

24

Some things about the South, and Appalachia in particular, were clichés. That didn't mean they weren't often true. After all, clichés didn't develop in a vacuum. And often, those clichés served the useful purpose of ensuring no one looked past the expected surface.

Popcorn Mantis's entire life, then, seemed to be a cliché.

He lived in a stereotypical mountain shack, the kind immortalized in countless black-and-white photographs taken by well-meaning outsiders. There were many similar homes across Cloud County, hidden in the hills and at the end of barely passable drives. Quickly slapped together sometime in the last century, often as temporary dwellings while moonshine was brewed nearby, they proved sturdier than even their builders had expected, to the point of being viable for the new century's moonshine, methamphetamine. They weathered the mountain climate, resisted fire and mildew, and ultimately became a part of the landscape around them, almost indistinguishable from the rocks and trees.

Unless their owners were determined to draw attention to themselves. Like Popcorn.

Mandalay walked up the little path paved with old hubcaps pounded flat by mallets, feet, and time. Even though it was cold, the crickets had begun to emerge for the spring, and they sang in the weeds that encroached on the yard. A single lantern burned in one window, but she wouldn't have cared if the house had been totally dark. On an occasion like this, rank had its privileges, and time was a factor.

"Popcorn!" she called out.

"Go 'way," a man's voice called from inside. "Cain't you read the damn sign?"

Mandalay glanced at the yard-long board propped up on the porch that said at the top, NO TRESPASSING! Beneath that, in smaller letters, it read, *What part of* NO *don't you understand?*

"It's Mandalay Harris, Popcorn."

"How I know that?"

"Open the damn door and look at me."

"How I know you ain't a revenuer?"

"Because no revenuer could ever find this place. I'm coming up now."

"I got two barrels packed with thin little dimes pointed right at you, you best stop where you are."

"You shoot me, Popcorn, you ain't never seen the haint like the one I'll slap on your sorry ass," Mandalay said as she climbed onto the porch. A fringe of dried groundhog skins hung around the edge of the roof. She knew they weren't decorative; Popcorn used them to make banjo heads.

Popcorn Mantis was the best banjo maker in Cloud County, and that meant he was one of the best in the world. But he never sought recognition for that. He made what he wanted, charged what he felt like, and ignored entreaties from the rich and famous. In fact, while his name was well known in those rarefied circles, few knew where to find him, and even fewer had actually met him. But his signature on an instrument caused grown men to bow their heads.

Legend said that country star Son Emerson heard about his skill and once showed up at his door, insisting that Popcorn build him a banjo. He promised him any amount of money. Popcorn supposedly told Son exactly where he could go, and slammed the door in his face. Emerson denied it, of course, and Popcorn couldn't be bothered to comment.

Mandalay rapped on the screenless screen door. "Come on, Popcorn, open up."

Popcorn eased the inner door back. Heat and the odor of tanning hides surged out. Silhouetted against the glow of an open iron stove, he held the double-barreled shotgun leveled at Mandalay. "I ain't got no truck with you, Mandalay. You just scurry on home."

"You do got truck with me, Popcorn." She raised her left hand, clenched into a fist, then made two short, simple gestures with her fingers and thumb. "Now stop acting like some hillbilly in a horror movie and let me in. It's cold out here."

He carefully uncocked the twin hammers and lowered the weapon until it pointed at the floor. "You can't be too careful."

"Yes, actually, you can."

"So what's so damn important?"

She pulled the four bones from her pocket. "I brought you something. And I need something from you, soon."

"You know I work when I want to. Don't nobody tell me what to do or when."

"You want to. Elsewise, I'll have to keep coming back and checking on you. Can we get out of the cold, please?"

Popcorn looked her up and down. "Wouldn't think someone like you would get cold."

"You'd be wrong."

"Then I suppose I have to make us some damned tea."

"I'd prefer the green kind," she said, but the sarcasm was lost on him. She followed him in, stepping over the homemade doormat that read, POPCORN SAYS FUCK OFF.

The decor inside the shack looked exactly as Mandalay remembered it. Her father had brought her here to get her first banjo, before she'd settled on the guitar as her preferred instrument. She'd been five, but of course, the vast history in her head had churned up other memories of Popcorn, from his time as a dapper young man to his sad decline into alcoholism, and finally to his partial rebirth as a sober but unpleasant old craftsman. Which explained why her first question to him back then, as a five-year-old girl, had been, "Are you still drinking?" Which, in turn, explained why he couldn't stand the sight of her to this day.

He put a kettle on the stove and then lit two lanterns. The great lifetime's-worth of clutter alternately shone and cast shadows, making the little foyer seem like some kind of incredibly complex labyrinth. She wondered where some of these pieces of wood, wire, and cloth had come from, and what Popcorn had in mind for them. But she knew better than to ask, since she needed a favor from him. She could pull rank, but it was always better to inspire people to be helpful than to command them against their will.

"I learnt about this tea over in Germany when I was in the service," Popcorn said as he put the loose leaves into a pair of rusty old infusers. "We used to go to this little tea shop because the owner had a half-dozen blond daughters, and they was all prettier than a sunrise without a hangover."

"Did you like Germany?" Mandalay asked, to keep the conversation friendly.

"Oh, hell yeah. Anytime we'd go into town, all the little kids would come up to us and wave, shout stuff, and so on. I asked my sergeant why they were so damn friendly. He said, 'If you got your ass kicked twice by somebody, you'd be friendly, too.'" He laughed, a big barking noise that frightened something alive in the clutter and made it scurry away. He blew the dust off two old cups and asked, "So what brings a little girl like you out here on a night like this?"

"Have you heard about what happened to Kera Rogers and Adam Procure?"

"Them the ones that pig killed?"

"That's right."

"That's all I've heard. Some pig killed 'em."

"There's more to it than that. At least for Adam."

"Like what?"

"I'm not completely sure."

"You? I thought the night winds tucked you in every night and brought you coffee every morning."

"Not quite."

He poured the tea before the pot whistled and put the cups on a table. "You can sit down."

"Thanks. Sugar?"

"Nope."

"Do you have any Equal?"

He snorted. "Not in this life."

"I meant sweetener."

He put a mason jar in front of her. "That's honey I harvested myself."

"Thanks," Mandalay said, retracting the dipper from the thick liquid and letting it drip into her cup.

"So what does that have to do with me?"

She put the bones on the table. They clattered in the silence. "I need these made into tuning pegs. And then I need you to make a banjo around them."

He picked up the biggest one and held it toward the lantern. "These ain't pig bones."

"No."

His eyes opened wide in his wrinkled face as he realized. "Well, damn, girl."

"I know," she said as she sipped the bitter tea.

"Do their folks know you have these?"

"No, and I don't plan to tell them."

He held one up and squinted at it. "I can signify that this is a young man's bone."

"How do you know that?"

"Hey, I got my secrets, missy, and you got yours." He looked at the others. "And those are a young lady's." He snorted sarcastically. "Gee, I wonder who they could belong to?"

"Don't get smart with me, Popcorn."

"It cain't be legal for you to have these."

"Is everything you do legal?"

"Who else knows about this?"

"Nobody."

He put the bone back down with the others. "Only got four."

"Then it'll have to be a four-string, won't it?"

"Don't *you* get smart with *me,* little missy. You're playing with some powerful stuff here."

"I know that. How fast can you do it?"

"You need me to build the whole thing from scratch, or can I put these pegs on one I've already got?"

"I need the whole thing from scratch. It'll get played once and never again."

"That big a deal?"

"That big."

He thought it over. "Give me a couple of months. I got some paying jobs ahead of it."

Mandalay started to protest, then caught herself. She could order him, of course, but she was already imposing. It wouldn't be polite to make it a demand, and given the nature of his work, it might pervert the final result. "Okay," she said.

He was still mad. "You know, you coming in here like this, demanding all my attention, I don't appreciate at all. I'd expect it from ol' Rockhouse, but not you."

"Popcorn, this is serious. Two people have already died, more could die, and we won't know the truth about it until you—" She pointed at him. "—give us the means."

"Who is 'we'?"

"All of us," she said with soft deliberateness.

Jack watched the glow at the heart of the fire, where it went from red to orange to white and back in random alternating patterns. All the patterns he'd counted on in his life had just come crashing down with the reality of what Bliss had told him, and then shown him.

Back in her robe, Bliss snuggled against him on the couch. "It's a lot to accept," she said.

"It is that," he agreed without turning to her. "So are all the Tufa . . . ?"

"Some more than others. It's a matter of how much true Tufa blood you have in you. I'm a pureblood."

Now he looked at her and waved his hand in the air where those beautiful, fragile-looking wings should be if what he'd seen was real. There was nothing. "Do they, like . . . retract?"

Amusement crinkled the corners of her eyes, but she didn't laugh at him. "It's more complicated than that. And subtle. I can't fully explain it."

"I can believe that." He paused. "Bronwyn Chess? Can she do this?"

"She can."

"I'm a scientist at heart, you know. I think that way. Everything exists for a reason, and fits into the world in a specific way. Nothing evolves for just the hell of it."

"You think we don't fit in?"

"Fairies?"

"That's one word."

"This *is* a lot to accept, Bliss."

"I know. If you need some time, or want to stop seeing me altogether, I'll understand. Not everyone can. Accept it, I mean."

"You're not worried that I might tell people?"

"Tell them what?"

She had him there. He had no proof, and if he went around claiming the Tufa were actually a bunch of fairies, he'd be shipped to the mental hospital in Bolivar before the sun went down. "Well, you've got me there."

"Do you think you *can* accept it?"

She looked so lovely in the firelight, he couldn't begin to get angry. He touched her cheek. "You're still you, right?"

"Always have been, always will be." She knew he didn't get the irony of that comment.

He pulled her close. "I may have other questions, as we go. But I do want to keep going." After they kissed, he added, "I assume you want me to keep this secret?"

"It's probably better for everyone if you do."

"Right. Well, then, I guess it's only fair if I tell you: I have a secret, too. If it gets out, it could cost me my job, my friends, everything."

"What's that?"

He looked at her with total seriousness. "I'm a Democrat."

She giggled. And she kept giggling even as he kissed her, scooped her off her feet, and carried her upstairs to her bedroom.

25

The crowd at the storytelling festival watched Janet's every move now, rapt in a way that only people fully emotionally invested in a story could be. Janet knew this story had it all: danger, romance, betrayal, a monster, and a sense of inevitable reckoning. It was why she'd chosen to tell it, and she wasn't surprised by the response.

She'd been noodling on her guitar throughout, and now she made eye contact with the sound man, who raised the volume gradually until it was loud enough to provide real accompaniment. She sang:

And the winter went by with its snow and ice
Until the spring spread its petals anew
And everyone with the truth in their blood
Knew something was coming, and soon.

I was just a girl, and I could only watch
I didn't know the threads in the skein
But as they drew tight to form the fabric of their
lives,
I knew the truth would pour like rain.

Because it doesn't matter how well you hide it
Or how many secrets your heart has beside it
The truth has a way of coming out on its own
Even when you stop, or try to postpone
Because only the fire can burn off the sh—

She stopped in mid-word, and everyone laughed, releasing some of the tension that had been building. Some, Janet thought smugly, but not all. Just like she planned.

"Almost forgot we had some kids here," she said, and the sound man took her cue and eased the guitar's volume back down.

Janet looked out at the crowd. She blinked sweat from her eyes and tried to see if any of the Tufa had driven over to catch the show. It wouldn't be like them, she knew, but then again, you could never tell. There were a few heads of jet-black hair, but none seemed to connect to her the way another Tufa would. This was a totally mundane audience, and she was giving them tons of Tufa secrets in such a way that they'd never, ever believe them.

Of course, in her head, the story unfolded as it had all those years ago, with the real people and their real names. Luckily she was good enough, and practiced enough, to redact on the fly.

"So, once again, we have to jump ahead a couple of months. Things progressed as they do: one girl grew more pregnant, another girl continued to plug away at both her music and her senior year of high school, the game warden and the paramedic found a lot of new ways to do the oldest thing in the world—"

She paused for knowing laughter.

"And the girl with the secrets in her head waited for the old luthier to finish his job. Some things can't be rushed, and a guy like that puts more of himself into his work than most of us do. Every curve of the wood re-created a woman he'd known as a young man. Every notch in the bridge was perfectly cut to hold his own dreams. It's a slow way to work, and to a lot of people, a ridiculous one. After all, most luthiers can bang out a banjo in a week. But for him, there was only one way, and it took as long as it took.

"And so all these stories began to draw together, on one day in the late spring. It began with the pregnant girl giving her troubled fiancé an ultimatum."

26

"Dude, I can't do this. I can't do this whole wedding thing."

Renny wore only a huge T-shirt that said, HI, Y'ALL on the front and BYE, Y'ALL on the back. She paced as much as she could, leaning back to balance the weight of the growing baby. Although she couldn't imagine it getting much bigger, the granny-woman acting as her midwife assured her that everything was fine, and that she wasn't having twins. "He's just a sizable one," she said, using the male pronoun.

Renny had been using it, too, ever since the old woman held a pendulum over her gravid stomach and it swung in such a way that indicated the baby was a boy. Renny accepted it, but she wasn't sure she wanted a boy. Hell, she wasn't sure she wanted a *baby.*

And now Duncan looked up from his computer and snapped, "Then what the fuck do you want to do? We've rented tuxes, dresses for your damn bridesmaids, catering—"

"Asking your mama to cook for everyone is *not* catering."

"You got a problem with my mama's cooking?"

"No!" she almost yelled; then she put her hands over her ears. "Can you please just let me say this, okay?"

"Sure," Duncan said. "You've been saying shit all along, why should this be any different?"

She closed her eyes and took several deep breaths. "Duncan," she said slowly, "I don't like who you've turned into these past couple of months. I don't like who I've turned into, either. We're the worst of both our parents, and it's because of this damn wedding, isn't it?"

Duncan knew he could never answer truthfully. "Yeah."

"Then let's just blow it off. What do you say?"

"And not get married?"

"No, let's just go do it. Drive over the county line and find a justice of the peace. Right now."

"Are you serious?"

"Yes, I'm serious!" she cried desperately. It wasn't like the way she normally raised her voice: there was real fear and real pain in it, and he saw a look in her eye that was new, and broke his heart.

"All right," he said, wrapping his arms around her and leaning forward to accommodate her belly. "It's fine with me. But you should put on some underwear."

"Are you sure?" she said in a small voice.

"Yes, you definitely need underwear."

That got a smile. "No, about eloping!"

"Of course. If it's what you need, it's what we'll do."

He couldn't tell if she was crying, but it wouldn't surprise him. She cried a lot these days. The tough, acerbic girl who used to slam him against the wall and undo his belt and pants with one hand had become weepy and pitiful.

"You know, it's all because of Adam," she said.

Duncan's whole body jerked at the mention of the name.

"If he was here," she continued, "it would all be okay."

"It'll still be okay," he said, stroking her long black hair, staring off into the distance of time to that day in Half Pea Hollow.

"It must be dead," Max McMaynus said. He sat opposite Jack's desk, sipping coffee. He scowled and said, "Man, no offense, but this coffee takes like ass."

"I'm not qualified to make that comparison," Jack said dryly. "So I bow to your superior knowledge."

"Ha fucking ha," Max said. "Look, Dolph spent all winter looking for it and never found it. I've been out there, and I assume that little Tufa honey has, too."

"Her name is Bronwyn," Jack said, annoyed. "And if she hears you call her that, she's liable to change your voice for you."

"My point is, we haven't found a sign of it. And really, has anyone actually *seen* it?"

"We all saw it that night on the trail cam. You saw it right there in front of you."

"I've been pondering about that. Suppose we didn't. Suppose we just saw a bunch of piglets, and one big—not gigantic, just big—sow? I mean, think about it: we were expecting to see a monster, so we saw one. But all we had to compare it to were the other pigs."

"And the trap. It was too big to get through the gate, remember? And you shot it."

Max frowned. "Yeah, that's a good point."

"And we weren't the only ones that saw it. That Gowen boy said he did, too."

"He was hysterical."

"I'm inclined to think the hog was the cause of that, not the effect. Look, I hope it's dead, too, Max. I really do. But until more time passes or somebody finds a carcass, I'm not willing to accept that. If you don't want to be involved anymore, I understand."

"No, that ain't what I meant, Jack. Yeah, it's hard to take off time from my practice, but I hate those damn pigs no matter how big they are. I hate the way they smell, the noises they make, the way they leave their shit everywhere. I hate the way they tear up the forest. I'm always up for killing a few more of 'em. I just don't like . . ."

"What?"

Max sighed. "Wasting my time, man. My patients are going to start looking around for another vet if I'm not in my office some more. Plus . . ."

"What?"

"You and I know it's important to get rid of these pigs. But it doesn't sound very good that a vet spends his spare time shooting animals."

"If we haven't found any trace, and nobody's reported seeing it, by the Fourth of July, I'll go along with you and call it. Fair enough?"

"That's three more months."

"Yes."

"And until then?"

"Dolph's looking. Bronwyn's looking. So am I. You have the longest commute, so you don't have to, if you don't want to. I won't call you until we have something solid."

"No," Max said with another sigh. "That's not fair to the others. I'm in for a pound."

"Thanks," Jack said sincerely. But he was troubled that, since the winter discovery of the den, no one had seen hide, hair, scat, or track of the monster even he had begun to refer to as Piggly-Wiggly.

Janet waited patiently while Don Swayback read over the story she'd e-mailed him earlier. She was a little annoyed that he hadn't already done so; that was the point of sending it, after all. But since she also insisted (politely) that she hear any critique in person, she guessed she couldn't complain.

She watched his eyes scan down his screen, his face studiously unreadable, and at last had to look away. Knowing he was reading her words was the most nerve-racking thing she'd ever experienced. How did full-time reporters stand it?

Then she remembered that night with Mandalay, and amended her thought. *Nope,* she thought. *Second most nerve-racking.*

She looked around at the accumulated detritus of the *Weekly Horn* office, wondering how old the newspaper was, and how long some of those pictures had been hung on the tacky '70s paneling. In the background, the office manager muttered her theory that all journalists were eternal, world-class slobs as she swept the back room.

Janet had moved on from the Piggly-Wiggly story, and had written off her adventures with Mandalay as a quirk in the girl's nature. After all, she'd heard nothing from her since that night, and that suited Janet just fine. School, the newspaper, and Little Trouble Girls kept her plenty occupied.

Don had approached her after a concert at the weekly barn dance, asking if he could do a feature about Little Trouble Girls. While interviewing her for that, they'd started talking about journalism, and she asked if he'd look at some of her work. It couldn't hurt to get a professional's opinion. And he earned her respect by getting the band's name right, and not calling them *the* Little Trouble Girls.

Besides, Don was part Tufa, and had been accepted by Mandalay into their group. He still lived outside Cloud County, but he covered it exclusively for the paper, and understood the need for discreet censorship. Like Alvin Darwin, he filled in the blanks so no one else came looking. Which was why Janet wanted him to be impressed with her work.

Finally Don said, "Well. That was interesting."

"Worth coming in on Saturday for?"

"Interesting," he repeated.

"'Interesting' doesn't sound like the best thing."

"It's the best thing about this. Who are you writing it for?"

She felt her cheeks burn. "Just the school paper."

"Not what. Who?"

"I don't understand."

"You've written this like you were talking to your best friend."

"I like to think of my readers as my friends."

"Not when you're writing a news story. For features, yeah, sure. But this is a story about an animal that's killed two people, and is still on the loose. Do you think it's a good idea to refer to it as 'the porcine predator'?"

"Seemed catchy," she said, trying not to sound defensive.

"That's not the issue. How many people in your school knew the boy and girl who died?"

"A . . . lot."

"Lot of them are family, too. Cousins and such. Right?"

"Yes."

"How do you think they'll feel when they read, 'On that day, she left home for the last time, not knowing she'd never see her family again'?"

Janet couldn't meet his eyes. "I guess it might hurt."

"Yeah. Look, Janet, I understand why you're here. I know what you're looking for."

"You do?"

He nodded. "Validation. And you're a good writer, there's no denying that. This isn't a criticism of your ability. But unless you're writing for a big-city paper or some Web site with an international audience, you *have* to take your readership into account. I'm not saying lie, or leave out uncomfortable truths. But those truths should serve a purpose. This," he said with a nod at his screen, "only serves the purpose of your ego."

Before she could reply, he held up his hand. "You know who Quentin Tarantino is?"

"Sure."

"He's pals with Robert Rodriguez. Know him?"

"I've seen the *Spy Kids* movies."

"Okay. So, here's the difference between them. Rodgriguez's movies say, 'Look how cool this is.' Tarantino's movies say, 'Look how cool *I am.*'" He looked at her steadily. "Which do you want to be?"

Janet made her good-byes and left as quickly as she could without running. In the car, she turned the radio up all the way and cried, letting out the humiliation she'd choked down. But when it was done, she headed back to Needsville with a new, clear-eyed determination.

Bliss and Jack sat in her living room. It was an airy, sparsely furnished space, the opposite of the clutter and knickknacks of her prior house. When that one burned down, there had been no way to replace so many of the personal objects and family heirlooms she'd lost. So she'd simply let it be, and gradually decorated it as she found pieces that seemed to have the appropriate feel.

Bliss sat at the edge of the couch, her guitar across her lap, playing S. J. Tucker's "Dream of Mississippi." When she finished, she looked back at Jack, who reclined with his sock feet tucked behind her. She asked, "Did you like that?"

"I did. Is it one of yours?"

"No. Sooj Tucker wrote it. She's from a different set of hills, over in Arkansas. You said you played piano a little; we could play together."

"I said I knew what one was. I haven't played in years."

She put the guitar aside and crawled back to snuggle with him. "I'm willing to bet I could motivate you to get back to the keyboard."

"Oh yeah? Exactly how?"

She was about to tell him when the doorbell rang.

"Excuse me," she said as she climbed off him. "Hold that thought."

When she opened the door, Mandalay stood there. She looked

particularly serious, so before she could speak, Bliss said, "Jack's here."

"I know. I saw the truck."

She called back inside, "I'll be right back, hon. See if there's anything on Netflix we can watch tonight."

She stepped outside to join Mandalay. The spring night was cool, and the breeze tangled Mandalay's dark hair. Bliss wore hers in a single braid down her back. "What's up?"

Mandalay said, "I'm here to warn you. I'm going to do something tonight that might have repercussions."

"On me?"

"Indirectly. On you *and* Jack."

"What are you going to do?"

"I can't tell you. I can't tell anyone. I don't want even the slightest little hint to get out on the night winds. But I'd make sure your phone's turned on tonight. Your professional skills might be needed."

Lots of people called Bliss for medical help or advice, the same way they'd once contacted Appalachian granny-women back before modern communication. Bliss was happy to fill that role, but this seemed far grimmer. "Okay, now I'm a little concerned. What's this about?"

"The deaths of Kera Rogers and Adam Procure."

"You sound as bad as Jack. I don't think it's off his mind for more than ten minutes at a time."

"In that case, yes, I am that bad."

"Have you found out something?"

"I'm going to."

"Using those bones you took?"

"Yes."

"Then I should come with you. Let me grab—"

"No. I have someone else in mind."

This brought Bliss up short. "Wait, you . . . what?"

"I have someone else in mind to help me with this."

Bliss had been Mandalay's advisor, protector, and confidante since the girl first learned to talk. "I don't know what to say to that."

"Bliss, you've always been there for me, and I know you always will. But right now, I need someone else."

"Luke?"

That made Mandalay laugh. "No. He'd do it in a heartbeat, but he's only thirteen."

Bliss nodded. She knew better than to respond, *So are you.*

"It's no reflection on you," Mandalay added. "I still need you."

"If you say so." She made a hand sign of respect and fealty.

Mandalay responded. "I have to go. Hopefully we *won't* need you tonight, and you and Jack can have a nice relaxing evening together."

"I don't think I'll be relaxing much," Bliss said, but the girl was already gone.

She stood alone after Mandalay departed, staring up at the stars. A few clouds driven by the winds scudded across her field of vision. She'd cared for Mandalay since the girl was born, protecting her and standing up for her while she learned her place in the world. And even though Mandalay had denied it, Bliss couldn't help but think this marked some kind of separation.

And she tried to think of whom Mandalay would turn to for help. Who else could do what Bliss did?

Janet's father knocked on the bedroom door. "You have company," he called.

Janet quickly stubbed out the joint, and Ginny sprayed some neutralizing air freshener around. They'd perfected the routine, so by the time she opened the door, Janet's room smelled like old sage had been burned.

Mandalay Harris stood beside Janet's father. She was dressed in jeans and wore an old denim jacket. "May I come in?" she asked.

"Uh . . . sure," Janet said, and stepped back. She caught her father's eye, and his unmistakable *Remember who that is and behave yourself* look.

Janet and Ginny both made the elaborate gesture that signaled their respect for Mandalay. She made the response. Once the door was shut, Mandalay said, "I need your help tonight."

Janet and Ginny exchanged a look. "What can we do for you?" Ginny asked.

"Not you, Ginny. Just Janet."

"Oh," she said in a small voice.

"It's nothing personal, Ginny. It's something only Janet can do, and it's dangerous, so I don't want to involve anyone I don't have to."

Janet remembered the terror of that night at the grave. "Dangerous how?"

"Probably nothing bad will happen to us. But I can only say 'probably.' And if something bad does happen, it's liable to be *real* bad."

"What is it you need me to do?"

"Drive me to two different places."

"You need a chauffeur?"

With a faint smile, Mandalay said, "No, but I don't think you could keep up with me any other way."

"That's a fair point," Janet agreed. She looked at the window. "Do we need to sneak out? It's fairly easy, we just shimmy down the—"

"No, it's okay. We'll use the front door."

"Well," Ginny said snarkily as she repacked her overnight bag, "can you guys drop me at home on your way?"

"Yeah," Janet said. "I mean, if that's okay."

"It is," Mandalay agreed. "And I'm sorry, Ginny."

"Let me guess: She won't even be able to tell me about it tomorrow, right?"

"Actually, I don't think she'll have to. I suspect everyone will know by sunrise."

27

Mandalay and Janet waited in Popcorn's living room. Janet sat in a recliner that smelled like cats, whiskey, and a few things she couldn't quite identify. Whatever it was, she was sure she'd never get the odor out of her hair. *It's all material,* she reminded herself as she shifted and heard something make a wet squelch. *All grist for the song and story mill.*

Popcorn emerged from the back room with the instrument shrouded in a heavy dark cloth. He placed it reverently on the table, then stepped back with a sigh.

"Is that cerecloth?" Mandalay asked.

"It is indeed," Popcorn confirmed.

"What's cerecloth?" Janet asked as she stood beside Mandalay.

"It's a burial shroud," Mandalay said. "It's coated with wax on one side. It's an old tradition that doesn't get used very much anymore."

"So the banjo's dead?"

No one responded to her joke. Popcorn picked up a mason jar of moonshine, screwed off the lid, and took a swallow. Even at this distance, the fumes made Janet's eyes smart as she extracted herself from the recliner.

What she'd assumed to be a pillow at the small of her back turned out to be a cat that scrambled free as soon as she moved. "Can we see it?" she asked, nodding at the banjo.

"Not so damn fast," the old man snapped. "This is more'n just an instrument. More'n just pieces of wood and skin and ivory. You think I don't know what you want this for?"

"I know you do," Mandalay said.

"You're right about that," Popcorn said with a snort. He took another swallow of the moonshine. "Great gosh a'mighty, that'll put hair on your innards." He offered the jar to Janet.

"No thanks, I'm hairy enough inside."

Mandalay shook her head as well.

He closed the jar and took a fiddle and bow from a nearby shelf. He handed them to Mandalay and said, "I ain't giving it away until somebody plays 'The Song of the Lost Soul' over it."

Mandalay held the instrument awkwardly. "Why?"

"Because I fucking said so. You don't like it, go see someone else."

"Why don't you do it?" Janet asked, and then said along with Popcorn, "Because I fucking said so." She smiled with flat humor. "I knew it the moment I asked."

"You ain't as stupid as some," Popcorn said.

"You charmer," she said, and he barked out a laugh.

Mandalay handed the fiddle to Janet. "You know that song?"

" 'The wicked man is dead, his wife goes to his tomb to pray'? French song?"

"That's the one."

She tucked the instrument under her chin and laid the bow on the strings. "Yeah, I know it. But I know a better song for this." And she drew out the first long notes of Joy Division's "Atmosphere."

As the sad song filled the shack and cast its spell, Popcorn's lower lip trembled. To the girls' amazement, tears filled his eyes. He wiped at them hard with his sleeve, then drew back the cloth covering the instrument. The metal gleamed, the skin shone, but all Mandalay could look at were the four yellow-white tuning pegs on the head.

Janet finished the song, lowered the bow, and said, "Wow."

"That's all you got to say?" Popcorn snapped, his voice still a little ragged. "Goddamn, girl, I've worked these old fingers so hard, I could've used my own bones for another set. This is a thing of beauty, a work of motherfucking art, and all you got to say is, 'wow'?" He sneered the last word with all the contempt of the old for the young.

Janet was oblivious to his abuse. "How does it sound?"

"How does it sound?" Popcorn roared. "You can just haul that tight little ass of yours right out my door, you disrespectful little MTV-watching bitch!"

"Popcorn!" Mandalay snapped, but Janet hadn't even been listening. She bent close and studied the banjo's construction with an expert's eye. At last she said, "Can I play it?"

"Yes," Mandalay said before Popcorn could respond. The old man *hmph*ed and took another sip of moonshine.

Janet reverently picked up the banjo. It didn't have a strap, so she sat on the nearest kitchen chair.

"Open back," she said to herself. "Low action. Who'd you build this for?"

Again, before Popcorn could answer, Mandalay said, "I'll tell you later."

Janet plucked expertly at the strings, and quickly adjusted the pegs to a standard C-G-D-A tuning. She played a little, and let out a low whistle. "Wow."

Mandalay glared at Popcorn, who said nothing.

Janet began playing Dale Ann Bradley's "East Kentucky Morning," and unlike the violin, this didn't swirl around and fill the space. Instead it pricked at the listener's skin, like the sensation of a sleeping limb coming back to life. Without realizing it, Mandalay and Popcorn both backed away from her.

Then she began to sing. She sang plainly, with very little inflection, letting the aching tragedy of the lyrics do the work. Her voice was strong, and her touch on the strings sure.

When she finished, the shack was silent. Then they all heard the unmistakable sound of two coyotes howling outside, sounding for all the world like they approved.

Janet looked at Popcorn. "You're really an artist, Mr. Mantis. I've played a lot of instruments, but I've never played anything that was as smooth and proper as this." She handed it back to him.

He took it and mumbled, "Thank you."

Mandalay held out her hands. "I'll take that now, Popcorn. And thank *you*."

He said nothing to her as he handed it over.

To Janet, Mandalay said, "Let's go. We have somewhere else to be tonight."

"We do?"

"Yes."

"Where?"

Mandalay gave her a knowing little half smile that was so mature, so filled with knowledge and history and power, that on her thirteen-year-old face it was like seeing the image of some ancient pagan goddess. "You won't believe me when I tell you."

Bronwyn Chess opened the door, wondering who would be stopping by this late. She was even more perplexed when she saw who it was. "Duncan," she said. "Renny. What's wrong?"

"Nothing," Duncan said quickly, unable to meet her eyes. Her position in Tufa society was so high, and so powerful, that he felt like a child meeting the police chief after being caught egging someone's house.

"We're sorry to bother you, Mrs. Chess," Renny said, and made a gesture of Tufa respect. "Hope we didn't wake your little one."

"No, she could sleep through a Metallica show."

"We're actually here for your husband."

Bronwyn gave them a dubious look. "Really?"

"Yes. Is he around?"

"Sure. Come in."

They followed her into the living room of the parsonage, located next door to the Triple Springs Methodist Church in Unicorn, just across the county line. Bronwyn's marriage to a non-Tufa had, briefly, caused a wave of outrage among the First Daughters: she was one of the dwindling numbers of Tufa pure-bloods, and it was expected that she'd marry one of the others, to help keep the Tufa together. The uncertain (to everyone else) parentage of her now-three-year-old daughter ameliorated it somewhat, since that big-eyed, black-haired, precociously kind little girl clearly belonged more to her mother's lineage than to that of her her sandy-haired, good-natured father.

But now that father rose from the couch to greet them. Dressed in a T-shirt and jeans, he looked more like an Ivy League frat boy than a minister. "Hello," he said easily, and shook Duncan's hand. To Renny he said, "I haven't had a chance to express my condolences for the loss of your brother, Miss Procure. I'm very sorry."

"Thank you," Renny said.

"Honey, y'all visit as long as you want, I've got some work I can do." He kissed Bronwyn on the cheek and started to leave, but she caught his hand.

"Actually, they're here to see you," Bronwyn said.

"Really? Well, what can I do for you?"

Renny looked back at Duncan, then said, "We want to get married."

"So I've heard," Craig said. He did not look at her belly when he said it.

"Right now," she continued. "Here."

"I see," Craig said calmly, as if this happened every night.

"I seem to remember Bronwyn saying that there was a big ceremony planned."

"There was. We've changed our minds."

Craig looked at Duncan. "'We'?"

"We," Duncan said.

"Okay. Well, let's sit down and talk about it a little. Honey, would you mind putting on some coffee?"

"Sure," Bronwyn said. "And I'll make decaf, so you can have some, too, Renny."

Duncan and Renny followed them to the kitchen. Renny noticed their wedding invitation pinned by a magnet to the refrigerator. She squeezed Duncan's hand for reassurance, but wasn't sure whether she intended to give or receive it.

In the kitchen, Craig gestured for them to have a seat. Duncan held Renny's chair until she was settled; he'd taken to using old-school manners around her, as if it would somehow add incrementally to the karma he was trying to build up to balance what he'd done.

As he took his own seat, Duncan was most startled by all the evidence of Craig and Bronwyn's daughter: drawings stuck to the refrigerator with magnets, sippy cups drying in the dish drain, a laundry basket filled with toys and stuffed animals tucked in a corner. Would his home soon look like that? The thought filled him with a mix of terror and something very like contentment, or at least similar to how he remembered contentment felt.

While Bronwyn set up the coffeepot, Craig joined them at the table. "So," he said gently, "can you explain to me why you want to be married now, instead of waiting?"

"It ain't because of this," Renny blurted, gesturing at her belly. "Everybody knows about this. At this point, I couldn't hide it if I wanted to."

"Okay," Craig agreed.

"It's just . . . what do they call it, the sword of Damien's Sleeves?"

"What?"

"You know, when you feel something's hanging over your head."

"Damocles," Craig corrected.

"Yeah, it's like that. I'm not having second thoughts or anything, but the waiting is driving me batshit." She caught herself. "I apologize for my language, preacher."

"Call me Craig," he said with an easy smile. "And I've heard the word before, you can be as blunt as you want. Duncan, is that how you feel?"

"Yes, sir."

Craig thought a moment before speaking. "I suppose you realize I'm a Methodist minister. I'm not a justice of the peace. If you ask me to perform your wedding, it's a religious ceremony, not a civil one."

"What's the difference?" Renny asked, her voice harsh from fear and worry. "We'll still be just as married, right?"

"If you've got the license, yes, you'll still be just as married."

"Then it's fine. Give him the license, Duncan."

Duncan took out his wallet and handed over the folded paper. It was printed on linen paper, declared itself a MARRIAGE CERTIFICATE OF CLOUD COUNTY, TENNESSEE, and the elaborate design incorporated music staffs and notes. Craig, of course, didn't know that the notes were not random, but were actually from the fourth bar of Leonard Cohen's "Dance Me to the End of Love." Craig looked it over, nodded, and put it on the table between them.

"Honey," Bronwyn called from the hallway. "Can you come here a minute? I need a hand."

Craig immediately stood. "Sure, hon. If y'all will excuse me?"

When he was gone, Renny looked down at the tabletop. "They're talking about us."

"Why?"

She snort-laughed, the way you do when you realize you might be the butt of the universe's joke. "Because we're two white-trash Tufas wanting to get married because you knocked me up."

"That's not true at all."

"Maybe not to us, but that's what it looks like to them. And it's all because of me being scared."

"Renny—"

"Just let it go, Duncan, okay? I don't need reassurance that you'll always be here." She closed her eyes and turned away from him.

In the hallway outside their daughter's bedroom, Craig said softly, "What's up?"

"Are you going to marry them?"

"I suppose so. I don't know them well enough to know if I need to talk them out of it. They're going to be parents, so they're already connected."

"No, that's not it," Bronwyn said. "Do you remember the boy and girl killed by that wild hog last fall? The girl was his girlfriend, and the boy was her brother. That's what brought them together."

"I see."

Even softer, she said, "I'm not convinced the full truth about that has ever come out."

"I don't follow."

"His girlfriend might have been sneaking around with her brother."

"Okay, wait, you've lost me. His girlfriend, the one who's sitting in there—"

"No, his girlfriend before, the one who died. Kera. Kera might have been sneaking around with Renny's brother. And he—" She nodded toward the kitchen, and Duncan. "—might have had something to do with what happened."

"I hadn't heard *that*."

"That's because there's no real evidence. If there was, he wouldn't be sitting in our kitchen right now."

They looked at each other seriously for a long moment. Craig trusted his wife completely, and she in turn knew not to abuse that trust. At last he said, "If you don't think it's a good idea, I won't do it. But someone will."

She nodded, thinking.

"Do you need to call somebody?"

"No. Technically, they're not my problem. They belong to Junior."

"Really?"

"Really."

"Those poor kids."

"I hear ya."

"All right." He kissed her. "Thanks."

"For what?"

"For your insight."

"It's not insight, it's just gossip. Are you going to do it?"

"They planned to get married anyway. They just want to do it sooner. I don't see any reason to turn them down."

"No, I guess there's not one."

"Certain you don't need to check with anyone?"

He meant Mandalay or Bliss, and she knew it. "No. If it was important, they'd have already contacted me."

"I'll need you as a witness."

"I thought you didn't need witnesses anymore."

"I didn't say they needed it. I said I did."

She kissed him. "I'll be right there."

He went into his study, picked up his book of marriage vows, and went back to the kitchen. The coffee was ready, so he poured cups from the carafe and set them in front of the others. "Anyone want cream or sugar?" They both shook their heads.

He sat down and took a sip from his own cup. "All right. If you two genuinely want me to perform your marriage right now,

I will. It'll be a Christian ceremony, though; that's what I am, and it's what I do. Have you written your own vows?"

Duncan and Renny exchanged a look. "No," they said together.

"Then I'll use the ones in the book. I'll redact them a little, since you're both Tufa. Are you okay with that?"

"Yes," Renny said before Duncan finished drawing breath to answer.

"Don't start yet!" Bronwyn called. She rushed into the kitchen with her mandolin. "Me and Magda—" she indicated the instrument "—have a song for you."

She sat down, picked a few notes, then said, "I think this is a beautiful song, and I hope you do, too." Then she began to play and sing Angus and Julia Stone's "The Wedding Song." She modified the lyrics a little, changing the line to "make *more* babies on the beach." When Bronwyn finished, Renny was crying openly, and even Duncan's eyes were full. Craig slipped a box of tissues in front of the girl, and waited while she composed herself.

At last Craig said, "Well, then. Should we stand?"

"I'd rather sit," Renny said, and took Duncan's hand. Her grip was like death. "If you don't mind."

"That's fine, too, under the circumstances."

Bronwyn stood to one side and began to softly play the standard "Cindy." He opened the book. "I'm going to skip the whole 'dearly beloved' part. Duncan and Renny—"

"Renata. My full name's Renata June."

"Mine's Duncan Boyle."

"Duncan Boyle and Renata June, I require and charge you both, as you sta—uh, *sit* here in the presence of God and the night winds, before whom the secrets of all Tufa hearts are disclosed, that, having duly considered the covenant you are about to make, you do now declare before this company, your pledge of faith, each to the other."

He caught Bronwyn's look of surprise. He'd modified the traditional vows to reflect the Tufa beliefs, something she'd never have expected. He'd explained to her back when they first married that he wanted to understand the Tufa and find common ground, not rail against things he didn't understand. His superiors would no doubt disapprove, but he'd managed to earn the trust of her people with this approach, and a few had even attended services at his church. That was a bigger testament than even he comprehended.

"Be well assured," he continued, "that if these solemn vows are kept unviolated as God and the night winds demand, and if steadfastly you endeavor to do their will, they will bless your marriage."

He paused, looked at them both, then said, "Duncan, look at your bride and repeat after me."

Duncan looked at Renny, who continued to clench his hand harder than ever. He wanted to be nervous, scared, excited, all the emotions he'd assumed he would feel on his wedding day. Instead, he was just numb, flailing and unmoored inside as he repeated the words, forgetting them as soon as they left his lips.

Then Renny repeated the same vow to him.

And just like that, he was a married man.

28

Janet drove so slowly, she was certain they could walk to their destination more quickly. Yet each time she asked, Mandalay just said calmly, "Keep going."

"I'm not sure we can get back out as it is." The road—really a pair of dirt ruts with an overgrown strip between them, sandwiched between saplings and thick undergrowth—closed in around them. Branch tips scraped the sides of the car and made nails-on-chalkboard screeches against the glass. For some reason, the most depressing songs she knew ran through Janet's head.

"And if I could move, I'd get my gun . . . ," she murmured aloud, the rough passage adding a vibrato to her voice.

Mandalay said, "What?"

"Sorry. Just a song stuck in my head. 'Ruby, Don't Take Your Love to Town.' Kenny Rogers." She frowned. "Now, why would I be obsessing about a damn Kenny Rogers song?"

"It's not your fault. It's because of where we're going."

"We're taking our love to town?"

Mandalay chuckled. "No."

"Are you going to tell me?"

For a long moment the only sound was the greenery battering all sides of the car. Then Mandalay said, "Rockhouse's cave."

Janet slammed on the brakes. Even though the car was barely moving, the jolt still flung Mandalay forward against her seat belt.

Janet stared at her. "I'm sorry, I must have earwigs or be in a temporal bubble or just be a really stupid hillbilly, because I *know* I didn't hear you correctly."

"Yes, you did."

Janet put the car in reverse and twisted to look out the back window. All she saw was a red glow on the cloud of dust raised by their sudden stop.

"Wait," Mandalay said calmly. "Let me tell you."

"They hang dead bodies to keep people out," Janet said, easing the car back along the path. "They have rape rooms. They brew meth and moonshine right in the fucking cave."

"Please, stop. It's important."

"Not to me." She barely stayed on the path and just missed backing into a tree trunk.

"I understand why you're afraid."

"Do you?" She slammed on the brakes. "Near as I can figure, you've never been afraid in your life. Everyone makes sure you're covered in Bubble Wrap and only bump into things with rounded corners."

"That's not true. I've been afraid."

"Oh yeah? When? What could possibly scare the great Mandalay Harris?"

In a small, flat voice, she said, "When the night winds spoke to me in human words from right behind me."

This brought Janet up short. She put it into park, took several deep breaths, and said, "Mandalay, I know you have a reason for this, and I appreciate your trust in me, but I'm about to pee my pants. I've heard way too many stories about what they do in that cave, and I don't particularly want any of it done to me. So I think maybe you should go get Bliss Overbay or Bronwyn Chess to come with you."

"I need you. I need your musical talent."

"For what?"

Mandalay looked out at the night, then turned back. "That banjo we got from Popcorn? The tuning pegs are made from finger bones."

It took Janet a minute. "Wait . . . *human* finger bones?"

"Yes."

"Whose?"

"Whose do you think?"

Janet barked out a laugh at the absurdity, then said, "You're really testing my bladder control here."

"Adam didn't die the way everyone says. I don't know if he was murdered, and if he was, I don't know for sure who's responsible. But I do know how to find out."

"By going to this cave and playing that banjo?"

"Yes."

"What song?"

"The song that comes to us."

"Comes to us from where?"

"Where do you think?"

There was just enough light for Janet to see Mandalay's eyes reflect like an owl's, big and round and silver.

Duncan drove Renny's truck, the one that had belonged to Adam, in silence. The radio was even turned off. The roads between Unicorn and his home were twisty and tricky, so he was careful. He had the most precious cargo in the world: his pregnant wife.

His wife.

His baby.

Holy shit.

He glanced over at her. She looked at the ring on her finger in the light from the dashboard. It wasn't anything spectacular—he'd never even gotten her a proper engagement ring, so the band was both plain and solitary—but she seemed happy with it.

"How you doing, Mrs. Gowen?" he asked.

"All right."

"And how's Baby Gowen?"

"He's fine. He seemed to take the whole wedding as a good sign."

"Smart kid."

She leaned against the window and closed her eyes. "Thank you. I feel much better now."

"Now that you're married?"

"I know, right? It's the dumbest thing. I used to make fun of girls who just wanted to get married and start having kids. It's like, 'Don't you have any dreams or goals in life?' But now look at me."

"I hope you still have some goals and dreams."

She laughed. "That's the thing, Dunk. I never really did. I mean, I knew I needed a job, and someday I'd probably get married. But I was never *driven* to do anything."

"You were driven to get married," he deadpanned. "I drove you."

She snorted. "Are all your jokes going to be that bad?"

"Probably."

She took his right hand and squeezed it. "Well, then, I guess I better get used to it."

"I guess you better."

She let go of his hand and looked again at her ring. "It just feels like everything is going to be okay now."

"Don't jinx it," he joked.

And then the giant pig was right there in the middle of the road.

The headlights illuminated its low-slung head and humped

back. It faced the truck head-on, and the image burned itself into Duncan's mind: eyes glowing red as the light reflected from the backs of its retinas, huge tusks sticking out yellow and curved from the lower jaw, and the mouth and nostrils wet with pig snot and saliva.

Duncan twisted the wheel reflexively to the right, but they were at the point of a curve to the left, so before he could turn back, they crashed through the slender trees at the shoulder. It seemed to happen in slow motion: one moment the trees with their bare lower branches were lit brightly, and then they slipped out of sight beneath the truck's hood.

The trees siphoned off most of the momentum, so that when the truck flew over the edge of the hidden ravine, it plunged straight down.

The front end slammed into the mud at the bottom with a loud squelch, burying the headlights, and the rear of the vehicle tipped forward. It leaned against the far side of the ravine, chassis exposed, cab almost upside down.

The air bag deployed on impact with the trees, and now Duncan struggled to get out of it. It felt like being stuck in mashed potatoes. "Renny!" he cried as he tried to see her. He reached for her, but couldn't find her.

At last the air bags deflated. She hung from her shoulder belt at an odd angle. He couldn't breathe at the thought that she might be dead, but her eyes opened and she said woozily, "What the *fuck,* Duncan?"

"That pig," he said. "That pig was in the road!"

"What pig? I didn't see anything."

"The one that killed Kera and Adam! It was right there!"

She tried to swing her arm around to undo her seat belt, but it wouldn't move. "Dude, I think my arm's broke."

"Hang on, I'll get you."

He tried to pop her shoulder belt, but it wouldn't budge. He undid his own, and spent an awkward moment twisting around for a better position. Then he tried again, but the mechanism was thoroughly jammed.

"Dude, have you got a knife? Just cut the damn thing."

"I don't," he admitted.

"A redneck without a pocketknife," she said with a mocking shake of her head. "What sort of man have I married?"

He looked around. The impact had stalled the engine, but the dash was still lit, and he turned on the dome light. It showed him Renny's pale face, and her right arm, twisted in a way it wasn't meant to. This was serious.

He dug out his cell phone. He got no signal. "Let me see your phone."

"It's in my pocket. You'll have to get it."

He reached into the back pocket of her jeans and fished it out. She got no signal, either.

"I'm going to climb up on the road and see if I can get a call through," he said.

"I'll just hang around," she joked, but he could see the veins on her neck and forehead bulging from her upside-down position. It couldn't be good for her, or their baby.

"I'll hurry," he said, and kissed her. "I love you."

"You have to now," she shot back with a smile. "I've got the hardware on my finger and the software in my belly."

Duncan worked his way out the driver's-side door, landing in cold mud as he fell on his face. He got up, shook himself off, and looked around. In the dim light, he saw that the gully's sides were twenty feet high, and the bottom was muddy from runoff coming from higher on the mountain.

He grabbed a protruding tree root and ascended toward the road. Cold water soaked through his shirt and jeans, since he had to press himself against the mud to climb. Just as he was about to reach the top, he remembered something.

The pig was still up there.

He hadn't hit it, and it certainly hadn't looked scared.

He was absolutely sure he had seen it. It had been right in the headlights, massive and dark and bristling with hair and fury. He'd seen it before, after all, from the same angle, that day it killed Adam; it wasn't like he'd mistake a cow or one of those emus for it.

He rose enough to peer over the top edge of the gully wall. He smelled wet leaves and dirt, along with the metallic odor of the wrecked truck. There were no streetlights this far out of town, but he could see the road fairly clearly.

It was empty.

"Duncan?" Renny called from the wreck. Her voice was shaky. "You still there?"

"I'm here," he answered as he pulled himself up onto the shoulder.

"I'm getting cold down here."

"I'm on the road. It won't be long."

He pulled out his phone and checked it. As he did, he noticed the battery icon in the corner was now a mere sliver of red. He got no signal, and he barely had any juice left.

He checked Renny's phone. It was completely dead.

He turned off his phone to conserve what he had. "I have to find some high ground to call," he told Renny.

"Don't leave me here, Duncan," she said in the most pitiful voice he'd ever heard.

He never imagined Renny capable of sounding so helpless, and it broke his heart. "I won't, honey. I just have to run up the hill."

He looked in both directions. Which way actually did lead closer to town, and to any cell signal he might pick up? He was disoriented in the darkness, and his head just couldn't sort it out. He'd driven this road many times, and should know exactly where he was. He looked back the way he'd come, and saw only highway twisting out of sight around a curve. Then he turned toward the way ahead.

And almost screamed.

Because there was the pig, looking elephantine in the darkness, silhouetted black against the lighter gray of the highway pavement.

He stared. Were his eyes playing tricks on him? Was it a shape made of shadows?

He had just about convinced himself that it was, when it grunted. The noise was so low that he felt it in his chest like a hit on a bass drum.

It took a step toward him, its hooves clacking on the road.

He turned and ran the other way. He heard it clacking on the blacktop behind him, gathering speed.

29

Mandalay said softly, barely moving her lips, "Janet, were you ever terrified before?"

In the same tone, Janet answered, "Yes, ma'am. Up to and including right now."

The two girls stood at the bottom of the steps that led into the moonshiners' cave. Every eye in the considerable crowd was now on them, and all music and conversation had stopped.

Janet had parked in the field with the other cars and trucks, worried that the soft ground would make it impossible for them to leave in a hurry. Carrying the banjo, she followed Mandalay right past the skeletons hanging at the entrance, the ones that might have been headless deer but looked awfully human to Janet. It didn't help that she had to pass them in the dark, with only the light from Mandalay's key chain flashlight to guide their way.

And then, about halfway down the narrow passage, they hit the *smell.*

Janet had encountered some rank things before—any girl growing up on a farm wasn't fazed by strong odors—but this was different. It was a combination of harsh chemicals, urine, the odd whiff of decaying vegetables, and over and under and around everything else, the miasma of unwashed bodies.

She stopped and gagged. "Oh my God, wait a minute."

"It's harsh, I know," Mandalay said.

"It's fucking awful. I'm gonna throw up on this banjo."

"It'll pass."

"Are you sure?"

"I'm sure. It's just one of their little tricks to keep out people who ain't supposed to be here."

Janet fought the nausea down. "Like us?"

"Most definitely."

With a final deep breath, mainly through her mouth, Janet stood back upright. Mandalay appeared totally calm.

"What will they do when they see it's us?" Janet asked.

"They'll listen to our song."

"The one we're going to make up on the spot."

"Yes."

"As plans go, this isn't one of the best I've heard."

"It's all we've got."

So they'd pressed on and emerged into the cavern, and found themselves face-to-face with thirty Tufa who'd just as soon kill them (or worse) as look at them. And, despite their sullen silence, they certainly didn't seem inclined to listen.

Mandalay said loudly, "Is Junior here?"

Her voice echoed in the immense cavern.

"Who wants to know?" a woman's voice said. The crowd parted to allow Flint Rucker, wearing sunglasses to protect her hypersensitive eyes, to move to the front. They closed in behind her.

"I do," Mandalay said.

"Oh, the little princess, shining bright," Flint spoke-sang. "You grace us with your disdain tonight? And who is that with you?"

"I'll speak to Junior," Mandalay said.

Flint lowered her sunglasses and looked Janet over. Janet felt suddenly sticky, as if something in the girl's vision had coated her with slime.

"Such a pretty girl," Flint said. "I wonder if she likes the dark?"

"She's with me," Mandalay said. "Back off, Flint." She made a forceful gesture, and Flint stepped back with a hiss like an angry cat.

"I'm here," Junior said, pushing his way to the front of the crowd. "What the hell is this?"

"You have visitors," Flint said.

"What do you want, Mandalay?" he demanded.

Mandalay could have silenced him with a gesture, but instead she smiled and said, "We need to play a song for you folks."

Junior laughed, and a ripple of amusement went through the crowd. "Is that a fact?" he said.

"It's a fact."

"Well, maybe we don't want to hear it."

"Do you want me to throw them out?" Flint asked. The request seemed ludicrous from such a diaphanous personality, but no one took it lightly.

"Wait here," Mandalay said to Janet. She strode down the steps and stopped before Junior and Flint. The crowd surged closer, threatening to encircle her. She looked even smaller and slighter with all the men and women towering over her, crowding in to intimidate and frighten her.

"Flint, back off," she said loudly, and the pale girl vanished into the crowd. Mandalay made a series of hand gestures, and everyone backed away, leaving her and Junior alone.

Janet couldn't hear what Mandalay said to him, but eventually Junior made a few hand gestures back, and Mandalay nodded.

When she returned, Janet asked very quietly, "Are we leaving?"

"No. I just needed to remind Junior yet again about seniority."

"That Flint girl gives me the creeps."

"That means you're a good judge of people. You ready?"

"No. How do I make up a song on the spot and have it sound like anything?"

"Trust in the night winds."

Janet was left dumbstruck on the steps and had to rush to catch up as Mandalay made her way toward the open space that passed for a stage. The crowd followed them, some still laughing.

Duncan didn't remember leaving the road, but when he stopped, exhausted and wheezing for breath, he found himself in the woods. He looked around, but there was no trace of the giant pig. He also saw no sign of the trail he'd made, or the path he should take to get out. The darkness was thorough: no lights showed anywhere, except the stars and the moon above.

His heart thundered like a Neil Peart solo as he gasped in the cool, damp air. Sweat trickled into his eyes. He tried to hear past the roar in his ears, for any sound that the monster might make as it approached. But except for a faint owl, he heard nothing.

He turned on his phone long enough to see that he still got no signal. *What the hell?* he thought. Outsiders got notoriously bad reception, blamed on the scarcity of cell towers and the intervening mountains, but a Tufa *always* got a signal. His battery was down to 10 percent, so he quickly turned it back off.

He cried out, "Hey! Hey! Anyone here? Please, I've been in a car wreck, I need help! Anybody?"

In the distance, he heard either a dog or coyote howl, but he wasn't sure if it was in response to his cry.

He had to find a way out. Renny and his unborn baby were trapped in that truck, helpless and injured. It was spring, but it got cold at night, and she wasn't dressed for it. For that matter, neither was he.

"Help!" he tried again. *"Help!"*

This time the coyote howl was right behind him. He screamed and fell on wet leaves as he spun around.

In the darkness he saw, not a coyote, but a young woman. She sat with her back against a tree, her knees drawn up to her chin. She was barefoot, and wore what seemed to be skimpy garments made of fur, like a Hollywood version of a cave woman. Her hair was twisted into dreadlocks, and her eyes shone with what little light reached them.

"Hello, Duncan Gowen," she said. Her voice was low, like a growl, but definitely not sexy.

"Please," Duncan said, "my girlfr—I mean, my wife's stuck in our truck. We ran off the road."

"Oh, Duncan Gowen, what of your first girlfriend?"

"Wh-what?"

"The lovely lass Kera."

"I didn't kill her!" he cried.

"No, ye didn't," she said, and stood. She was petite, lithe, and yet somehow she terrified him. She moved with a slinky grace, her body swaying in a way that would have been arousing in any other circumstance. "But ye did kill thy friend over her."

"No, I didn't! That giant hog did it!"

"Oh, Duncan Gowen, we see all that happens in the forest. Ye could've saved him, and didn't. His soul is restless because of thee."

Duncan took a deep breath and forced down his panic. "Look, I don't care about that, okay? It's not important right now. My wife is in trouble. Can you help me?"

She threw back her head and laughed, a yipping sound more like the calling of a wild dog than a sound of human amusement. "Do ye know whom I serve?"

And suddenly he did, but he couldn't believe it. As much as the Tufa populated the stories of the people who lived in the surrounding area, so these beings—the King of the Forest, an immense stag (or stag-headed man), and his coyote attendants (or beautiful girls who shifted with ease into canine form)—frightened the Tufa children at bedtime. In those tales, the unfortunate souls who saw them were forever changed, and the ones who interacted with them were often never heard from again.

Yet here was one of them, apparently real, or else someone yanking his chain at the worst possible moment. But why would some girl be dressed like this, in the middle of nowhere, just as some sort of role-playing joke?

Impulsively he grabbed her arm. "Look, I don't have time for this, take me to your family's—"

The girl snarled, and he felt teeth sink into his hand. He released her with a cry, and when he looked back, a coyote stood there, hackles raised and teeth bared in a snarl.

Duncan felt blood run down his hand and drip on the ground. "Please," he begged, "help me. My wife's pregnant."

The coyote threw back its head and howled. Another answered from deep in the woods. Then the animal turned and trotted off into the darkness.

Duncan fell to his knees. "Please, I didn't kill anybody," he called out, almost sobbing. Then he screamed, *"I didn't kill anybody!"*

Janet pulled a stool from the row along the wall and settled onto it. She put on her banjo picks, one for each fingertip on her right hand. The banjo didn't have a strap, and it was hard to find the proper balance, since she'd played it only once before.

Mandalay lowered the microphone to her height and said, "Hello." Her voice echoed around the cave.

"Y'all know what the difference is between a banjo picker and a nose picker?" someone asked. "You can't wipe a banjo on your pants!"

"Show us your jailbait tits!" someone else yelled.

"Hey, now," Mandalay said coolly. "Don't be mean. We don't have to be mean. Because remember, no matter where you go . . . there you are."

There was a general muttering of "What the fuck?" Mandalay's lips turned up in a tiny, superior smile.

"Mandalay!" Janet whispered. "What the *hell* are we playing?"

Mandalay turned away from the microphone and said softly, "Close your eyes."

She looked around at the crowd. "I'm not sure that's safe."

"It's safe. Trust me. Close your eyes . . . and listen."

Janet gave the crowd one last look, then closed her eyes. Almost at once, a sense of calm came over her. The darkness of her eyelids was illuminated with soft, faint bursts of color. She still heard the mocking laughter, but there was something else, a sound or presence between the crowd and her, a kind of psychic buffer. She no longer felt afraid.

And then she heard the *voice.*

Start with C sharp minor, it said.

It was neither male nor female, loud nor soft, urgent nor lackadaisical. If she had to characterize it, the only word would've been "omnipresent." It seemed to come from everywhere, contain every thought and feeling, and act as both a reassuring pat and a commanding shove.

She settled her fingers on the neck, found the chord, and began to play, midtempo and with an easy rhythm.

Open your eyes.

When she did, Mandalay watched her with approval. She felt her hands move almost on their own, creating a melody that had that aching inevitability of the best songs. The chord progression came to her an instant before she needed it, and once she'd gone all the way through the verse and chorus, she knew it by heart.

Mandalay stepped up to the microphone and began to sing. Her voice was pure, and high, and weighted with a sorrow no child her apparent age should be able to convey. It stunned everyone into rapt silence.

In every man there dwells a dark and unforgiven place
Where no amount of light could show redemption, or
replace
The desperate weight of sorrow with the peace before it
grew
And no chance of absolution clears a path that proves him
true. . . .

Janet looked out at the now-silent crowd, studying their faces. She was so thoroughly in the pocket that her fingers moved unconsciously, keeping up effortlessly with Mandalay's singing as she went into the first chorus.

My love she found her ending under these same callous
stars
That follow us unblinking knowing everything we are
A liar with two lovers or a traitor steeped in pain
They'll stand sentinel against the black 'til nothing else
remains. . . .

Now that she had the melody, Janet began to improvise, adding little fills and extra flourishes. She kept glancing at the tuning pegs, knowing what they were, wondering if, wherever they now existed, the people who provided them could hear this song.

With a jealous heart of malice beating reckless in my chest
I led my prey uncaring to the trap my anger set
Though my reason held me steady when it came my time
to act
I stood still against the raging wild and cannot take it
back. . . .

Janet tore into the bridge, bringing the song's anger and outrage to the forefront. If she'd looked up, she would've seen the crowd riveted, many with their mouths open. But one man's face was not smiling, not gaping; it was red with fury.

Then Mandalay began the final verse.

Oh my darling I have loved you out of guilt and out of shame
For the sake of what I did not do, I promised you my name
But there's no forgiveness coming for the man who owes this debt
Just the watching winds who saw it all and won't let him forget.

Janet finished with a flourish. The crowd was still, but the anger she'd sensed earlier remained, except that it was no longer directed at the two girls.

A few people clapped, mainly because they didn't know what else to do. It quickly faded.

"Thank you," Mandalay said calmly, then stepped over to Janet and whispered, "Let's get the hell out of here *now*."

"Wait!" someone yelled from the crowd as Janet stood. The red-faced man she had noted, his longish hair falling in his middle-aged face, pushed his way to the front of the crowd. "Is that true?"

Janet recognized him as Adam and Renny's father, Porter Procure. He was drunk and bleary-eyed, but his outrage was hot enough to sober even the dead.

Mandalay said, "It's a true song."

"Don't make jokes about this, you fucking cock-teasing bitch!" he bellowed. He nearly fell as he lurched toward her, but two friends held him up, and back. "Did Duncan Gowen kill my son?"

"I'm not joking, Porter. The song is true."

People murmured as they realized what that meant.

"Tell me where he is," the drunken man said. *"Tell me!"*

Janet clutched the banjo tightly, worried that she'd have to use it as a weapon. "That ain't up to me," Mandalay said.

All eyes turned to Junior Damo, who looked like an ant with a thousand magnifying glasses pointed right at him. Even Flint stepped away.

"Let's go," Mandalay whispered, grabbed Janet's arm, and pushed her toward the exit.

When they were outside, Mandalay took a deep breath of the cool night air and said, "*Man,* do I need a shower."

Janet kept looking back and forth from the cave entrance to Mandalay. "What just happened in there?"

"We acted as the agents of the night winds," Mandalay said.

Janet stared at her. "Then . . . that voice I heard, it was . . ."

Mandalay nodded.

"I think I'm going to throw up," she said.

Mandalay took her free hand. "I don't blame you, but let's get as far away from here as we can before you hurl."

30

Duncan was exhausted. He'd pushed through the woods, watching all around for both the giant hog and the strange coyote-woman, but had seen neither. He'd also seen no sign of civilization. He was sweaty from the exertion, chilled from the night air, and mocked by the winds that tousled the treetops above him.

He knew all the stories of slow time, tales of people who spent hours or days lost in the woods, only to emerge and discover years had passed. But the Tufa had always been immune to that; some, in fact, could slip in and out of it at will. Was he being punished that way, like that old rockabilly singer who appeared out of nowhere, not a bit older than the day he'd supposedly died sixty years ago?

Each time he stopped and checked his phone, it was no different. He got no signal, and the percentage of power went down: 10, 8, 5, now 3 percent. He quickly turned it off, wondering how many more tries he'd get before it died for good.

And as the phrase "died for good" went through his mind, he thought about Renny, and their unborn child in the truck. And he pushed on.

Janet drove faster than she should have, and she knew it. But it felt like the cave, with its ghastly smells and sights and atmosphere, refused to recede into the distance. She repeatedly glanced into the rearview mirror to assure herself that it wasn't still right behind them, the skeletons glowing red in their taillight.

Mandalay rode in the passenger seat, one foot again propped up on the dashboard. They hadn't even turned on the radio. At last the girl said, "Turn just ahead."

Janet slowed down and turned off the highway onto another rugged road. They bounced along until Mandalay said, "Stop here."

She did. Ahead the road continued into the darkness beyond the headlights. To one side was a bare field, recently turned prior to planting. On the passenger side, a wire fence blocked off the forest.

Mandalay got out. She reached into the backseat and grabbed the banjo as Janet turned off the car. "Follow me," Mandalay said, and didn't give Janet time to respond.

"Are we going to burn the banjo?" Janet asked as they climbed over the fence.

"Don't talk," Mandalay snapped without looking back. Janet obeyed, because something in the girl's voice struck her like a slap.

They hiked through the dark woods. Mandalay never stepped wrong, and it was all Janet could do to keep up. She wanted to ask all the basic journalist questions: where, what, why, who, and how? But she knew better.

Then Mandalay stopped, and Janet almost knocked her down. The younger girl held up her hand for silence.

Janet looked around. They were in the middle of the forest at night, with no references in any direction.

Then they heard a sharp yipping cry. A coyote.

"This way," Mandalay said, and started off again. Janet rushed to keep her in sight, and only tangentially realized they were heading *toward* the coyote.

Unbidden, the memory of a folksinger killed by coyotes in Canada came to her. It had happened several years earlier, but now she wished she'd paid a lot more attention to the details. Hell, she'd never even *seen* a live coyote, only dead ones on the side of the road.

It yipped again, closer and from behind them. The one ahead answered. There were two.

"Mandalay—"

"Hush!" Mandalay said urgently.

They emerged into a small circular clearing. The trees around it were all deciduous, and the area reeked of their freshly surging sap. Janet leaned against one to catch her breath, and her hand came away sticky.

The coyote ahead yipped, and it sounded like it was just beyond the clearing. Behind them, the other also sounded close. Janet stood beside Mandalay, ready to flee. In the darkness, the moonlight cast harsh shadows and turned the grassy ground silver.

Something stepped in the forest. It was no coyote: it was far too large. Janet imagined a bear, recently awakened from its hibernation and hungry for anything, even teenage girls.

Then she thought of Piggly-Wiggly, the giant hog. She began to tremble, wishing she knew where they were so she'd know which way to run.

But neither a bear nor a hog strode out of the darkness. Instead it was a tall man, naked except for a small animal-skin girdle and a kind of cap decorated with a rack of immense stag horns. The horns made him nearly eight feet tall, and his chest was broad, muscular, and hairy. Janet had, in fact, never seen anyone so overwhelmingly masculine.

From the other side of the clearing, a young woman emerged.

She also wore a skimpy fur outfit, was barefoot, and her hair was twisted into dreadlocks. She walked over to the man and, without exchanging a word or a glance, crouched at his feet. These two newcomers watched Janet and Mandalay with knowing, faintly amused expressions.

Then Janet yelped as another barefoot woman appeared directly behind them and sauntered casually toward the other two. Like him, she wore only a loincloth, and like the other girl, her hair was twisted in dreads. She crouched at his feet on the other side.

Mandalay made a complex hand gesture, and the antlered man responded. Then Mandalay walked forward and stood looking up at him.

"This has served its purpose," she said, indicating the banjo she held. "The spirits it binds need to be released to their rest."

The big man replied, but his voice was so deep, Janet felt it in her chest, rather than hearing actual words.

"Of course," Mandalay answered.

And then the antlered man, all eight feet of him, went down on one knee. Mandalay handed him the instrument, touched his bearded cheek, then turned and walked away. The banjo looked like a toy in the man's hands as he stood upright.

The two girls at his feet also rose and scurried with surprising silence into the forest. The man turned and followed them. Moments after they disappeared, two coyotes howled from the direction they'd run.

Mandalay walked back to Janet. "You can talk now."

"Who . . . what . . . why . . . ?" She was still so stunned, it was difficult for the words to come out.

"He has that affect on people sometimes," Mandalay said. "Especially women. Makes you wish you had a boyfriend."

"Well, I wouldn't say *that*."

Mandalay nodded knowingly. "You and Ginny."

"What? No! Why would you think that?"

Mandalay looked surprised. "Well, the two of you—"

Janet held up her hand. "Stop right there, okay? Ginny and I are just friends. In fact, I'm just friends with *everybody.* I have no boyfriend; I have no girlfriend. I have no interest. Can we go home now?"

"I didn't mean anything by it," Mandalay said. "And I certainly wouldn't judge."

Janet looked around at the dark woods. "I've *never* felt the way you're supposed to. The way the songs say. I don't think I can. There's a word for it, but . . ."

Mandalay put a hand on her arm. "There's no need for it here. You are who and what you are, and the Tufa don't care. It's your music that matters to us."

"Seriously?"

"Seriously."

Janet took a deep breath. A weight had come off, one she didn't realize was there until it left. "Wow." She chuckled, took a few more deep breaths, and said, "So who was that? The big guy?"

"If you think about it, you'll know who he is."

She remembered the whispered tales around campfires, at swimming holes, and in the dark outside the barn dance. "But I thought he was . . . I mean, just a story."

"We're all just stories, Janet. Or songs."

With that, Mandalay walked past her and back into the forest, although now there was a wide, clear trail. It led quickly back to their car, through a gate in the fence that was conveniently left open. She said nothing as Janet backed them back onto the highway and started the drive to Mandalay's house.

At last Duncan emerged into a different clearing and collapsed onto the damp grass. Above him the sky was cloudy, and the hidden moon cast a dim, grayish glow that diffused across the whole vista. He was thoroughly spent, and rested until his pulse no longer pounded in his ears. Then he got to his feet.

He looked around. He saw the cars and trucks. He smelled the rank odor.

Wait a minute, he thought. *I know this place.* And then he realized.

He was outside the old moonshiners' cave, the place his people gathered and celebrated, the place where even now, he might find help. He checked his phone again, but its battery was totally drained.

He ran to the entrance, stumbled down the tunnel, and emerged with a cry.

"Somebody, please!" he shouted. "Kera's stuck in my truck at the bottom of a holler. That big-ass hog ran us off the road, and she's hurt."

There were a lot of people in the cave, most of them men, all gathered around Flint and Junior Damo. They fell silent and turned to look at him. Their gaze was cold and hard.

"What's wrong?" he said. He was so tired, he could barely stand, and had to lean against the nearest cave wall for support.

No one spoke. They just stared.

"Come on!" he exhorted. "Move!"

No one did.

"All right, then please, someone, anyone, just call 911 for me. My phone's dead."

Their total silence scared him more than anything. Then Porter Procure pushed his way to the front of the group. Procure was red-eyed and red-faced, and pointed an accusing finger at him.

"You!" he yelled, his voice charged with emotion. "You let my son die when you could've saved him!"

Duncan's legs collapsed, and he slid down the wall. He closed his eyes in defeat and disbelief. How did the man *know*?

"Aw, no," he whimpered. "No, not now . . ."

Porter Procure wasn't the only one. Everyone glared at him with the same hatred, the same knowledge. Fuck, did they *all* know?

"No, it wasn't like that," he said, eyes still closed. "It was just—"

"We know what you did!" Porter screamed, his face distorted with alcohol and rage. "We know! *We know!*"

Tears ran down Duncan's face. Hearing the truth spoken by someone else drove home anew what he had done, and gave it a reality that he couldn't ignore. He wanted to curl up and die.

But Renny still needed him. He opened his eyes and pushed himself back upright. The crowd was now all around him, blocking any possible escape. Porter Procure stood in front, Junior Damo and Flint just behind him.

Duncan forced himself to look at his father-in-law. "Please, Mr. Procure, your daughter is hurt, we have to—"

But Porter was drunk, and enraged, and headed a mob that loved nothing more than an object at which to fling its ire. "We know!" Porter kept repeating, and soon the whole bunch chanted it. "We know!"

And then a song began. It was one Duncan had never heard before, but it had a kind of awful familiarity just the same, a connection with him that made each note, each lyric, as inevitable as the sunrise.

In every man there dwells a dark and unforgiven place
Where no amount of light could show redemption, or replace . . .

Duncan felt himself grow smaller, weaker, more pitiful. This must be his own dying dirge, the song that could take his life and return his spirit to the night winds for their disposition. He couldn't stop it, and he had no song to counterpoint it.

He slid back down to the floor and drew his knees up to his chin. "Please," he begged again and again. "Please, help Renny, she's hurt. . . ." He looked up and made eye contact with Junior, whose face was a mask of disapproval and amusement, but whose eyes revealed the fear that his own role in what had happened might be brought to light.

Duncan got to his feet, pushed his way over, and grabbed Junior by the shirt. "Please," Duncan begged Junior. *"Please."*

Then Porter Procure hit him with a piece of lead pipe, crushing in one side of his skull. As his people, his tribe, descended on him, he died in a shower of blows and kicks, his dying dirge swirling around him.

*Though my reason held me steady when it came my time
to act
I stood still against the raging wild, and cannot take it
back. . . .*

31

In the truck, Renny was starting to go into shock. Her broken arm was numb, and she could now see her breath by the faint, fading light from the dashboard. She wasn't sure how long Duncan had been gone, or how long she'd been hanging upside down, but her head pounded with every heartbeat, and she sensed that she didn't have long.

She kept her good hand over her belly. "I'm sorry," she whispered, "I'm so sorry, my baby, I should've been stronger, you deserve so much more. . . ."

And then came the unmistakable, disgustingly wet sound that has always been written as "oink."

She went absolutely still. The odor reached her then, faint at first but growing stronger as she heard the noise of several small bodies moving through the leaves that lined the floor of the gully.

She kept listening, until suddenly a pig's snout and head pushed their way into the open driver's-side door. Then she screamed.

She began to thrash, ignoring her arm, her baby, everything. The horror of what had happened to her brother filled her and choked out everything else. "Help!" she cried. "Jesus Christ, somebody, *help me*!"

The pig cocked its head and looked at her oddly, mystified by her sudden movement and noise. Another pig tried to shove the first one aside. They squealed at each other and fought for position.

Renny tugged at the jammed seat belt with her good hand. "Help me! Help me!"

One small pig awkwardly worked itself all the way into the truck cab. It nosed in the debris for anything edible, then looked up at Renny. Its snout, wet and wrinkled, was inches from Renny's face.

She punched it.

The animal squealed and drew back, then turned and tried to get out of the cab. It struggled through a hole in the shattered windshield, shrieking as the jagged edges tore at its thick hide.

Renny stared past it, at the herd of pigs rooting along the bottom of the ravine. They were mere shapes in the dark, emitting sound and odor, crunching anything that was remotely edible.

Then, looming over and above its brethren, came the monster that had killed her brother.

"Oh God," she whispered. "Oh God, don't eat my baby, please, no . . ."

The monster came forward, slow and inexorable, toward the truck. Its smaller herd mates squealed as they were pushed aside. Renny wanted to scream, but fear paralyzed her.

Janet drove while Mandalay checked her phone. The night was silent, and the only sound was the road noise. Janet should have been exhausted, but instead she was wired with stress, adrenaline, and relief of a secret revealed.

Mandalay saw that Bronwyn Chess had called while she and Janet were in the cave, where no cell signals penetrated. Bliss had called as well.

As she was about to call Bliss back, Janet blurted, "Okay, what really did happen back there?"

Mandalay jumped and dropped her phone onto the floorboard. "Whoa! You scared me to death."

"I'm sorry, but back in the woods, that man with the two girls. *Was* that who I think it was?"

"The King of the Forest," Mandalay said softly, looking straight ahead.

Janet gripped the steering wheel with both hands. "Wow."

"That's the right response."

"Do you see him often?"

"No. He and the Tufa aren't always on good terms. I see him only when it's necessary."

"And this was necessary?"

"Oh yes. That banjo had to be disposed of in a very particular way. I could've done it, but by asking for his help, I hope to make him more sociable to us."

"And now?"

"Now we're done. We've sung our song. Now the decision is up to the night winds."

"Was that really who whispered to me? In the cave, I mean. Was it really the night winds?"

Mandalay was about to answer, when she suddenly said, *"Stop!"*

"Hey, don't get your knickers twisted, I just want to know—"

"No, the *car,* stop the car!"

Janet slowed and pulled to the side of the road. There was a tight curve ahead, and if anyone swung wide coming around it, they'd plow right into them, so she turned her headlights on high and set her emergency flashers. By then Mandalay was already out of the car.

"What is it?" Janet asked as she followed.

"There's been a wreck here. Look."

In the high beams, the path Duncan and Renny's truck had

taken through the saplings was plain, as was the dark opening of the ravine below it.

"Stay here," Mandalay said. She carefully picked her way to the edge and looked down. Then she ran back, her phone to her ear. "Bliss? Is Jack still with you? Get out to Stack's Pike as fast as you can. That curve just before Maggie's Mill Road. There's been a wreck, and there's a bunch of those wild pigs nosing around it. Yes, I'm here with Janet Harper. We'll wait for you."

Janet went to the edge and looked down. She saw the wreck, and the pigs visible in the truck's fading headlights. She called out, "Hello, is anyone down there? Are you hurt?"

The pigs squealed, startled, and scattered back down the ravine into the darkness. Nothing human answered.

An hour later, Duncan's truck rose from the ravine, pulled up by Doyle Collins's wrecker. Alvin Darwin's car, its blue lights counterpointing the yellow ones on the wrecker, blocked the road at the top of the curve. Road flares did the same thing at the bottom. Neither had been needed so far; there had been no one on the road who wasn't summoned to the wreck.

When Jack and Bliss first arrived, they'd gone down to check for survivors. The registration identified the truck as belonging to the late Adam Procure, but no one had been inside.

"Was it stolen?" Jack asked.

"I don't know," Bliss said. "I'll try to call his parents." But there was no answer.

Darwin showed up, called Doyle to bring his tow truck, and joined Jack in looking up and down the gully. Neither man saw any sign of people, only the unmistakable damage inflicted by the pigs. The slippery mud stank of pig manure.

Eventually Doyle arrived, and he and Jack rigged the crashed vehicle so it could be pulled up to the road. Darwin went to sit in his car and stay out of the way.

As Doyle did his job, Mandalay quietly told Bliss what had happened at the cave. When she finished, Bliss said, "I can't believe you went there alone."

"I wasn't alone."

"You might as well have been," she said, glancing over to make sure Janet didn't hear. The girl leaned against the fender of her car, her face bathed in the flickering gold from the tow truck's light bar.

"You're right, she wasn't you," Mandalay agreed. "But she didn't need to be. I needed her talent."

Bliss's phone rang. She walked away down the road, so she could hear over the truck's winch. When she returned, she said, "That was Adam's mother. She said Renny's been driving it."

"Did you see any sign of her?"

"No. Not her, not Duncan Gowen."

"We don't know that he was with her."

"Yes, we do. They showed up at Bronwyn's house earlier tonight and got Craig to marry them. Bronwyn called and told me about it when she couldn't reach you. This would be the fastest way home for them." She looked up at the starry sky. "I can't believe the night winds claimed them both."

"All three, you mean. You know Renny was pregnant. If she died, the baby died."

Bliss folded her arms and bit down the reply she wanted to snap out. Mandalay put a sympathetic hand on her arm.

In the gully, Jack stayed out of the way as the truck rose up the side. He had a powerful halogen flashlight, but even with its help, he couldn't make out much. The thoroughly churned-up ground confirmed that a herd of wild pigs had been here, but he saw no human tracks except his own.

There had been blood on the windshield, but he wasn't sure if it was human or porcine. It would take lab work to tell if this was a mere traffic accident, or something worse. Duncan and Renny might have left the truck before the pigs arrived, and their tracks had been obliterated. But if so, where were they?

He methodically shone his light around, studying the mud for any additional clues, and it wasn't long before he found one: the clear, deep print of the monster.

So once again, the Gowen boy was present when the monster appeared. If this were a horror movie, he'd think that the boy had some way of summoning it, or that it was a supernatural being manifested by a guilty conscience. But no, he reminded himself, it was just a wild animal, dangerous and in need of disposal.

The truck reached the top and dug a chunk of mud out of the edge as it was pulled free. Jack jumped aside as it sluiced down and landed with a splat where he'd been standing. When all was clear, he climbed back up to the road. He opened the truck's door and shone his flashlight around the wrecked cab: the air bags and seat belts were mangled, and the stuffing had been chewed from the upholstery. But he saw no blood except that on the edges of the shattered safety glass.

He turned off the flashlight and walked over to where Bliss and Mandalay stood talking.

"Any sign?" the girl asked, once again sounding older and more in charge than any of them.

"It's too hard to track at this time of night, but I did find the prints of our monster. So it was here."

"Did it eat them?" Bliss asked, verbalizing what they all were thinking.

"I don't know. I only found a little blood, but it's hard to tell at night."

"How long would it take?" Mandalay asked. "To eat a person, I mean."

Jack thought. "Depends on how many people, and how many pigs. And how hungry the pigs are."

"Could they have eaten them and left no traces?"

"I'm sure there are traces. We just can't see them. Once the sun comes up, I'll be able to tell more."

Janet leaned against her car's fender, watching the other three deep in conversation. She'd called her parents, assured them she was with both Bliss and Mandalay, and that she'd be home soon. But she wasn't about to leave the site of possibly her greatest story yet for the *Raven's Caw.* She'd taken dozens of photos on her phone, trying to see the dramatic moments in what had, so far, been a pretty uneventful thing. Without injured victims, or bodies, it would just go into the blotter section of the *Weekly Horn,* if it even got mentioned.

She paced along the edge of the highway, humming "Didn't Leave Nobody but the Baby," which had become her go-to song for killing time.

Go to sleep, you little baby,
Go to sleep, you little baby. . . .

She trailed off, but in her head, she heard the next line, "Mama's gone away and your daddy's gonna stay. . . ."

Then she realized she heard it *outside* her head, too: faint but clear, somewhere in the darkness, audible over the noise of the tow truck.

She walked to the edge of the gully and used the flashlight on her cell phone to scan the bottom. The light was too dim to see any detail. Nothing moved except the water slowly seeping into the hole left by the truck.

She turned away, and then heard, high and keening enough to penetrate the tow truck's idling, "Didn't leave nobody but the baby. . . ."

She hadn't imagined it.

"Hey!" she called to the others. "Hey, I hear somebody down here!"

Jack, Bliss, and Mandalay rushed over. But the voice had fallen silent.

"I don't hear anything," Mandalay said.

"Are you sure you didn't imagine it?" Jack asked.

"I'm sure," Janet snapped, trying not to sound defensive.

"Do any of the rest of you hear anything?"

Mandalay and Bliss both shook their heads. "Maybe Doyle had the radio on in his truck," Bliss suggested.

"Look, I'm not making this up," Janet said. "I heard someone down there singing."

Jack shone his flashlight down into the gully. It was much brighter than Janet's phone, and showed the torn and trampled ground in much more detail. But there was no sign of anyone.

Bliss leaned close to Mandalay. Very softly, she said, "Could it be a haint?"

Mandalay shrugged. "Hell, maybe. I don't know."

"I don't see anything," Jack said as he turned off the light.

"I swear I heard it," Janet said, but she sounded far less certain now. Had she imagined it?

Mandalay touched Janet's sleeve to get her attention, then nodded for the girl to follow her. They walked away from the adults, outside the area of light.

"I'm not making it up," Janet insisted.

"I believe you," the younger girl said quietly. She stepped close and took Janet's hands. "Close your eyes," she said calmly.

"Not again."

"Yes."

"Why?"

"Just trust me, like you did earlier. Listen to what's around you. Then, when I tell you, open."

Janet did so. She heard the grinding of the tow truck winch and its chugging diesel engine, and the trilling of insects and animals awakened by the noise in the cold spring night. The wind blew in the background, and for a moment she dreaded that omnipresent *whisper* that had spoken to her in the cave. But it never came, and she heard no other voices, until Mandalay said, soft as a breath, "Open."

She did.

And she found herself in the air, floating on the night winds, looking down into the ravine with a clarity she'd never experienced even on the brightest, sunniest day.

Every twig, every bud, every insect and animal stood out in sharp relief, their life forces producing a spectrum of colors that no human words could ever describe.

And there were people, too: of all ages, sizes, and eras. They were ethereal, passing through the trees and rocks, even occasionally through each other. The shades wandered aimlessly, not singing or speaking, showing no sign that they saw each other, or her watching them. These were spirits still tied to the ground by unfinished business or a sense of belonging. "Haints," they were called in local parlance, and Janet could only stare in sympathy and dread.

But it was the sounds that overwhelmed her. The haints were silent, but everything alive, and even the rocks themselves, *sang* to her. Even with her laser-sharp musical memory, she knew she wouldn't be able to recall and reproduce these melodies, so all she could do was let them wash over and through her.

She drifted, like a feather or a dandelion seed, held aloft by the merest current. She wanted to look everywhere at once, absorb all the beauty around her, but then she heard a woman's voice, clear despite all the other sounds.

Go to sleep, you little baby. . . .

And she saw the woman, then, too, as plain as anything. She huddled against the muddy wall, far down the gully, curled up so small that no one would spot her until morning, and maybe not even then. Her face was hidden by her muddy black hair. And somehow Janet could tell that she was hurt, and sick, and dying.

"Come back down," Mandalay's voice said gently, and at the next blink, Janet was back.

Surprisingly, her knees didn't wobble and she didn't fall over. Instead, she just stared into the younger girl's eyes. In a whisper, she said, "Was that what riding the night winds is like for you?"

"I don't know," Mandalay said honestly. "What did you see?"

"Everything. And I heard—"

And then the pain struck.

She grabbed either side of her head. "Oh *shit*! Oh, fucking hell—"

"Did you see any sign of Duncan or Renny?"

"Not so loud! My brain feels like it's having a baby."

Mandalay rubbed Janet's temples. "Shh, it's okay. You went a little farther into it than I expected."

"Renny's down there," Janet said as the pain eased a little. "Or at least, I think it was her." She forced her eyes open and said, "How can you *stand* it?"

"Bliss! Mr. Cates!" Mandalay called. To Janet she said, "Can you show them?"

"If we go slow."

"She knows where Renny is," Mandalay told the two adults.

"You do?" Bliss said.

"Yeah," Janet said.

"Are you all right?" Jack asked.

"No questions, please. They make my brain baby kick."

Jack and Bliss exchanged a puzzled look. Mandalay tried not to giggle.

"Never mind," Janet said. "Follow me." She led them away into the darkness. After several minutes, Mandalay heard her say, "There! Look!"

Mandalay let out a long breath. Sharing her vision with Janet was a spur-of-the-moment thing, and one she'd have to remember not to try again. Janet didn't have a lot of Tufa blood in her family, but even a pureblood like Bliss or Bronwyn would be unable to bear the full intensity of the night winds for long. Above and beyond the girl's musical talent, she was tougher than anyone thought. Because of that, her future would be, as the apocryphal Chinese curse said, interesting.

She was tired, and she wasn't needed here any longer. When she was certain no one was watching, Mandalay closed her own eyes, and a moment later, she was gone, the night winds carrying her wherever she wanted to go.

32

“I won’t keep you in suspense,” Janet told the storytelling festival crowd. Then she stopped noodling on her guitar and paused for a drink of water. A few people laughed as they got the joke; the rest sat riveted. She deliberately put the cap back on the water bottle and placed it on the floor, before leaning close to the microphone.

“They found the lost girl, and she was fine. Her baby was fine. They gathered her round and rushed her to the hospital in Unicorn, where they patched her up. And they found her newlywed husband dead at the bottom of a cliff near the old moonshiners’ cave. The official story was that he wandered over the edge while trying to get help. But most folks knew the truth. And now you do, too.”

She began to strum again. The tent was silent, the crowd almost afraid to breathe too loud, lest they disturb the fragile spell. The sea of sweaty faces hung on her every move, every inflection.

“That wasn’t quite the end, though. There was still the matter of the monster. Only that didn’t end how anyone expected, either. . . .”

33

Jack walked around the carcass. The pig had died sometime during the winter, but Dolph had only just discovered it deep in the undergrowth of Half Pea Hollow. Not much was left: most of the bones, some leathery strips of skin, and of course, the massive skull. The rest had been processed by nature's garbage disposals.

"Been dead about a while," Dolph said.

"Not enough left to tell what killed it," Bronwyn observed.

"Look closer," Dolph said. "Check out the skull."

Jack knelt and turned the huge cranium. There was a round hole, obviously from a bullet. "Somebody shot it in the head."

"Yeah, but that's not the interesting part. Look closer."

Jack gave him an annoyed look, then bent close to the skull. "We're not in a biology lab. You could just tell me."

"Where's the fun in that?" Dolph said. He caught Bronwyn's amusement, and winked.

"Hell, I can see it from here," Max said. "There's new bone tissue around the edge of the hole."

"It had started to heal?" Jack said.

"Bingo," said Dolph.

"So somebody shot it in the head and it didn't die?" Jack asked.

"At least not right away," Max said.

"At least it can't hurt anyone else," Jack said. He turned to face his team. "Thank you, folks, for staying so motivated on this. I'll sleep easier, knowing that this monster, at least, is gone."

"Not exactly a win for WHOMP," Bronwyn said.

"Not a loss, either," Max said. "It's a draw, like Vietnam."

"What do you know about Vietnam?" Dolph said sharply.

"Hey, I wasn't trying to offend anyone. Sorry."

"Don't make jokes about what you don't know."

"Wonder where it came from originally?" Bronwyn said, trying to change the subject. As a veteran of the Gulf War, she knew that nothing good came from bringing up military conflicts. "I mean, it can't just have magically appeared, can it? Obviously it crossed paths with someone else."

Jack turned to Bronwyn. By now he understood that she, like Bliss, carried pure Tufa blood, along with everything that implied. "I don't think so," he said. "I still think that a pig like this couldn't grow that large in the wild. But anything's possible."

"It didn't start out in the wild," Max said. "See its bottom incisors? The way they're spread out? You only see that in pigs raised domestically."

"He's right," Dolph said. He tossed something small through the air to Jack. "Found this with the bones."

Jack caught it and looked at it. The implications ran through his mind like lightning. He pocketed it and said, "Well, that helps."

Jack rang the doorbell at the old farm. The house was run-down, in need of both a new roof and a paint job. In that way, it looked like many other farms trying to eke out a living in the mountains, using the few nearby acres of relatively flat land to grow corn, squash, or beans. There was an equally decrepit barn, with a small corral and a pen for pigs. Only one pig, small and mottled, nosed around in it.

Heavy steps approached, and then the inner door opened. A bearded, bleary-eyed man of around fifty looked out through the screen. He wore old coveralls and heavy boots. He looked at Jack, and at Trooper Alvin Darwin standing beside his car. "Yeah?"

"Mr. Dale Bolander?"

"Who're you?"

"I'm Jack Cates, with the state wildlife office. I'd like to talk to you about Bruce."

"Who is it?" a woman's voice called.

"Vacuum cleaner salesman," the man answered.

Jack's voice turned hard. "This is official law enforcement business, Mrs. Bolander," he said, loud enough for the woman to hear. "I'd like to ask you and your husband some questions."

"She don't know nothing," the man said. "And I don't know no one named Bruce." He started to shut the door.

"Then I'll have my friend back there go round us up a warrant." He looked back at Darwin, who touched his hat to show he'd heard everything. "Is that what you want?"

The man opened the door again, but didn't invite Jack inside. Instead, still speaking through the screen, he said, "So what makes you think I know this 'Bruce'?"

Jack held up the ear tag Dolph found with the hog's remains. An identification number was stamped into it above a bar code, and the word BRUCE had been written on a piece of duct tape on the other side. "Apparently Bruce is running around with your address on his ear."

He saw the fear in the big man's eyes. "I don't know—"

"Look, we know you raised him, and we know you must've sold him. How big was Bruce when you did that?"

He looked down, scratched under his beard, and said, "Right at a thousand pounds."

Jack nodded. "And who did you sell him to?"

"That fella over at Fast Creek Farms. Runs them, what do you call 'em, pickled hunts?"

"Canned hunts."

"Yeah, that's it."

"You ever been there?"

"Naw, I can't afford that fancy shit. I just sold the man a pig."

Jack asked a few more questions, but he already had the information he needed. He walked back to Darwin's car. "You get what you need?" the trooper asked him.

"Yep. Got another stop to make. You up for it?"

"Hell, you couldn't keep me away with a rabid polecat," Darwin said.

"It's all legal," Freddy Bourgeois said with a smile so smug, it took all Jack's self-control not to punch it through the back of his head. "I've got all the paperwork on file. I'll get my lawyers to send you copies if it'll help you sleep better."

"It's not legal when one of your animals gets out and kills people," Darwin said.

The three men stood on the porch of Bourgeois's beautiful ranch house that looked out over his immaculate lawn. Flower beds marked the corners of the long drive, and a mailbox in the shape of cartoon revolver stood watch. Two enormous pickup trucks, each recently washed and shining, were parked near the house. The view, from halfway up the slope of a mountain, was spectacular. Like Bruce's former owner, Bourgeois had not invited Jack inside.

"That's not possible," Bourgeois said. "You've got the wrong hog."

"How do you figure that?" Jack said.

"Well, the hog I bought from ole Dale was killed before any of those attacks."

"Yeah? When?"

"Oh, last year sometime. I'd have to look it up."

"I'd appreciate it if you'd do that," Darwin said.

"Who killed it?" Jack asked.

"A twelve-year-old boy from Cookeville. Birthday present from his daddy. It shoulda been in all the papers, but the boy got all upset afterwards, and the daddy wouldn't let me publicize it. He didn't even want the meat. But word got around; when that kind of thing happens, it always does. I sorta count on it," he added with a chuckle.

"What did you do with it, then, after it was killed?"

"We just buried it."

"You didn't have it butchered?" Darwin asked.

He laughed as smugly as he smiled. "Good Lord knows I got enough pork in the freezer to do me till doomsday."

"Show us," Jack said.

"Show you my freezer?"

"No, show us where you buried it."

He gestured down at his polo shirt and pressed khakis. "Mr. Cates, Officer Darwin, I ain't dressed to go traipsing around the woods today. I got clients coming, and—"

"Show us, or we'll come back with a warrant, and we'll make a bigger mess than you, or your lawyers, probably want," Darwin said, and imitated his smug smile.

"Is that a threat, Officer? You're standing on my porch, threatenin' me?"

Jack recalled the cave where he'd recovered Adam Procure's remains. He'd had about enough of this smug bastard, and said, "Mr. Bourgeois, for the slightest provocation, I'd beat you senseless on your porch."

"And I won't see a thing," Darwin added.

Bourgeois saw that they meant it. "Excuse me while I get some boots on, then."

"You do that."

Bourgeois had them climb into one of the big trucks. He drove them out to the spot where the hog was buried, at the far edge of his property, behind a stand of pine trees and near the perimeter fence. They startled a herd of "wild" pigs on the way, scattering them from the rutted path.

"How many pigs have you got?" Jack asked.

"Not sure. Changes depending on how many hunts we have."

"Any ever get out?"

"Of course not," he said with the diffidence of a practiced liar.

The burial site looked legitimate; the ground had clearly been dug up and refilled in a size appropriate for a pig as large as the one they'd found. They got out and looked around.

"Why'd you bury it way out here?" Darwin asked.

"This is where that boy killed it. It's too big to drag to my dump or anything, and I didn't want it to attract coyotes or bears."

"What did he use?" Jack said.

"The boy that killed it? One of them Smith and Wessons with a laser sight on it."

"A handgun? How many times did he hit it?"

"Nine or ten."

Jack's rage must've shown on his face, because Bourgeois backed up. "Hey, now, he was just a kid, can't blame him if he ain't much of a marksman."

"And there was nobody with him?" Darwin asked.

"Sure, his pappy, a guide—"

"Not you?"

"I don't generally go out on the hunts."

"Why didn't someone finish the damn thing off?" Jack demanded.

"The pappy wanted the boy to do it."

"So you let that pig run around hurt and bleeding for how long, exactly?"

"A few hours. Like I said, I wasn't here."

Jack walked around the grave, then stopped. "What happened over here?"

Bourgeois and Darwin joined him. "I don't know. It looks like—"

"I know what it looks like. Do you have a backhoe?"

"Yes, why?"

"We're going to open this grave."

"What, now?"

"Yes, now. Either you do it, or we do it. And we'll be a lot messier than you, and it'll take us a long, long time."

It took the better part of the morning to get the backhoe out to the location and then dig up the grave. Jack wasn't surprised at what he found: an empty hole. But clearly something had been buried there once, even if it wasn't there now.

"Well, if that don't beat all," Bourgeois said as he climbed out of the backhoe cab. He seemed genuinely puzzled. "Where the hell is it?"

Jack had spotted the disturbed dirt at the back of the grave, where earth had been pushed aside before falling back into a secondary hole. That had completed the puzzle: the giant pig had not been dead after all when they buried it, only stunned, wounded, and weakened. And after catching its breath, it dug itself out and escaped.

Bourgeois and two of his workers looked on in dumb surprise. "So you assholes buried it alive," Darwin said.

Bourgeois looked up. "There's no need for that sort of language."

"And it got loose, despite your state-of-the-art technology," Jack said, rattling the loose fence. "And two people died."

"I don't know what you—"

"You might want to get them lawyers you're so fond of mentioning on the phone," Darwin said. "I expect they've got some billable hours in their future."

The smugness finally drained from Bourgeois's face, which

didn't satisfy Jack nearly so much as putting his fist in the middle of it would have. But he'd settle for it.

"Oh my God, Jack, that's awful," Bliss said as she snuggled against him. They were in his small, sparse bedroom this time, and he'd just told her about the events at the hunting farm. When he'd opened his front door and seen her standing there, he found he suddenly wanted to do something other than talk. And so did she.

"Happens more and more," he said. "Somebody puts up a fence, stocks their land with a bunch of game, and charges people to come in and hunt it. Some even guarantee results. It's not illegal, but . . ."

"That's not hunting," Bliss said. "It's just *killing*."

"I agree."

"What will happen to him?"

"Some sort of fine, unless they decide to charge him with being an accessory to those two kids' deaths. But given how lawyered-up he claims to be, probably just a slap on the wrist."

"I'm sorry. After all the work and time you've put in, I know that must be a disappointment."

"More people get away than get caught—that's in the nature of the job."

"And yet you keep doing it."

"Somebody has to."

"It doesn't have to be you."

He turned and looked at her. She was so beautiful to him at the moment, all words stuck in his throat. He just wanted to look at her, to drink in her hair and her lips and the little crow's-feet at the corners of her eyes.

"At least," she continued, "you and Alvin seemed to have reached a truce."

"I understand him better now that I know . . . some of the things I know." He kissed her and said, "I'm tired of shoptalk."

"What would you like to talk about, then?"

"I'm really tired of talk, period."

This time she kissed him, and pulled him on top of her. And they didn't talk again for quite a while.

After Jack fell asleep, Bliss lay awake staring at the ceiling. The wild hog was dead; it turned out to be a mere animal after all. And yet, what had prompted it to dig itself out of its grave and come all the way to Half Pea Hollow in the first place? Instinct? Or the urgings of a certain six-fingered haint searching for a way to cause still more trouble for the people who'd celebrated his passing?

If Mandalay couldn't say, then there was certainly no way for Bliss to tell. She hoped it was exactly as Jack said it was, and that the discovery of its carcass signaled the end of the story. But what if it wasn't?

They could only wait. And watch.

Janet lay next to Ginny as well. They'd grown up this way, snuggling into each other's bed since they were children. Janet blew softly on a harmonica as Ginny expertly rolled a joint.

"Are you blowing the blues for Piggly-Wiggly?" Ginny asked after she licked the paper.

"No," Janet said, and tapped the harmonica on her palm. "I wrote his obituary for the *Raven's Caw.* He can rest in peace now."

"Then what is it?" She lit the joint, took a drag, then said, "You're not still obsessing over that night, are you?"

"How can I not? The night winds *whispered* to me, Ginny. In an actual voice. And then I saw the world like Mandalay does."

"That only happened because Mandalay was there." She handed the joint to Janet.

"How do you know?"

"Has it happened again?"

Janet tucked the end of the joint into the far left hole and drew in her breath. It made a D note. She held it for a moment, then let it out, a faint C note accompanying the smoke. "Well . . . no."

"There you go. You got a special gift that night, Janet, but it was a onetime thing. Accept it and move the fuck on."

Janet turned to look at her with mock outrage. "'Move the fuck on'? That's your advice."

"Best advice you'll ever get," Ginny said smugly.

Janet put the joint in the ashtray on her nightstand, then jumped on Ginny and began tickling her. They both screamed and laughed until they fell off the bed, and were still laughing when Janet's mother stuck her head in to ask what all the racket was about, and why they were burning sage again.

Renny Procure—she'd had no trouble getting the marriage annulled—stood at the foot of Duncan's grave. It was in the small Gowen plot, behind a weed-choked wrought iron fence at the end of a short trail behind his grandparents' house.

She still wore a sling, although the physical therapy had restored almost all her movement in her arm. Her belly was now huge, and she was due in less than a month.

"This would've been our wedding day, if I hadn't chickened out that night," she said to the grave. "Right about now, I would've been lumbering my fat ass down the aisle. You'd have been waiting for me in a cheap rented tux, with my brother as your best man. Oh, wait. You'd already killed him by the time you proposed."

She didn't cry. She had no tears left. And even her rage had muted to a kind of constant noise in the back of her mind. She walked around the grave and kicked at the new marble headstone. "I just wanted you to know that your son will never even know your name. As soon as he's born, I'm moving to Asheville. Yeah, I know all about what happens to Tufa who leave, but I'm willing to take that chance, for his sake. I don't want him hearing stories about how funny and sweet and kind you were. I don't want his friends telling him about how their parents said you died trying to save me, and him. Because none of that balances out what you did."

She kicked the headstone harder, and winced at the pain in her foot. The wind began to blow through the trees, and her eyes scanned the shadows, looking for a human shape. But she saw nothing.

"By the way, I heard that Miss Azure saw your haint being chased by the ghost of that giant pig. I hope that's true. I hope it's true, and that the pig never catches you, just chases you until fucking doomsday. Because that's what you deserve, you son of a bitch."

She spat on the grave, then walked back down the trail to her car.

34

Janet walked off the stage, the rapturous applause continuing as she stepped out of the tent and into the backstage area. "Dang, honey, that was amazing," the announcer said, having to shout it into her ear.

She signed autographs for the small crowd waiting for her, accepted the well wishes from the other storytellers, then got a fresh bottle of water from the cooler by the stage steps. As she guzzled it, she heard the announcer say, "And now, ladies and gentlemen, let's hear it for our final storyteller, Sheila Kay Adams."

The applause was even louder. Janet smiled to herself; one of the things she liked about coming back for this festival was that it kept her humble.

A dozen people, spouses and friends, business managers and personal assistants, milled about in the outdoor green room. The change from the humid, still tent to the relatively cool night was bracing and very welcome. Two small children slept curled up in canvas chairs, blankets tucked up to their chins. Beyond the open flaps, various vehicles parked, including the rental car that would shortly carry her to her parents' house in Needsville.

She closed her eyes, grateful for the breeze. Beneath the starry sky, Ginny Vipperman sat in a canvas chair and looked up from her phone. "Sounds like she got a bigger response than you did."

"This is her crowd. I'm just kibbutzing. And the announcer got the band's name wrong *again*."

"You're the only one who still gets a weed up her ass about that."

"It's never been—"

"*The* Little Trouble Girls, yeah, I know," Ginny finished. "You know, you should've taken my suggestion: Nine Hundred Ninety-nine Megabytes."

"But then we'd never get a gig," Janet said, and they both cracked up at their old inside joke.

"So you told the pig story?" Ginny asked.

"Couldn't you hear?"

"I wasn't paying attention." She got up and stretched. "Besides, I've heard you tell that one plenty of times."

"I should've let you tell it, then."

"Your mother texted me. She wants to know when you'll be home."

"Probably not till dawn. I want to go jam in the café after everyone finishes." After a pause she added, "Aren't you going to ask me if I saw him?"

"I figure you must have. Where was he this time?"

"Where he always is. At the back of the tent. Just standing there, watching."

"And you're sure it's not someone who just looked like him?"

"No, of course I'm not sure. I never am. But it's a hell of a coincidence that every time I tell that story here, somebody who looks just like Duncan Gowen is in the audience."

"I thought his haint was still being chased around Half Pea Hollow by the ghost of that giant hog."

"Maybe he gets time off for good behavior."

"Does it bother you?"

"No. Not exactly. I just wish . . ."

"What?"

"Every time I start telling that story, I wish that he'd made a different decision that day. That he'd shot the hog, or warned Adam, or just not even gone hunting in the first place."

"He could've made a *worse* choice."

"What do you mean?"

"He could've shot Adam Procure right in the head."

Janet smiled, but she was too tired to laugh. "Murder, suicide, dismemberment, or coming back from the dead."

"What do you mean?"

"That's how you know if it's a love song."

"In these mountains, that's a fact," Ginny agreed.

Janet looked up. The sky above Jonesborough was clear, and the air, while warm, moved with just enough breeze to be pleasant. The urge to leap into that sky, spread wings like glass, and ride the wind beneath the stars was strong, as it was whenever she came home. But for this night, she was grounded by choice, and she'd have to wait for another time.

SONGS LIST

All song lyrics are original, except the ones listed below.

CHAPTER 1

"Somebody's Tall and Handsome," composed by "J.R.M." in 1884, https://www.loc.gov/item/sm1884.03529.

"Handsome Mary, the Lily of the West," traditional Irish folk song, later Americanized, https://en.wikipedia.org/wiki/Lily_of_the_West.

CHAPTER 3

"Old Bangum," traditional, https://maxhunter.missouristate.edu/songinformation.aspx?ID=1499.

CHAPTER 4

"The Nightingale (The Soldier and the Lady)," traditional, extant copies as early as 1682, http://www.stolaf.edu/people/hend/songs/Nightingale.html.

CHAPTER 6

"The Fairy Lullaby," found in *Seventy Scottish Songs* by Helen Hopekirk, first published, 1905.

CHAPTER 8

"The Dead Brother's Song," composed in Asia Minor during the ninth century, https://en.wikipedia.org/wiki/The_Dead_Brother%27s_Song.

CHAPTER 20

"Young Orphy," anonymous retelling of the Orpheus legend, found in the Auchinleck manuscript from the fourteenth century, https://en.wikipedia.org/wiki/Sir_Orfeo.

CHAPTER 23

"The Two Sisters," number 10 of the Child Ballads, collected in the nineteenth century by Francis James Child.

CHAPTER 29

"Against the Black," written by Jen Cass and Eric Janetsky, © 2015, used by permission.